CARLY PHILLIPS

New York Times bestselling author Carly Phillips
tossed away her legal briefs and a career as an
attorney to become a stay-at-home mom. Within
the year, she turned her love of reading into an
obsession with writing. Over twenty-five published
novels later, Carly writes sexy contemporary
romances, striking a balance between
entertainment and emotion, and giving her
readers the compelling story they have come
to expect and enjoy. You can find Carly online
at www.carlyphillips.com.

New York Times Bestselling Author

CARLY PHILLIPS

Lucky Streak

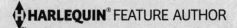

Recycling programs
for this product may
not exist in your area.

ISBN-13: 978-0-373-60621-4

LUCKY STREAK

Copyright © 2009 by Karen Drogin

Printed in U.S.A.

Dear Reader,

I am thrilled to bring you *Lucky Streak,* the second book in a trilogy featuring the sexy, charismatic Corwin cousins, men who are dogged by a centuries-old family curse. According to legend, any Corwin man who falls in love is destined to lose his love and his fortune.

So what does fate have in store for cousin number two—Boston cop Mike Corwin? An impromptu trip to Las Vegas for his partner's wedding takes him on a wild ride of his own, including winning a fortune, marrying a woman he met the night before and waking up alone— no wife, no cash. The family curse has hit him hard. Or has it? Amber Rose isn't my typical heroine, as Mike quickly finds out.

I can't wait for you to read this fun story! The series concludes with Jason Corwin's story, *Lucky Break,* and began with Derek's story, *Lucky Charm.*

Visit www.carlyphillips.com for release dates and so much more. You can write to me at P.O. Box 483, Purchase, NY 10577 or email carly@carlyphillips.com.

As always, thank you for buying my books, and happy reading!

Best wishes,

Carly Phillips

This one's been used before but bears repeating!

To Phil, Jackie and Jen—I love you always!

To Bailey and Buddy—my daily companions. Life wouldn't be complete without you.

To Mom and Dad—thanks for setting the best example in life and in romance. I love you, too!

To Brenda Chin, my longtime editor—keep doing what you do for me. We make a great team!

And last but not least, to the Plotmonkeys— Janelle Denison, Julie Leto and Leslie Kelly. As usual, I couldn't do it without you and I wouldn't want to try. XXX OOO

LUCKY STREAK

INTRODUCTION

IN THE LATE nineteenth century, in the small village of Stewart, Massachusetts, 1.5 miles west of Salem, site of the now-famous witch trials, fear of curses and witchcraft ran rampant. During this time, William Corwin fell in love and eloped with a woman who was already betrothed to another. The man William wronged, Martin Perkins, was the oldest son of the wealthy Perkins family from the neighboring village of the same name. To William Corwin's misfortune, Martin's mother, Mary Perkins, was a witch.

And she immediately sought revenge on her son's behalf with this curse: Any Corwin male who falls in love will be destined to lose his love and his fortune.

No male Corwin has walked away unscathed...

CHAPTER ONE

AMBER ROSE WANTED out of the con-artist life. Counting cards in Vegas high-stakes poker games was not the way she wanted to live—even if it did bring in money she desperately needed to pay for her Alzheimer's-stricken father's medical bills and keep him in a top-notch nursing home. But now she'd saved enough to find another way. She glanced around the crowded, smoke-filled casino, where she'd arranged to meet Marshall Banks, her soon-to-be ex-partner. The Bellagio was his favorite hotel on the Strip and she hoped the atmosphere would put him in a good mood for when she delivered the news. Amber glanced at her watch. Though it felt like hours, only five minutes had passed since she'd arrived. Relax, she ordered herself, when she finally caught sight of Marshall across the room.

She couldn't help but notice many appreciative female eyes followed him as he cut through the crowd. With his black slacks and colorful striped dress shirt, and dark, slicked-back hair, he epitomized Vegas glitz and studly Andy Garcia-like appeal. Women had always been drawn to Marshall. As a young, impressionable teenager, Amber had been one of them. How could she not have a crush on her father's top protégé?

Sam Brenner had been a gambler extraordinaire, a man Amber had been in awe of. He was everything Vegas—big and large, dynamic and exciting. He'd adored his daughter and he'd seen to it she had everything she'd ever needed. Since he was often traveling the gambling circuit, leaving Amber with his parents, she'd extended her awe and love to her dashing father to her hometown, Vegas. She reveled in the glitz and glamour that emanated from it in waves.

The shine had long since come off Marshall, though, and these days she saw her soon-to-be ex-partner for the man he really was. A middle-aged con who made his living by gambling and cheating, simply because he could. Amber's reasons for getting into the life had been less self-serving, yet she couldn't deny they shared a mutual investment in their partnership.

"Hey, beautiful." Marshall stepped up beside her and pressed a cool kiss to her cheek. "How are you this morning?" he asked, interrupting her introspection.

"I'm just fine." She pressed her fingers together to keep from fidgeting or tipping her hand before she was ready.

"Can I get you a drink?" Marshall asked.

She frowned at his question. "Isn't noon a little early for cocktails?"

"Come on, babe, relax. It's Friday. The start of the weekend." He flagged down a waitress. "Johnnie Walker Black for me. And a chardonnay for the lady."

Chardonnay was Amber's drink of choice when she and Marshall were acting the part of gambler and his bimbo. Amber didn't want anything to do with the charade now.

She waved her hand in the air. "Nothing for me."

With a nod, the cocktail waitress turned and walked away.

Marshall immediately cocked his head to one side. "Something wrong?" he asked Amber.

She shook her head. "No, it's just that it's awfully early in the day." Even for a Friday.

He pinned her with his astute stare. "What's your problem? You usually don't give a damn what I drink or when as long as we have a gig planned that'll bring in some cash. And I already told you we're set for tomorrow night. Relax." He reached out a hand to smooth her long curls.

She forced herself to release a calming breath. He was right. She'd never questioned him about his drinking before. From the moment she'd asked him to join her in her mission to raise big money by revisiting the tricks her father had taught her in her youth, she'd always let him do his own thing. Amber didn't want him drinking now because the more alcohol he downed, the more volatile he could become when he heard her news.

She might as well get it over with. "About tomorrow's game." Amber clenched and unclenched her fists. Her palms were damp and she resisted the urge to wipe them on her dark dress.

His wary gaze turned his irises coal-black, but Amber wasn't afraid. He usually possessed enough charm to cover his explosive temper. Usually.

"What's wrong?" he asked again.

"I won't be there."

"That's a bad joke." He frowned, the scowl marring his features. "You know I can't win without that photographic memory of yours. What could be more important than the game?"

How to explain honesty, morality and guilt to a man who didn't worry about those things? Amber bit the inside of her cheek, wondering how to phrase things so he'd understand.

She met Marshall's unnerving gaze. "I'm not coming tomorrow because I'm finished with card counting. With this life."

She'd always loved the highs and challenges that high-stakes gambling offered, but she also needed to like the person she viewed in the mirror each morning. And she had, until she was forced to leave the career she loved to look after her father. As a concierge in Beverly Hills, Amber had had a legitimate job that offered her enough challenge to satisfy her reckless streak. She'd found the best in life and she wanted it back. And since she'd saved enough money to take time and find another way to pay for her father's care, she intended to do just that.

"Finished? Come on, baby. Be real." Marshall laughed from deep in his chest as his eyes wandered over her. "Like I just said, we're a team, you and I."

"Not anymore." At twenty-four years old, she'd learned that she preferred to come by her excitement honestly.

"Oh, really?" He folded his arms across his chest, his body language telling her he wasn't buying one word. "Where else are you going to get the tax-free cash to pay for that fancy place your old man is in?" He leaned in closer as he spoke.

The suddenly too-strong scent of his distinctive cologne assaulted her senses and she pulled back. "That's my problem, not yours. I'm just telling you our days as partners are over. I'm out."

"The hell you are." He grabbed her arm tight.

She shook him off and shot him a deadly look. "Do not touch me like that again. Ever." She rubbed her sore arm. "I've made my decision and nothing you say…or do is going to change my mind."

"Sorry, babe. I have too much riding on tomorrow night to indulge you," he said through gritted teeth. He took a step toward her, clearly intending to scare her into changing her mind.

No sooner had he wrapped his hand around her forearm again than someone stepped beside them. "Is something wrong here?"

Amber jerked toward the sound of the sexy male voice and was literally blown away. *Good-looking* was too mild a word to describe the dark-haired stranger whose gaze bore into hers with genuine concern.

"Everything's fine." Amber didn't want this man to get into an argument with Marshall, who seemed primed for a fight. As long as they were in public, her ex-partner wouldn't do more than make a show of manhandling her.

"Doesn't look fine to me." The stranger deliberately stared at Marshall's hand on her arm.

Amber would have shoved Marshall away, but she knew she'd only set him off and cause more trouble for the stranger who seemed determined to play white knight.

"I don't see what business it is of yours," Marshall said, all bluster and machismo.

"I'm making it my business." Her rescuer shoved his hand into his back pocket and pulled out a wallet, flashing a badge. "I heard the lady ask you to keep your hands to yourself. So either you're deaf or just plain stupid. Care to tell me which?"

He shoved the small leather billfold back into his pocket just as fast.

Marshall immediately released his grip on Amber's arm. "Hey, no harm," he said, raising his hands in a gesture of surrender as he took a step back.

"Really?" The other man squared his shoulders, which seemed to grow broader beneath his navy T-shirt. "Why don't we ask the lady if that's true. Did he hurt you?" His caring voice softened as he spoke to her, wrapping around her like a warm caress.

She met his gaze. "I'm fine now." She bit the inside of her cheek to keep from saying anything that might incite more trouble between the men.

Marshall nodded in agreement. "See? Just a lover's quarrel. Isn't that right, babe?"

Nothing could be further from the truth. Her goal had been to extricate herself from Marshall. She wasn't about to let him pull her back in. Or lead her sexy savior to the wrong conclusion about them.

She shook her head. "Actually we are…I mean, we *were* business partners. But we aren't anymore," she said.

The stranger's blue eyes narrowed. "Then I guess there's nothing left to discuss, is there?" he pointedly asked Marshall, dismissing him.

Marshall shifted on his feet.

Amber knew no one could make him leave if

he wanted to stay, but the stranger had flashed a badge.

So Marshall turned away, but not before sending Amber a warning glance.

He wasn't finished with her yet.

MICHAEL CORWIN watched the dirtbag walk away, making sure the other man left the casino before turning his gaze toward the beautiful woman he couldn't help but rescue.

"Are you really okay?" he asked.

She cocked her head to one side. A cascade of blond curls fell over her shoulder as she glanced at him. "I'll live," she said wryly. "I could have handled Marshall myself. But thank you for stepping in." Appreciation and what looked like admiration glittered in her clear blue eyes.

As a detective, it was in his nature to be protective, but as a man he'd been drawn to the alluring woman who'd obviously needed his help. "You're welcome."

She studied him intently. "You aren't a *Las Vegas* cop, are you?"

He raised an eyebrow at her astute observation. "Boston, Massachusetts. What makes you ask?"

"The accent clearly says you aren't a local. Marshall would have realized it himself if he'd been composed enough to breathe." She extended her hand. "I'm Amber. Pleased to meet you."

"Mike Corwin." He shook her hand and felt the jolt all the way through his body, settling right in his groin. Unexpected, but not unwanted, he thought. "Do you have a last name, Amber?"

"It's Rose. Amber Rose."

He raised an eyebrow at the exotic-sounding name. Added to the short black cocktail dress that draped her slender body, revealing ample cleavage for such a slight woman, he had to admit she made for an enticing package. One he couldn't ignore if he'd wanted to.

He didn't.

"I know it's an unusual name," she added.

"Actually, I was going to say it sounds like it belongs to a Vegas showgirl. No insult intended."

Her porcelain skin flushed beneath the tacky casino lighting. She grinned, showing off one dimple in her cheek. "You're half-right. Rose was my mother's maiden name. Celia Rose. She was a showgirl."

"She's retired?"

A shadow passed over her eyes. "She died when I was born. So, what brings you to Vegas?" she asked, changing the subject as she looked down and noticed their still-intertwined hands.

He'd been holding on, drawing lazy circles around her wrist with his thumb, enjoying the connection that felt so right, so fast. Obviously she didn't want to discuss her mother and he let the subject go. "I'm here for a wedding."

"Yours?" She jerked her hand back, a horrified expression on her face.

"Hell, no, not my wedding. Do I look like the kind of guy who'd hit on a woman if I was getting married?" he asked, quickly setting things right. "It's my partner's."

"Oh." She exhaled hard. "So you *are* hitting on me?" she asked, sounding extremely pleased at the notion.

"Most definitely." He stepped closer. Despite the acrid smell of cigarette smoke in the air, he caught a whiff of her floral scent and grew immediately more aroused. "I'm not married or involved," he said, further reassuring her.

Her lips turned upward in a smile.

Any normal, red-blooded man would be attracted to her. Mike had worked so many hours lately, he couldn't remember the last time he'd gotten laid. He didn't normally go around picking up the women he rescued, but Amber was different. Sexual attraction wasn't her only appeal. She was intelligent and obviously had morals—she'd made it clear she wouldn't have been interested in him if he'd been someone else's husband.

He was here enjoying a long weekend before he had to be back in court early Monday morning to testify in a case he'd closed last year. He'd planned to have fun, unwind and celebrate with his friends. This woman was an unexpected bonus and he realized he wanted to do all of the above with her by his side.

He wasn't normally so impulsive, but what the hell? Where else but Las Vegas could a man indulge and not feel guilty? If the desire was mutual.

"So." She ran her tongue over her glossed lips. "What are you going to do now that you've hit on me?" she asked in a husky voice.

"Oh, I'll think of something," he said, gauging her interest.

Her smile widened and his gut churned with desire the likes of which he hadn't felt in a long time. He wrapped his hand around hers and once again the connection sizzled between them. Touching her like this made him feel as if he'd known her for longer than a few minutes. Without a doubt, he needed more time.

"So, are there any more Marshalls I should know about?" he asked.

She said he'd been her business partner. Past tense. And he believed her.

She shook her head. "Lucky for both of us, I'm unattached." Her grin expressed unmistakable interest. In him.

"Corwin, we're heading to the Hard Rock. Are you coming?"

At the sound of his partner's voice, Mike turned.

"Be right there." He refocused on Amber. "That's my partner and some other cops from back home."

She glanced at the men and women who stood waiting for him. "You should go," she said. But she didn't sound like she meant it.

He wasn't willing to leave her, either. "Come with us. We're celebrating. Sort of a traveling wedding party. It'll be fun." He paused. "Unless you have something else planned?"

"Nope, no other plans," she quipped. But she cast a wary eye between Mike and his group of friends.

"There are women in the group," he said, guessing at her hesitancy to walk off alone with them. "Some of them are even cops, too."

"Well, then, I couldn't get better escorts," Amber said, laughing.

He nudged her with his elbow in case she needed more convincing. "Come on. Get away from your life for a little while."

Amber smiled. He didn't realize how tempting his offer actually was. Over his shoulder, she caught sight of Marshall's sleazy best friend, J.R., lingering by the bar.

Watching her.

She'd known Marshall wouldn't give up so easily. Putting J.R. on her tail ensured he could find her—and get her to change her mind later. So, disappearing from this casino sounded like a good idea to Amber right now. Doing it in the middle of a group of cops was even better. And spending time with her sexy savior was like a cherry on top of an already overly frosted cake.

"Besides, how can I continue to hit on you if you don't come along?" he asked, his breath warm against her cheek, his musky cologne making her weak in the knees.

He had the most potent effect on her and she couldn't resist his rationale or his charm. Given her circumstances, a new man in her life was the last thing she needed, but the pounding excitement in her veins told her *this* couldn't be wrong.

"Lead the way," she said, hooking her arm in his.

A surprised but pleased look in his eye, Mike led her over to his friends. He introduced her to his partner, Dan Sullivan, and his new wife, Natalie, whose wedding last night they were currently celebrating. Mike ticked off half a dozen more names and Amber took a mental photograph of each.

People, places, names and numbers were her specialty, making her not just good at her former job as a concierge, but one of the best. She wasn't overly modest, she just understood that her photographic memory was an asset in the service industry. Charisma was another and she'd inherited hers from her father.

The expected stab of pain settled in her chest

as she recalled the vibrant charmer Sam Brenner had been, compared to the often vacant shell he'd become once his illness had progressed. Amber didn't share her father's last name because he'd wanted to protect her from his con-artist lifestyle. Since taking her mother's maiden name had helped memorialize a woman Amber would never know, she'd always been honored to have it. And it had certainly made her father happy. At least until his illness had taken hold.

She and her father had always been close, which was why she'd decided to leave her grandparents behind and go on the road with Sam while he did his cons. She'd gotten her GED in place of a traditional high school diploma, and talked the head concierge of the Crown Chandler Hotels in Vegas into taking her on as her assistant and teach her the ropes at the age of eighteen. Amber had traveled the country, viewing all the hotels in the chain and ultimately earning the head job in Beverly Hills at the unheard-of age of twenty-one.

She'd remained there for three years, until six months ago, when Amber had moved back from L.A. to her father's Vegas apartment in order to care for him. She'd taken a job as a cocktail waitress at the bar of an old friend's, who'd promised her time off if her father had an emergency. That was something she couldn't count on even if she transferred to a Vegas hotel. Yet after only three months of living with her father, she'd had to step up her plan to find him a decent nursing home. The day she'd come home from work to find Sam had wandered off was the day she knew things had to change.

The first few facilities she'd viewed, homes she could have afforded on a concierge's salary, had been seedy dumps she wouldn't even consider leaving her father in. Old buildings run by people who clearly weren't compensated enough to handle elderly-patient care; the smells and sights had left Amber close to tears. She knew then she had no choice but to find a way to raise big money quickly, and often, so she could afford a higher standard of living for her father in a privately owned facility.

That night she'd gone in search of Marshall. Within a few days, he'd found them their first game and she'd taken home enough cash to ensure her father was looked after properly.

Shaking off the memory, she refocused on Mike and his friends. Mike had wrapped his arm around her shoulders for each introduction and everyone she met took his body language as a cue to welcome her into their group warmly and without question.

Before they took off for the next hotel, they loaded up on drinks. Someone handed Amber a Bloody Mary, which she discreetly switched for her own choice, Grey Goose Orange, club soda and a slice of orange. If she was going to indulge, at least she'd enjoy it.

Mike took her hand and they made their way out of the casino and into the muggy Vegas streets. Her Vegas, the place she'd grown up knowing and loving. The glittering lights, the excitement, the constant exhilaration. A rush of adrenaline flowed through her as she walked the streets of her city with a man who excited her just as much.

She wasn't involved with anyone and hadn't been for a long time. She felt as though she'd been waiting. For him. And she found herself wishing their time together never had to end.

She wasn't going to let anything kill her sudden sense of joy.

Not even her gut instinct that Marshall and his pal J.R. weren't far behind.

AS THE DAY WORE ON, the drinks flowed as freely as Amber's laughter and her easy touch—her hand on Mike's arm, his back, it didn't matter. She obviously felt comfortable being demonstrative, and during the long, playful day he spent with her, she kept him in a constant state of arousal. She seemed happy to remain with him and he was having too much fun to question why or ask what she'd normally be doing.

His friends didn't have a set agenda, they only wanted to party and Amber was happy to be their tour guide. They visited the premier hotels, viewing them from the unique perspective of someone who'd grown up there. Along the way, they stopped in each of the bars and casinos along the Strip, including one owned by Amber's friend Paul, where Amber said she worked part-time.

Mike lost count of the amount of beer he'd consumed, but he had a healthy buzz going on, while Amber had kept up with the women, drinking her orange vodka. They spent hours touring Madame Tussaud's Wax Museum in the Venetian Resort Hotel and documented the trip with photographs on someone's digital camera. They ate dinner at Grande Lux Cafe where they gorged on cheesecake and returned to the casino afterward where everyone split up, agreeing to touch base the next morning.

"Looks like we're alone," Amber said.

He nodded. "Does that bother you?"

"Actually, I'm relieved. How else can I get to know you better?" she asked, slipping her arm around his waist. Warm and feminine, she wrapped him in seductive heat. "Come."

"Where are we going?" Not that he cared. Anywhere she wanted to take him was fine by him.

Her eyes glittered as she walked him through the entryway leading to the shops. "We're going on a gondola ride." Laughing, she nudged him forward until they ended up at the back of a short line.

He glanced over a railing to see a canal running through the hotel, complete with bridges that led to other upscale stores. "I heard Vegas was incredible," he said in awe.

Growing up in a small town on the Massachusetts coast hadn't prepared Mike for the glamour and excitement here, beginning with this woman.

"Here comes one now." She leaned over and pointed in the distance. "An authentic Venetian gondola complete with singing gondolier." The long, graceful boat glided beneath a bridge, through the water and toward them.

Five minutes later, they were seated in their own private gondola, taking a scenic tour of cobblestone streets filled with cafés, balconies and shops.

The boat glided through the water and Mike leaned back, wrapping his arm around Amber and pulling her close. She snuggled into him, her soft curves fitting against his hard chest and thighs. Her hair smelled fragrant and fresh, tickling his neck as she settled in.

"Your friends, the ones that got married. They look so happy."

"They are. They even bucked office politics to be together. We had a no-fraternization policy until Natalie got the other women to petition for a change." He shook his head, laughing at the memory of her determination. "She was so adamant, even the men ended up backing her."

Including Mike. He'd even had a moment of envy during the ceremony yesterday…until he reminded himself of his heritage. First comes love, then the Corwin curse kicked in. For as many generations as Mike could remember, and even those that he couldn't, any Corwin man who'd fallen in love had suffered the repercussions. His reclusive father, Edward, was living, breathing proof the curse existed, as were his uncles, Hank and Thomas.

"I admire a woman who goes after what she wants," Amber said just as the gondola glided beneath a long, dark bridge.

She slipped one hand onto his thigh and she tilted her head back. Her lips parted, her desire as clear as the dual meaning of her words.

Unlike his male relatives, Mike refused to let the curse rule his life. Instead, he made it a point to avoid the *right* kind of woman. The kind who believed in happily ever after. The type who wouldn't take a chance on a cop who faced being killed each time he walked out the door. A woman who'd take one look at his family, his history, and run screaming the other way.

What a prize package he was, Mike thought wryly.

But he wasn't here to fall in love, he was here to have fun.

And Amber seemed more than up for that.

CHAPTER TWO

VEGAS HAD ALWAYS instilled a sense of adventure in Amber and with the flowing drinks throughout the day, today was no different. Her surroundings faded away as she leaned closer to Mike, gathering her courage.

"Kiss me," she said, going after what she wanted.

He stared into her eyes, tracing a finger down her cheek. Her head spun. From her alcohol-induced buzz or from him? He'd had a potent effect on her from the beginning. Throughout the day he'd allowed her to forget her problems and be carefree in ways she'd had to suppress since returning to care for her dad. Mike was generous, and over her protests, he insisted on paying for her drinks, lunch and everything in between.

He seduced her with his easy wit and charm and with the sex appeal she couldn't ignore. Between working all the time and then dealing with her father's illness, romance hadn't been all that important to her. But the electricity that crackled between them made her wonder if she'd just never met a man who affected her the way this one did.

He was solely focused on her. Nothing else around him seemed to matter except her. By the time the moment arrived, kissing him seemed natural.

Necessary.

She touched her lips to his and he responded, slipping his fingers into her hair and cupping her head in his hands. She responded to the possessive way he took control, opening her mouth to let him inside. The kiss immediately turned hotter and more urgent. He drew insistent circles with his tongue, gliding as smoothly as the gondola they rode in, leaving no place untouched. He took her to heaven. Her heart pounded in her chest and she didn't want the dizzying sensations to end.

"Ah, the beauty of young love."

The sound of the gondolier's voice brought Amber back to reality and she regretfully pulled back.

"The ride's over," the man said. "Unless you'd like me to keep going?" he asked in a knowing voice.

She couldn't be embarrassed over something so right. Besides, the man was probably used to people making out under his watch. She glanced at Mike. Though she'd love to continue their ride, she had other plans for him.

"We'll get out here," she decided for them.

Mike raised an eyebrow, obviously surprised, but he stepped out first, then helped her do the same.

"Ready for some more fun?" she asked him.

He nodded. "Though I can't imagine anything being more fun than *that*." He tipped his head back toward the gondola, his eyes glittering with unslaked desire.

Her stomach fluttered with answering need. "I'm not finished showing you my Las Vegas." She grasped his hand and led the way.

She didn't question the impulse that demanded she share the city as she knew it. She wanted him to know her better and this was the perfect way to do it. Because she and Las Vegas had the same spirit.

From the Venetian, they traveled to Circus Circus where she took him to the Adventuredome. "My dad used to love roller coasters and we'd go to carnivals all over the U.S. I grew up loving a fast ride."

Mike heard the wistful tone in her voice. "Did your father pass away, too?"

"No. He has Alzheimer's and it's progressed fast. Sometimes it feels like…" She shook her head, unable to continue.

He squeezed her hand tighter. "I'm sorry. I know what it's like to have a father who's not all there."

And he did. Edward Corwin had always been off

somehow. Before his parents' divorce, Edward had been withdrawn and eccentric, making it hard for Mike to bring friends home. Afterward, the older man's behavior only got worse.

"Is your dad sick, too?" Amber asked.

"He doesn't have Alzheimer's, he's just…not all there." He tapped his head, unsure of how else to describe the eccentric oddity who was his father. They weren't close. Couldn't be, considering his father was a man mired in the curse and the past. But Mike loved him, despite it all.

"Well, we have that in common. So do you like roller coasters?" she asked, obviously eager to change the subject. "They have the most amazing rides here. The Canyon Blaster goes fifty-five miles an hour with a full loop." She circled her arm wide. "Or there's the Sling Shot or Chaos… We could even get wet if we went on the Rim Runner," she said, bursting with enthusiasm. "Which one will it be?"

He glanced in the direction of the huge rides and frowned. "None of them. I really don't like roller coasters. In fact, I hate them." He wasn't comfortable admitting weakness, but better than having to get in one of those contraptions held together by nuts and bolts.

"What do you mean you don't like roller coasters?" She perched her hands on her hips and cocked her head to the side, clearly shocked. "Everyone likes roller coasters!"

"No, they don't."

"What? Did you fall out of one when you were a kid or something?" she asked, nudging him playfully in the ribs.

"No, I just can't take the sensation of having my stomach turned upside down and inside out." The reality was that they reminded him too much of his childhood, the incredible highs and devastating lows.

Mike would ask Edward to come to his baseball games and too many times, he'd take the muttered *maybe* as a hopeful sign. He finally learned not to count on his dad. Now it was Mike who had to care for his father, even though it had never been the other way around.

"Oh, really?" Her eyes glittered in disbelief.

"Really."

She raised her eyebrows and stepped closer. The perfume that had been getting to him all day caused his gut to clench again now.

"Well, I bet I can turn your stomach upside down and inside out and not only will you like it, you'll be begging for more," she said, her meaning deliberately, seductively clear.

He wrapped his arm around her waist and pulled her against him. "Oh, yeah?"

"Yeah." She rose onto her tiptoes and kissed him full on the lips.

He found her absolutely irresistible as she wove her web and pulled him in like no other woman ever had. He dated on occasion, but between his dangerous job and his unwillingness to bring anyone home to his father, Mike had never let anyone get close enough to become serious. He'd become somewhat of a loner himself, at least in the relationship department. Sex was fine, when the need arose. Anything else brought with it too many complications.

Now there was Amber. Desire pounded hard and fast inside him as she tangled her tongue with his and took him on that wild ride she'd promised. Fast and furious, better than any roller coaster could be.

She ended the kiss too soon and grabbed his hand.

"Where to now?" he asked.

"Well, I still can't believe my big brave cop is afraid of roller coasters," she said, teasing him. "But I'll settle for the arcade."

The next hour was spent mixing old-fashioned games and long, heated kisses, resulting in his losing a fair amount of money in an attempt to win her a ring with a big fake diamond. No matter how much he spent, no matter how many darts he threw, the ring remained elusively out of reach. Yet they couldn't stop laughing and she didn't stop touching him. It felt as if everything about their time together was right.

He got caught up in the sheer pleasure of the carnival-like atmosphere and he savored being with a woman who wanted to be with him, without the stigma of the Corwin curse hanging over his head. No expectations, no games, just plain fun. And though he knew nothing could come of this, he found himself wishing they had time for something more, something real and lasting.

They walked from stand to stand, always coming back to the dart game where Mike would once again attempt to win the ring. Amber cheered him on until her voice was hoarse. He bought them both cold beers and they laughed over the ugly bear he'd traded the smaller items in to win.

But the ring remained out of reach, frustrating him because he knew how much she wanted the small token of their afternoon together. And he wanted her to have it.

"Let's head back to the Bellagio," she suggested after a while.

"Are you ready to call it a night?" He turned to meet her gaze, wondering just how their time together would end. He knew what he wanted, but he wouldn't pressure her.

"I'm ready to leave here." She paused a beat. Ran her tongue over her glossed lips.

He never caught her reapplying makeup, but

she'd kept that shimmer on her lips all day and night. The gloss had a hint of vanilla scent and each time he kissed her, he wanted to devour even more.

"Let's take a cab." He held on to her hand and started through the arcade in the direction of—he thought—the exit.

"Mike, wait."

He turned.

"I don't think I'm ready to leave you."

He exhaled the breath he hadn't been aware of holding. "The feeling's mutual." He squeezed her hand.

His body was strung tight and only one thing would alleviate the need pulsing inside him. But on the way to the taxi, they passed the dart game and Mike paused. He reached into his pocket and tossed his last five dollars in change on the counter.

"You *are* determined." The guy running the game handed him five darts. "Tell you what. Three out of five and I'll trade the bear for the ring," he said, looking at Amber and winking.

Mike picked up the dart and eyed the balloons, sparsely placed to make it difficult to hit the target.

"No matter what, I just want to be alone with you," she whispered.

He threw and missed.

She laughed, her breath warm in his ear. "No pressure. Really."

He tossed again, popping one balloon.

Beside him, she squealed in excitement, patted his back and stepped away so she didn't break his concentration.

A direct hit.

Another squeal.

He rolled his shoulders. Just one more....

"Relax," she said as if reading his mind. "You have two more chances," Amber said.

He shot her a warning glance. "Quiet."

She grinned.

He picked up the fourth dart, aimed and tossed. The balloon popped easily and Amber cheered, rewarding him by wrapping her arms around his neck and pulling him into a tight hug followed by a long, lingering kiss. One that gave a steamy hint of what was in store for him once they returned to his room.

"Here you go, buddy." The guy behind the arcade stand handed him the ring with the large fake diamond.

Amber held out her hand. An eerie sensation— as if his wish for something more with her had magically come true—struck him as he slipped the too-big ring on her delicate hand.

Top heavy, it rolled to the side. "I'll make it smaller with tape later," she said, laughing.

"If you ask me, a pretty lady like you deserves a real diamond," the arcade guy said.

If he and Amber were really involved, the man would be right. "Let's go," Mike said to her.

She nodded, a wide smile on her face.

"Wait. Since you seem to be on a lucky streak, take this." The arcade guy handed him a silver dollar. "You never know what coin will strike it rich in those slots," he said.

Mike shook his head. "Keep it," he said to the guy. "I already struck it rich."

Amber blushed.

He couldn't wait for them to be alone.

AMBER HELD Mike's hand as they wove their way through the arcade. They'd worked up a thirst and had stopped to buy drinks. She finished her glass of wine as quickly as he polished off a beer, adding to the light buzz she'd maintained all day. They walked through the casino on the way to the taxi area at the front of the hotel.

She'd enjoyed being with Mike so much, she'd almost forgotten about Marshall and the scene back at the hotel. Even though she'd never completely shaken the feeling that she was being followed, she'd been able to put the unsettling notion out of her mind. Until she saw J.R. in the hallway where they stood inside the hotel, Circus Circus.

Damn, Marshall was persistent. But that's what her ex-partner did when he considered something— or someone—his. Luckily for Amber, this was one of the easiest hotels to get lost in, with its awkward layout and confusing maze-type locations.

Yet somehow, J.R. still managed to keep track of her.

With his shaved head and broad shoulders, he intimidated her on a good day. Coming off her argument with Marshall, today wasn't one of those. She didn't want to deal with a confrontation and she definitely didn't want Mike to get into a fight with J.R. So she did the only thing she could think of on short notice. She pulled Mike into the nearest alcove and into a hot, distracting kiss.

One she felt from the tips of her toes all the way through her body. With each sweep and swirl of his tongue, her stomach fluttered and everything around her faded as his lips worked magic. He cupped her cheeks in his hands and his body pressed into hers, urging her against the wall for support. She felt his erection swell beneath his jeans and press into her stomach. This man aroused her on so many levels she couldn't think clearly all.

"We've got to get to my room," he muttered.

She swallowed hard, the reality of her situation returning to her and creating a sick feeling in the pit of her stomach. She couldn't return to plain sight just yet. She glanced around and realized they weren't in an entryway but a large, floral-lined room.

"Are you ready to go?" Mike asked gruffly.

She stroked her fingers down his razor-stubbled cheek, scrambling for a reason to stall leaving for a few precious minutes. "I am, but—"

"Are you two next?" a male voice asked.

"Next?" Mike asked.

A gray-haired man holding a clipboard glanced at them. "Come come. If you're going to change your mind about getting hitched, do it out in the hall."

"Hitched?" Amber's voice squeaked as she repeated the question.

"What else would you do in a wedding chapel?" the man asked.

"I don't know." She tried not to stammer. She glanced at Mike.

He raised an eyebrow, his expression thoughtful.

"Everyone's nervous the first time," the other man said, cracking a smile at his own joke. "Sally, get them something to drink," he called over his shoulder. "It'll calm their jitters."

The man's assistant, an overly made-up woman, handed them each a plastic flute filled with champagne.

Mike threaded his hand through Amber's, but said nothing.

The fact that he hadn't run for the hills made Amber wonder what he was thinking. She took a large gulp of the bubbly drink.

"Which package do you want? All of them in-

clude a small bridal bouquet, music, souvenir certificate and holder, garter and minister. That'd be
me." The man spoke by rote and clicked his pen
with each item on the list. "The least expensive one
is the Traditional. For two hundred and eighty-one
dollars, you also get a bigger bridal bouquet and
a boutonniere for the groom." He almost sounded
bored.

"What about photos?" Mike asked, speaking up
for the first time.

Amber nearly choked. "What?"

Mike shrugged and leaned closer to her. "It's
Vegas. Let's just do it," he said, his gaze delving
into hers intently.

She licked her lips, which had suddenly gone
dry. "Come on," she said, certain he was teasing.
"Even the tables in Vegas have limits," she said in
an effort to see how far he'd take things.

Because the notion of marrying him on the spur
of the moment held too much appeal.

"That doesn't mean we can't set our own." He
raised an eyebrow, challenging her. "You've said
it's a place where anything can happen."

"But...you don't live here!"

He met her gaze, holding on. "We'll figure it
out later."

"I don't got all day," the man said.

Mike turned back to him. "A bride should have

full-color glossy memories of her wedding day," he said.

"One photo is included. Anything else is extra."

Mike shot Amber a look. "Are we doing this?" he asked.

She'd grown up a gambler. And she liked him. *Really* liked him. His sudden adventurous streak appealed to her reckless nature. And he made her feel so good...

"Why not?" she asked, suddenly into this as much as he was.

"Throw one more photo into the package," Mike said, reaching for her right hand.

"Are you sure?" she asked him.

Mike met her stare, his eyes warm and sexy. "Make it legal?" He toyed with the large stone on her finger. "I'm sure. Are you?"

Amber hadn't a clue what his reasons for pursuing this were, but she knew her own. She liked him, he obviously liked her and a big man was waiting to have a talk with her somewhere right outside the door. But more important, their impossibly romantic day had cast a spell over her, leaving her in a happy, dizzy haze.

Besides, these wedding chapels existed in the casino for a reason. Even her parents had married in one. Her head spun and she no longer knew whether it was alcohol-induced or if she was losing her mind. Nor did she much care.

She glanced up at his handsome profile. Her white knight. Her cop savior. "Why not?" she heard herself repeating.

"Credit card," the minister said.

She wondered if Mike would declare it a joke now.

He whipped out silver plastic.

Everything else—the organ played by Sally, the bouquet wilting at the edges thrust into her hand, signing the wedding certificate—happened in a blur of cheap champagne and I do's.

"I now pronounce you husband and wife," the minister said. "You may kiss the bride."

Unlike the fast wedding, the kiss was as clear as the rest of her day with Mike. Full of passion and desire, it was over way too soon. Before they knew it their chaplain had clapped his hands and dismissed them, already on to the next couple.

Amber's heart pounded hard in her chest as the reality of what they'd done settled around her. "Did we really just get married?" Amber asked, laughing as they walked out of the chapel, license and photograph in hand.

"I believe we did…Mrs. Corwin." It was almost impossible to comprehend, Mike thought.

He normally wasn't impulsive. As a cop he couldn't afford to be. Day to day, he relied on training and instinct. When a quick decision was called for, it was always founded in a combination of both.

Now he was married.

The initial impulse had been just that, yet somehow he knew the decision had been rooted in his connection with Amber, one he knew he couldn't lose. Even now that the deed was done, he didn't regret a thing. In some odd way, getting hitched to Amber made sense.

For a Corwin man.

He and Amber weren't in love.

No love, no curse.

Although for Amber, Mike sensed he'd be willing to tempt fate. For the first time, Mike thought he understood his cousin Derek's recent marriage to his high-school sweetheart, the woman he'd once pushed away to avoid setting the curse in motion. Amber was addictive and Mike discovered he liked being hooked. Enough to want to keep her by his side.

"What do you say we head back to my room and consummate this marriage?" he asked his bride, pushing thoughts of fate and the curse far from his mind.

She smiled at him, her blue eyes dancing with energy and excitement. "I like the sound of that."

So did Mike.

MIKE WAS MARRIED and he liked it, he realized as Amber snuggled close in the cab ride back to his hotel. With her hanging on to his arm, he headed straight to the large bank of elevators that led to his room. While the Bellagio suites had an opulence that had made him uncomfortable when he'd checked in, the thought of taking Amber up there now and undressing her surrounded by all that elegance pleased Mike and made the extravagant price he'd paid worthwhile.

He shoved his hand into his back pants pocket to make sure he had his key and a coin fell onto the floor.

"What's this?" Amber asked, bending to retrieve it. "A token for the slots?" She studied it on both sides.

He nodded. "Everyone in the wedding party got one."

"You should use it," she said, handing it back to him. "It looks like it's worth ten dollars. You can win big with one of those."

He raised an eyebrow. "The slots are as rigged as the arcade." He'd blown over one hundred dollars before that guy had handed the ring over for another five. "Not that I minded, but the guy could have given us the ring anytime he wanted."

"But what fun would it have been?" she asked, nudging him. "Come on. Don't be such a skeptic. I've lived here long enough to know it's a crapshoot. But someone has to win every once in a while." She took his hand and led him back through the casino to the higher-end machines. "Pick one," she urged.

She obviously wasn't going to give up until he lost the token. "You choose," he said.

She shook her head. "Oh, no. I'm just along for the ride. This is all yours. Come on. What are you going to do with the token anyway? Take it back to Boston as a memento?"

"I already have a memento," he said, stroking his hand down her cheek.

"Are you referring to the photograph? Or me?" she asked, laughing. "Come on. Get it over with."

He shook his head at her persistence. "Did anyone ever tell you that you can be a little pushy?" he asked, teasing her.

"Many people, many times. Now choose." She splayed her arms wide.

"Fine. This one," he said, indicating a machine that promised a million-dollar payout. "But if the impossible happens and I win, half is yours." He walked over, stuck the token into the slot machine and pushed the spin button. "Satisfied?" he asked, turning away just as bells, lights and whistles went off around them.

"You won!" Amber tugged on his arm and glanced at the machine. "You actually won a hundred and fifty thousand dollars!" She screamed and threw her arms around his neck, squealing in excitement.

The surreal moment played out like a movie, with the head of the casino and security showing up and paying him. *Cash*. Mike couldn't believe it, not even after they'd been escorted back to his room by a security guard via a private elevator.

When the man left and Mike locked the door behind him, he turned to his wife. He and Amber were finally alone.

First thing he did was to kneel in front of the safe in the closet, placing the money inside. "I need a code number I'll remember."

"How about the date? Our anniversary?" Amber suggested. She stood behind him, her hand on the back of his neck, her fingers softly threading through his hair.

Her touch was so arousing he could barely think straight. He punched in the numbers, hit Lock and turned to her.

Without further thought, he swept her into his arms. She shrieked and looped her arms around his neck.

"What are you doing?" she asked.

"I couldn't carry you over the threshold with the security guard standing there, but I can do the next best thing." He stepped toward the large king-size bed he thought he'd be sleeping in alone and laid her down on the mattress. "Today was unbeliev-able. You're my very own lucky charm. I can't be-lieve we just met."

She nodded in agreement. "I feel the same way. It's like I've known you forever."

He grinned and held up her hand with the big, gaudy ring on it. "This and our marriage license says you will."

Her eyes glazed with delight while his heart caught in his throat. She was so beautiful, with her wild blond curls falling over the pillow and her lips moist and welcoming. An angel sent to him from who knows where, someone who wasn't a part of his past, but would be part of his present and future. He couldn't say he minded.

Lowering himself beside her, he bent his head to kiss his bride. They'd been building up to this moment all day and the long, leisurely kisses that had sustained them during the afternoon no longer satisfied him now that they were alone. He kissed her mouth, her cheek, and followed a trail down her jawline, pausing to nibble on her delectable earlobe, grazing her soft flesh gently with his teeth.

She groaned, a husky sound reverberating from low in her throat. Her body tensed and writhed beside him, demanding more. He inhaled the floral scent that had been testing his restraint all afternoon and nearly came right then. But he needed more. Needed to see her naked and exposed just for him.

He reached for the zipper on the back of her dress at the same time she pulled his shirt from the waistband of his jeans. Clearly their first time wouldn't be slow.

She turned and he lowered the zipper, revealing her creamy back. He licked the exposed line of skin and blew gently, a cool stream of air that caused her to arch her back and treat him to another lusty groan. She openly expressed her need, and knowing he caused those hot, sexy sounds drove him insane.

While she shrugged out of her dress, he took off his shirt, jeans and briefs, tossing everything onto the floor beside his shoes. When he turned back, she was naked and waiting. Her little black dress had been deceiving. She had generous curves he hadn't imagined.

Amber trembled as his gaze raked over her, his eyes darkening with approval.

He laid back against the pillows and crooked a finger. She came willingly, settling her body on top of his. Her skin burned with an internal heat that had been building inside her all day. She fit into him, her breasts crushing his chest, his thighs cradling hers, and her wet core settling against his hard, rigid length.

She sucked in a shallow breath. There was nothing soft or giving about his body and yet everything in his expression told her he'd give her everything she asked for and even some things she didn't.

He pulled her hair back from her face, holding it

behind her as he looked into her eyes. "Do you feel how hard you make me?" He lifted his hips and let his erection thrust between her legs.

She closed her eyes, letting the rolling wave wash over her. "Oh, yes."

He slid his hand between them, slipping his index finger into her moist heat. "You're wet," he murmured. "And I'm going to make you wetter." He traced a long path with his tongue, a thorough exploration of her body with his hands, his mouth and light grazing of his teeth. And when he reached her breasts, he dipped his head for a taste, drawing one tight nipple into his mouth.

Amber felt the pull from her aching breasts straight down to her toes and everywhere in between. She glanced down. His dark hair brushed against her bare chest and an overwhelming sensation of rightness swept over her. She'd let him do anything and then do it again.

His hands parted her bare thighs and when he touched her *there,* all rational thought fled. Her focus narrowed until nothing mattered but the exquisite sensations he created in her body. He knew just where to touch her and how.

He held on to her thighs and the sheer eroticism of what he was about to do caused a quickening of excitement in her belly. He laved his tongue over her mound. Long loving strokes followed by quick flickers that brought her closer and closer to release. The pressure built higher and faster until she couldn't take it another minute.

Her hips bucked beneath him and suddenly she cried out, her climax catching her off guard as the waves assaulted her one after another, seemingly without end.

She was barely aware of him leaning away from her and then returning. Just as she began to come back to reality, he tore open a condom and settled himself over her.

"I can't believe you had one on you," she murmured in relief. Protection had been the last thing on her mind and it should have been first.

"It's been in my wallet forever." A flush heightened his cheekbones.

Amber appreciated the admission. "It's been a while for me, as well," she said honestly. "But I'm glad you're the kind of man who likes to be prepared."

"In my family, it pays to be." His eyes shuttered closed, blocking his secrets.

"You'll have to tell me why one day."

"At the moment, I can think of better things to do than talk." He drew her arms up above her head, distracting her with his naked body.

He was sexy, handsome and very, very male. And he was hers.

"What are you grinning about?" he asked.

"I didn't realize I was." Obviously thinking

about him made her smile, but she wasn't ready to admit that just yet.

Although her father had been her guardian, she'd had to be independent and she'd raised herself in his unorthodox world. She'd been alone and on her own for longer than she cared to remember and she liked the notion that she had someone to share things with now. The logistics between them didn't matter. They'd work those out in time. Right now, the ring and the license proved they were a couple.

"I'm just thinking, if my first…um, climax was so amazing, the next one will be off the charts."

He brushed his thumb over her moist lips. "Because I'll be inside you." As he spoke, he nudged himself between her thighs.

He was rock hard and she wanted, needed, to have him fill her in the most basic, primal way. She bent her knees to help him ease his way. Without breaking eye contact, he thrust deep inside. Her entire body felt the penetration as she accepted all of him and she drew in a shallow breath.

"Hey, are you okay?" he asked, glancing at her with concern.

She nodded. "I told you it had been a while."

He leaned forward and pressed a kiss to her lips, silently telling her he appreciated that fact. "Let's make it easier on you." With a slick motion, he rolled to the side, taking her with him and settling her on top, straddling him. "Now you're in control."

He placed his hands on her waist and rolled his hips upward, causing a rippling swell of rising need in her as their bodies ground together all too briefly before the tide eased.

She moaned at the sensual assault and picked up his rhythm, rocking her hips from side to side, reveling each time their bodies touched at just the right spot, and the pressure inside her built higher. Together they created the perfect ride and it wasn't long before she was moaning aloud as she clenched her inner walls harder around his rigid length.

His grip tightened on her waist and his pace grew more frenzied. Unable to hold herself up any longer, she stretched forward, leaning across him and letting her chest press hard against his. Heat assaulted her from the intimate contact and her nipples puckered tighter, pressing into him, the friction adding to the spiraling heights to which she was ascending.

Suddenly he let out a low groan, thrust his hand into the back of her hair and kissed her hard, his body frantically pumping upward, as he pulsed inside her and took her along with him. Her climax was all consuming, rippling through her with lightning speed. As one glorious wave ended, another began. Finally, she lay on top of him, spent and oh so satisfied.

MIKE AWOKE to a pounding headache the likes of which he hadn't felt since his college days and the smell of coffee brewing. Disoriented, it took a few minutes to remember. Las Vegas for Dan and Natalie's wedding, rescuing the beautiful blonde from the guy manhandling her, spending the day partying, winning a hundred and fifty grand and—*holy shit*—getting married?

He ran his hand through his hair and sat upright in bed. The quick movement was hell on his fuzzy head, but the events of yesterday were suddenly crystal clear. He had married Amber Rose.

He already knew he was alone in bed, but the smell of coffee told him she was up, and the sound of the fan indicated she was probably in the bathroom. He drew a deep breath and let the reality settle in.

He was married.

To Amber.

Surprisingly, he wasn't upset by the notion.

He'd grown up watching his father descend into reclusive madness because of love lost and the damn curse. With Amber, he'd had fun. And if they could make the logistics work, maybe they could have a decent life together without invoking the notion of his losing everything like the rest of the men in his family.

Although his cousin Derek was currently married to the love of his life, everyone around them felt as if they were walking on proverbial eggshells waiting for something bad to happen. Which made

Amber, who made him laugh and whom he enjoyed, something of a perfect catch. Even if they'd tied the knot in a Vegas chapel the same day they'd met.

He rose to check on his *wife,* eager to see her again and repeat the amazing sex they'd had last night. Just thinking about her warm body and the incredible noises she made had him hard and ready in an instant.

A full pot of coffee sat on the counter in the sitting area, but she wasn't there. The bathroom door was ajar and he could see she wasn't standing by the sink, either. He didn't hear the water running, but he stepped into the bathroom anyway, his gut churning as he took in the empty shower stall.

He was alone in the hotel room. Telling himself not to panic, he slowly walked to the closet and opened the door, praying he was wrong.

But the safe was open and the money gone.

All one hundred and fifty thousand dollars of it. And so was his new wife.

CHAPTER THREE

"I'VE GOT YOUR father."

Amber hadn't believed Marshall when she'd picked up a call from him on her cell phone while she was making coffee for Mike. She'd immediately hung up and dialed the nursing home, asking them to put her father on the line. He no longer had a phone in his room, since there really was no need. Carole, the day nurse, told her that Marshall had taken him out for lunch to meet Amber.

In the early days at the home, all her father had asked for was a weekly outing with Amber or Marshall, something to make him feel he still had the freedom to visit his favorite places with people he enjoyed. It had seemed a small thing to put Marshall's name on the list of people allowed to remove him from the home for outside visits. Only Amber, Marshall and Amber's closest friend, Paul, the bar owner who'd been her best friend since childhood, were allowed access. Paul was the second emergency contact.

As the days wore on and her father seldom

roused himself from staring vacantly into space, the outings stopped. She only came to visit and talk, hoping to catch a spark of something in his expression. She'd forgotten about the list she'd given the home of people allowed to take her father out.

Marshall hadn't.

J.R. had told him about Mike's winnings and that's what Marshall wanted. Mike's one hundred and fifty thousand dollars in exchange for her father.

Sweating in the un-air-conditioned taxi, she grit her teeth on the half-hour ride to the restaurant where Marshall had brought her father, wondering how her life had turned around so quickly.

One minute Amber had been feeling that everything was right in the world. She'd met Mike at the right time, when she was not only ready for a change, but needed one desperately. Marshall and the card-counting life she so despised were behind her. Instead, she'd go home to Boston with Mike, get settled and bring her father to a local nursing home nearby. She could get a job at a Boston hotel, get hired on as a concierge again, and somehow between them, she could make things work.

But as soon as her cell phone rang, she knew she'd been spinning fantasies that could never come true. Unless she got the chance to explain and make Mike trust her again when this was all over.

Her thoughts were interrupted when the cab

came to a stop in front of the restaurant. Amber tossed the driver a generous amount of money, grabbed the hotel laundry bag full of cash and jumped out of the car.

She started to run, then caught herself. Marshall thrived on his opponent's fear. If he sensed weakness, she'd lose whatever little bit of leverage she might possess. It was bad enough she was dressed in yesterday's rumpled cocktail dress, her hair a tangled mess. She could, at least, act calm and unruffled.

Drawing a deep breath, she walked inside and headed to the back of the restaurant where her father sat in his favorite chair, staring at nothing in front of him.

Ignoring Marshall, Amber walked over to Sam and kissed his cheek. "Are you okay, Daddy?" she asked him.

No reply. Not that she expected one. It was enough that he was here and safe.

"Of course he's okay. Mezze Luna is his favorite restaurant. As you can see I ordered him pasta Bolognese, his favorite meal. Join us." Marshall gestured to the seat next to him.

Amber sat stiffly. She didn't want to have an argument in front of her father because he tended to get upset if the dynamics around him were unfriendly. Until she had him safely back in the home and Marshall's name removed from the list of visitors, she had to play the game.

"Would you like something to eat?" Marshall asked.

"No, thank you."

"Really? I'm sure you and your new husband worked up quite an appetite last night," he said, not bothering to hide the disdain on his face.

She narrowed her gaze. "How did you know about that?" She thought she'd lost J.R.

"The same way I knew about the money. J.R. was keeping an eye on you and he's good at his job. You're not just my meal ticket, Amber. I care about you and I promised your father I'd look after you. Didn't I, Sam?"

Amber didn't look at him. Whenever she'd thought of getting married, she'd always imagined her father walking her down the aisle of a beautiful church, packed with family and friends. Not a quickie Las Vegas ceremony. Ironically, it wasn't the lack of frills that bothered her, it was the seedy way Marshall made her actions sound in front of her only parent. That and the fact that Sam couldn't have been there, but she'd come to terms with his illness. She just resented Marshall's using him as a pawn in his game.

"I'm not hungry, so let's get on with it. I brought what you want. Now I'd like to take my father back to the home." She placed the white bag on the table and rose.

"Not so fast," Marshall said, ice in his voice. "Your father is still eating. Is it good?" he asked Sam in a softer tone.

Amber wasn't fooled. Marshall obviously had more on his mind than her father's meal.

"Besides, I'm not finished with you yet," he added coldly, proving her hunch correct.

Her stomach rolled, but she refused to let her panic show. She lowered herself back into her seat. "You got your money. What else could you possibly want?"

"You. Me. One more game."

She shook her head. "Oh, no. I already told you I'm out." Her voice rose to an unsettling pitch.

"You made my favorite meat loaf tonight?" Sam interrupted, from beside her. But he wasn't talking to Amber.

He was talking to Amber's mother, the woman he loved, and the days he returned to when he spoke at all. At times like this, he was having what the nurses called a bad day. Something—or in this case someone—had rattled him.

"It's pasta," Amber said in a soothing voice.

She shot a frosty glare at Marshall.

"It was your tone that got to him. Don't blame me." He held up both hands as if he had done nothing wrong.

Her jaw hurt from clenching her teeth to keep the vile words inside her from spilling forward.

"One more job," Marshall said pleasantly. "That hundred and fifty grand is my stake. I owe some nasty men two-fifty. Once I pay that back and I know my legs and other body parts will remain intact, you can go and never see me again."

She should only be so lucky. "And if I refuse?"

He patted Sam's hand. "Your dad and I go for a ride." He leaned in closer to Amber and whispered in her ear, "And you never see him again."

Amber knew she was cornered. But she wasn't giving up without going for whatever she could, first.

She snatched the money bag back. "Half now and half before we buy in tonight. I want to get my father situated and safe first." She'd have to find another nursing home, she thought. One where Marshall had no access to him. She couldn't risk something like this ever happening again.

"Not a problem. When your father finishes eating, we'll go together. We'll take your father back, then you can go home and get cleaned up for tonight. I'll watch TV and wait, then we can head out, get a few drinks first to loosen up, and do our thing." He smiled at her.

She forced a smile back.

In other words, she was screwed. He wasn't letting her out of his sight and she'd have no chance to contact Mike until this mess with Marshall was over. By that time, she doubted he'd ever want to hear from her again.

MIKE HAD BEEN CONNED. Hours later, after combing the coffee shops, restaurants and the casino of his hotel, after he'd spoken to the few remaining hotel staff who'd been on duty last night, and after he'd spent the better part of the day scouring all the places he and Amber had visited together in the hopes of running into her again, Mike had to face the truth.

She was gone.

He still shook his head in disbelief. He'd acted like a gullible kid, not a trained cop who knew better than to pick up a strange woman, drink enough to dull all his senses except his hormones, marry her, share the combination to his safe with her and sleep with her. In that order.

He'd had a good buzz going, but he hadn't been completely intoxicated. He'd thought, really believed, he'd seen something honest in her eyes and felt something real between them.

If he was superstitious, he'd say that was the problem. He'd felt something for her, something he'd wanted to explore more deeply. And because he had, his father would say the damn curse had kicked in. He'd lost his fortune and his future love.

If he were superstitious.

At the moment, though, he just felt damn stupid.

Once he got home, he'd have the resources to track Amber down. Until then, he settled for asking Jillian, back at the station in Boston, to run a check on the name Amber Rose from Vegas. A few hours later, Jillian reported back. All he knew was that there was no Amber Rose in the criminal system. Either she'd been clean until she wiped out his hotel safe or she was *that good*.

Any further information would have to wait. Mike wasn't about to explain about Amber to anyone else, a necessity if he wanted any cops in Vegas to do him the professional courtesy of digging into her past. That would mean sharing his stupidity. And he damn sure wasn't ready to do that. Not with strangers and not with the friends he'd come to Vegas with.

But he wasn't finished with *his wife*. Not by a long shot, he thought, fingering the marriage certificate on the table. The next time he had a few days off, he'd return to Vegas and do some digging on his own. He'd find Amber, if that was her real name, and get himself a quick explanation and an even quicker divorce. But both of those things depended on his finding her.

Unfortunately, he had to be in court first thing Monday. Amber Rose would have to wait.

WITH AMBER BY HIS SIDE, Marshall used Mike's money to buy into the game, located in a penthouse

suite at an upscale hotel. As Marshall exchanged
Mike's money for chips, Amber tried to console
herself with the thought that Mike had promised
her that if he won at slots, half would be hers. So
in reality she'd only stolen half his money. Bor-
rowed would be a better term. But changing her
words didn't ease her guilty conscience.

It was all Mike's money and she hadn't intended
to take any of it. But she and her *partner* had an
agreement. And if tonight went the way it was supposed to, she'd be able to pay Mike back every last
cent and hopefully buy herself a second chance
with him.

Marshall had his slick image going tonight. He'd
greased back his hair and donned a white jacket
so he'd look like Andy Garcia in *Ocean's Eleven,*
at least in whatever mirror he viewed himself in.
When Amber looked at him, she only saw a lying
bastard.

"Since everyone's here, let's get started," Marshall said.

Bobby Boyd, a used-car dealer from Texas with
a ten-gallon hat and enough bluster for one hundred
men, nodded. "Texas hold 'em, boys. No one beats
King Bobby at his favorite game."

He'd called himself King Bobby at least a dozen
times since their initial introduction. Bobby Boyd
owned a number of used-car dealerships throughout Texas or so he claimed along with the title of

millionaire. Google would tell all…if she cared to find out. She didn't.

"Remember, little lady, if your boyfriend here wins, King Bobby will hook you up with your choice of one of the finest vehicles in all of Texas," he said to Amber.

He let out a huge guffaw of laughter, presumably because nobody beat King Bobby at Texas hold 'em. Ergo, she'd never see one of his cars.

"Ain't my man sweet?" Emmy Lou, a Dolly Parton look-alike, only older, asked.

"He's a…king," Amber managed to say with a smile.

Emmy Lou preened and hugged King Bobby tight. "Give me room, woman. The King needs to breathe if he's gonna win."

What happened next passed in a blur of shuffling, dealing and big and little blinds. Amber needed to pay attention so she could signal Marshall, but she was having trouble focusing on anything but Emmy Lou. The woman had probably been beautiful once, even if it had been in an overdone way, but age and lifestyle had obviously taken their toll. Her eyes were bloodshot, her face lined and dry, makeup caked in the cracks, while her breasts drooped so low, her cleavage had long ago stopped being an asset. She appeared oblivious to all these facts as she clung to her man, one who obviously took her for granted.

Whether she was his permanent squeeze or his bimbo of the night, Amber didn't want to know. Either way, the woman's life was sad and pathetic. And as Amber looked from her own cleavage across to Emmy Lou's and met the other woman's red-rimmed eyes, she saw a glimpse of what her future would have been—would be—if she didn't stick to her plan to get away from Marshall as soon as this one last game ended.

"Whoo-wee! King Bobby caught himself a nine on the river!" Bobby swooped forward and gathered the pot of winnings from the middle of the table.

Amber cringed. When she glanced around the table, she realized she'd spaced out on more than just one hand.

During a break, Marshall stormed over and grabbed her arm. "Get your shit together or this is over. And if I go down, you don't get your hundred and fifty grand to pay your husband back, either," he ground out under his breath.

"I'll be fine." She jerked her arm away, her stomach cramping.

"You'd better be or your father won't." He tossed out that little reminder before rejoining the table.

The game restarted and Amber kept her attention where it was supposed to be. Soon, Marshall was raking in chips. He didn't take every hand or else King Bobby and the rest of the table would

know something was up. She didn't overdo her sig-
nals to Marshall until the men grew drunker and
louder and the stakes rose higher.

Grateful they'd passed the halfway mark and
knowing she was due for a performance, she strode
to Marshall, "Baby, you're winning!" she cooed.
"Don't forget that gorgeous diamond necklace I
saw in Aladdin's. Just think how that piece will
look around my little neck." She wrapped her arms
around him, letting her cleavage nearly spill from
her slinky dress to display exactly where the necklace belonged. And to distract the other men from
their hands.

"It ain't over yet, little lady. King Bobby's just
warming up." The heavy man rubbed his hands together and tipped his hat backward off his ruddy
face.

"Come on, King Bobby, give a lady a break."
Amber deliberately pouted at him.

Marshall cleared his throat. "Move over, baby.
Let the men play."

Sulking, she stepped back.

"Hey, you look familiar." Howard, one of the
men at the table, said, staring at Amber. "I recognize you from Beverly Hills."

For a split second Amber froze. She and Marshall
had one hard-and-fast rule. If something seemed
off, they cut their losses and ran. The money wasn't

worth their lives if they crossed the wrong people. Nothing that extreme had happened. Yet.

Catching herself, Amber gave her best bimbo giggle and said, "Isn't that funny? He thinks I'm from Beverly Hills. I must look like a *star!*" Amber said in her ditziest voice.

Marshall rolled his eyes. "I'm laughing, baby."

"Because I don't look like a movie star?" she asked, insulted.

He shook his head. "Because you've never been outside Vegas." Marshall turned to the dealer. "Are we going to play?"

Howard didn't appear satisfied, but the antes began and he refocused on his cards.

She let out a huge sigh of relief. When she saw a chance for Howard to win, Amber let Marshall's opportunity pass in order to keep Howard's mind on his cards and not where he'd met her once before. She didn't need her real world colliding with her fake one. Not tonight, when the stakes determined both hers and Marshall's future.

Over the next half hour, Marshall's pot grew larger, King Bobby grew nastier, and Howard kept passing her covert glances that made her uneasy.

A quick tally in her head told her Marshall had won what he needed and she was halfway to paying back Mike. They were almost there.

"Bobby, honey, were you able to get us into the Country Club for dinner?" Emmy Lou asked. The exclusive restaurant in the Wynn hotel was world famous.

"Damn, woman, can't you see I'm busy? Call the concierge and find out if she made us a reservation if you want to. But let King Bobby be." He tossed her his cell phone.

"That's it!" Howard rose from his seat.

"Don't tell me this yahoo won again," King Bobby muttered. "It's enough that guy's messing with the King's mojo tonight." He gestured to Marshall.

A skittering of dread rushed through Amber and the hair on her arms stood on end.

"No, I just remembered where I saw her before." Howard pointed to Amber. "I may not remember the name, but I never forget a face. You were the concierge at some hotel in Beverly Hills."

Amber breathed in deep and forced a silly giggle. "Me, a concierge?" She turned to Marshall. "Baby, he thinks I'm smart enough to be a concierge."

"Lord, a man can't concentrate tonight what with these women gaggling like geese and this guy worried about where he met some two-bit whore before," Chuck, another man from somewhere in the Midwest, said angrily.

"He's got a point. I fold," Marshall said, tossing down his cards.

Amber didn't need to count again to know they

didn't have all the money they needed. At least, not enough for her to return to Mike with a semi-clean conscience, an explanation and a plea for forgiveness.

"That's it for me." Marshall rose.

"But honey, the necklace—"

"Maybe another time." He gathered his chips, cashed in, ignoring her tapping foot behind him and King Bobby's loud complaints that Marshall wasn't giving him a chance to win his cash back.

Once he was finished, Marshall grabbed her arm hard enough to leave a bruise and guided her out the door while saying his goodbyes all at the same time.

It wasn't easy, but Amber held in her angry explosion until they were safely in the car and out of earshot of anyone from the game.

"How the hell could you walk before we won what we needed?" she yelled at him.

He started the car. "In case that genius brain of yours missed it, I won what I needed." He dug into her large purse, pulled out the wad of big bills he'd stuffed in there and counted out the bundles. "Here." He slapped seventy-five thousand dollars onto her lap.

"That isn't enough."

"Too bad. You were fingered and we had an agreement. Cut and run at the first sign of trouble."

Amber was so furious she could barely think

straight. "That idiot Howard wouldn't know what to do with the information anyway. It didn't matter. There was no danger. You just wanted to play chicken with *my cut!*"

He turned toward her. "Chicken?" He shook his head. "I'm just being damn smart. *I'm* out of hot water. But what are you going to do? Go back to your husband with half his money and explain why you ran out on him?" He laughed at her predicament. "Or are you going to hide out here in Vegas? I don't much care. But I wasn't about to make your life any easier. Not after you screwed me by walking out of mine. And after all I've done for you." He shook his head and put the car in Drive.

She clamped her mouth shut tight. He'd left her twisting in the wind on purpose. Giving her the option to return to Mike with half the money or run away from him for good, assuming he didn't track her down and press charges. The man was a cop, after all.

She squeezed her temples with her hands. Neither option held much appeal.

AMBER KNOCKED on Mike's hotel-room door, her stomach churning with cold fear. Facing him again wouldn't be easy, but even if he turned her away, she owed him an explanation. That and another seventy-five thousand dollars, she thought, wonder-

ing how in the hell she'd raise that kind of money
while paying for her father's care.

Maybe Mike took MasterCard.

Or maybe he'd understand and let her pay him
back over time. She seemed like a different woman
than the one who was spinning fantasies of a new
life with Mike just this very morning.

Five minutes later, someone from housekeeping
arrived with a cart to clean the room, and informed
her the guest had checked out. Amber returned to
the elevator, disappointed but not completely de-
feated.

She had his full name and knew he was a cop
who lived in Boston. She stepped through the
lobby, engrossed in devising a plan to find him,
when she caught sight of a ten-gallon hat and the
big man wearing it.

King Bobby Boyd stood at the concierge desk
talking to Amber's friend Caroline. Beside him
stood Emmy Lou. Their game had been in a room
in another hotel. None of the high-stakes players
knew where anyone else was staying. For all she
knew, King Bobby could be staying at the Bellagio, too. It suited his larger-than-life taste. He
hadn't been pleased at the outcome of the night and
Amber didn't want to have a conversation with him
now, not with seventy-five thousand dollars hanging from the large handbag on her shoulder.

Not wanting to be seen, Amber ducked behind

a pole, and when a large group of people passed by, she strode out among them, hoping to get lost in the crowd.

"Amber, honey!"

Amber recognized Emmy Lou's distinctive Texas drawl and her stomach rolled in a panic. Gut instinct told her to run, so she did, ducking past all the people in the cab line, slipping a twenty into the valet's hand and grabbing the first open taxi, ahead of the line of people waiting.

"Just drive," she told the man, not sure where she wanted to go yet. Her heart pounding, she needed to calm down and think.

First she had to find out why King Bobby had been at the hotel. Had he been asking about her? She pulled out her cell phone and searched her contacts for the direct line to Caroline at the concierge desk in the Bellagio. Although it had been a while since she'd had to utilize them, Amber had friends like Caroline all around the country, especially in L.A. and here in her hometown. In her former job, she had to be connected to anyone who could find anything at all hours of the day or night. She'd prided herself on the ability to hunt down the most obscure item any guest desired. If she couldn't find it, she had a network of other concierges who might. All she'd had to do was send out an SOS and she'd have hundreds of people helping her out.

The person who found the item was owed a favor.
Amber had thrived on those challenges.

She missed her old job and her old life. A life
she'd worked hard for, one she'd been proud of instead of the one she lived now.

Caroline answered quickly. "Caroline du Zutter,
Bellagio concierge, how may I assist you?"

"Caroline, it's Amber Rose. I know its been a
while but—"

"Your ears must have been ringing! I've had the
most interesting day involving you."

Amber leaned forward in the cab. "Keep driving," she said to the taxi driver. "I'll let you know
where to go soon. Sorry, go on," she said to Caroline.

"Two people came by looking for you today. The
first was a gorgeous hunk of a man who asked if
you were registered at the hotel."

"Mike," Amber said aloud.

"Detective Michael Corwin of the Boston P.D.
to be exact."

Amber swallowed hard, memories of the man
still strong in her mind. "What did you tell him?"

"Nothing. He didn't ask me. He asked Nikki,
who was just finishing her shift from last night.
She's new. She said she didn't know you. He left
his card and said if she heard anything to contact
him. Then she asked me when I came on duty. I
played dumb."

"I owe you, Caroline."

"Hey, until I spoke to you and knew what he wanted, I wasn't giving you away. But I have to tell you, Nikki pointed him out as he was leaving. That is one gorgeous guy. Any chance you want to share information on him?"

Amber forced a laugh. "Not yet. Who else was asking about me?"

"A big loud Texan. He was booking dinner reservations when his wife started calling your name. I turned and didn't see you, but she was upset you didn't stick around. That's when the Texan asked her what she expected, considering he'd been fleeced. I didn't know what he meant and I don't much care. The man's so full of hot air, you can't believe anything that comes out of his mouth, little lady," Caroline said in a poor imitation of King Bobby.

This time Amber laughed for real. "Good call. A friend of mine pissed him off. Nothing to worry about." She crossed her fingers to cover her lie. "So nobody gave anything away, that's a relief."

"Well…" Caroline's voice rose in pitch. "The man started ranting about how he was *connected,* that if he didn't get answers, he'd call in favors and we'd all be in trouble. I didn't believe him. He blows too much smoke."

Amber's stomach cramped because King Bobby *did* strike her as dangerous. If he had any kind of underworld connections, she'd be in big trouble if he blamed her for his losses last night. "Then what happened?" Amber asked.

"Remember Danny Heath?" Caroline said the man's name with disdain.

"The bellboy from hell." Amber recalled him too well from the old days, when Danny had worked at the Crown Cladler.

"One and the same," Caroline said. "He heard the Texan talking and insinuated he knew something about you. Before I could blink, the big guy slipped Danny a fifty and Danny told him you used to be a concierge in Beverly Hills. I sent him off on an errand before he could give anything more away."

"You're a lifesaver. You have my cell number, right? Can you keep me posted if anyone else comes looking for me?"

"ASAP," the other woman promised.

"I owe you," Amber said again.

"Hey, you're the best at digging there is. I'm sure I'll collect."

"Anytime," Amber promised, disconnecting the call.

Deep in thought, she pinched the bridge of her nose. King Bobby knew her first name and her former occupation. And after Howard had told everyone she was from L.A., Amber knew Bobby could eventually track her down. But it would take a lot of time, money, patience and a reason for him to waste them all.

Pride was a darn good reason and King Bobby was loaded with it. What did he suspect? And who was he after? If he even sensed that she'd been in on Marshall's scam… She shivered at the thought.

She pulled out her marriage license and smoothed out the wrinkles on the paper. "Michael Corwin born in Stewart, Massachusetts, residing in Boston," she read to herself. She bit the inside of her cheek, conjuring up her sexy savior.

Just the thought of him set her body tingling.

Her first priority, as always, was her father and keeping him safe. She needed to settle him into another nursing home immediately.

When she'd chosen his current home, she'd also strongly considered another residence that was as clean, safe…and affordable. She'd move him there. And she'd make sure that the only visitors allowed would be herself and her friend Paul.

Paul had lived in the house next door to her grandparents when she'd lived with them as a teen and they'd been best friends ever since, keeping in touch over the years. He was like the brother she'd never had and he'd be more than willing to take care of her father for her. Most important, she could trust him to keep her whereabouts a secret.

With the cash resources she had saved and allocated for her father's immediate care, Paul would be able to handle getting her dad settled while she got herself out of town.

Once she was safely on a plane to Boston, she'd have plenty of time to figure out how to handle Mike.

SHE'D BE BACK. It was only a matter of time, Marshall thought. Not because Amber loved the life the way he did, but because they were a team. She'd been raised at her father's knee and she'd learned all the tricks of the trade, but she had something extra. She'd been blessed with a memory as gorgeous as the rest of her.

And she was his. Oh, sure, she'd married that cop and at first that pissed Marshall off. But he realized she needed a wake-up call. She'd done the same thing once before, gone to live her life in L.A., but she'd come back.

To him.

As soon as she needed someone to lean on, she returned to Marshall. She'd be back again when that stupid, straight-as-an-arrow cop broke her heart. And he'd be waiting with open arms.

CHAPTER FOUR

COURT HAD BEEN a breeze thanks to a green public defender straight out of law school. The guy didn't know what he was doing, which meant Mike got out in time for lunch. He headed directly to the café near the station to meet his cousin Derek, who'd called early this morning, needing to talk.

Mike had a gut feeling his father, Edward, was causing trouble again, in one of his unpredictable irrational attempts to protect the family from the curse. It didn't seem to matter that the curse had originated centuries ago and those who had perpetuated its belief were no longer wreaking havoc in his hometown.

The Perkins family had settled on the coast and made their money in real estate and shipping. Just recently, Mary Perkins, the descendant of the original so-called witch who had placed the curse on the Corwin family during the era of the Salem witch trials, was in jail for blackmail, conspiracy and a whole host of other crimes. Meanwhile, her granddaughter and namesake was in a mental institution until she was deemed fit to stand trial for arson. She'd burned down the Wave, a nightclub that had been an institution in the town of Perkins. Both women had used the Corwin curse to hold on to power in the town. With them out of commission, the younger Corwin generation, Mike, twenty-seven, Jason, twenty-six and Derek, thirty-two, hoped the old stories would die out. Unfortunately, their fathers wouldn't let it. The older generation still believed in the curse.

Mike's father most of all. Or at least, he was the one who'd taken fear of it to the most extreme.

After Mike's experience in Vegas with Amber— meeting and marrying, half convincing himself he could have something special with this woman, a *stranger,* because of some connection he'd felt, only to lose both her and his winnings—he could almost begin to see why his father believed in such nonsense.

Almost.

He arrived at the café to find Derek already there. The cousins were similar in looks, with dark hair, but Derek kept his short while Mike avoided the barber's chair.

"Hey, cousin, how's life treating you?" Mike asked, sliding into the plastic-cushioned booth across from Derek.

"Pretty damn good considering." Derek grinned,

the same smile he'd been sporting since marrying his high-school sweetheart, Gabrielle Donovan.

"Considering the curse?" Mike asked knowingly.

Unlike Mike, who just didn't deal with the curse, Derek had openly avoided it, breaking up with Gabrielle before college to avoid the fate of the rest of the Corwin men. Later, he'd gotten another woman pregnant, married her hoping to have a family and a child without invoking the curse because there'd been no love involved. The marriage had failed anyway. And Gabrielle, a successful author, had returned to prove to Mike's stubborn cousin there was no such thing as a curse—just coincidence and bad choices. She was still proving it, every day of their almost year-long marriage. Though Derek was wary, he was too much in love to live without her.

Derek leaned forward on the table. "Considering your father is making us insane."

"Can I take your orders?" a waitress asked, interrupting at just the right—or wrong—moment.

Derek shut his menu and ordered a hamburger and fries.

"Make that two, please," Mike said.

They both ordered colas and the waitress left, leaving Mike to return to the subject at hand.

"Okay, what's the old man done now?" he asked.

Derek's gaze darkened. "He's into voodoo."

Mike wasn't surprised. In the last few years, his

father had taken to alternative religions to ward off the curse. Juju dolls hung from the trees lining the path leading up to his secluded house and he'd erected ancient totem poles for protection. Mike didn't understand Edward's reasoning and didn't want to try. The farther he stayed from the insanity, the better.

"What's going on?" Mike reluctantly asked.

"He's spooking Gabrielle and you know that isn't easy to do."

As an author who made a living dispelling paranormal beliefs, Gabrielle wasn't easily scared. If Edward was upsetting Gabrielle, he must have gone too far. "Tell me." Mike gestured to Derek to continue.

"Well, we wanted to keep it quiet, but about six months ago, Gabrielle had a miscarriage," Derek said, his voice low.

"Damn." Mike shook his head, absorbing the news. "I had no idea. I'm sorry," Mike said to his cousin.

Derek inclined his head, acknowledging the words. "According to the doctor, it was a freak thing. There's no reason to think it will happen again or prevent us from having a healthy baby."

"Thank God." Mike expelled the breath he'd been holding.

"And we're trying again." Derek grinned once more. "But your father found out about the miscarriage. We figure he overheard Gabrielle and her friend Sharon talking about it in town." He shook his head. "Ever since he's been obsessed with protecting her."

Mike muttered an expletive under his breath. "I'm sorry. All it takes is the slightest problem when a Corwin man is in love and my father loses it."

Derek shook his head. "He's already lost it, Mike."

Mike knew. He just hated facing it because, too often as a child, he'd feared ending up like his father. As an adult, he prided himself on how well he had things together. He had a job as a cop, a career that enabled him to protect others, something he never quite felt he'd been able to do for his father. Edward fought his own demons. Mike fought other people's, at least in a way, and remained sane.

"Look, we know my father has issues."

"Right. The problem is, he's spreading the insanity now. Gabrielle came home the other day to find red dust sprinkled outside the front door."

"In Boston or Stewart?" Mike asked, since his cousin and his wife had a house in their small hometown village of Stewart and a Brownstone in downtown Boston. Gabrielle had lived in Boston before she'd gotten back together with Derek and they'd kept her place as a city retreat or an office in case Gabrielle was on deadline and needed peace and quiet.

"Stewart. But thanks for reminding me. I'm going to have to check the brownstone before I leave. I'd hate for Gabrielle to find a present from your father next time she visits."

"I'm sure your place in Boston is fine. I can't see my father going too far, can you?" The man rarely went into Stewart, let alone ventured beyond the town lines.

Derek shook his head. "But you never know. The red dust was followed by a string of juju dolls across the doorway. Gabrielle said she was damn near decapitated by the fishing line he used."

"I'll talk to him," Mike promised. "I'll call him tonight."

"I think he disconnected his phone line. Afraid of traveling spirits or some such nonsense."

Mike raised his eyebrows in surprise. "Are you sure? I just spoke to him before I left for Vegas on Thursday."

"Did you call him or—"

"He called me from his cell."

"No wires." Derek shrugged. "Don't ask me. It makes sense to him, that's all I know. I paid him a visit on Saturday and he explained to me. I told him as nicely as possible that Gabrielle appreciates his concern but she doesn't want his spirit-invoking items left in surprise places." Derek spread his hands in front of him. "I just don't think it sunk in."

Mike nodded. "I can't imagine it would. He's too obsessed. I'll see what I can do," he promised.

But Mike didn't hold out much hope. Renee, Mike's mother, had threatened to leave Edward when the craziness became too much for her to handle, and when nothing changed, she followed through. Since then Edward hadn't changed, only sunken deeper into his own world.

The waitress arrived with their burgers. While she put their plates on the table, Mike silently thought about his parents' so-called cursed marriage.

Renee had fallen for Edward in the early days when he'd been fairly normal. But before she'd met him, Edward had been in love with another woman, Sara Jean. And Edward's brother, Thomas, had fallen in love with her, too. When Sara married Thomas, something in Edward died. Rumors she'd been Edward's second choice and Edward's own hard-to-live-with personality, which only grew worse over time, led Renee to finally leave him.

Mike's mother was now happily married to a doctor and living a normal life. Mike envied her.

Mike would do what he could for his cousin and his wife, but knowing Edward, once he had his mind set on a course of action regarding the curse, nothing would change his mind.

Mike turned his attention to lunch. "I'm starving. Long day in court," he said, taking a large bite of the burger without bothering to add ketchup first.

"So on to more exciting things. How was Vegas?" Derek asked, taking a bite, as well.

At the mention of the subject Mike had been trying not to think about without any success, he lost his appetite.

"That good a time?" Derek asked into the silence.

Mike knew if there was anyone he could trust with the truth, it was his cousin Derek. "You know that expression 'what happens in Vegas stays in Vegas'?"

The other man inclined his head. "Yeah…?"

Mike drew a deep breath and told his cousin the entire story.

"So basically both the woman and the cash stayed in Vegas," Derek concluded for him. He shook his head. "Holy shit. Why don't you press charges? You're a cop, after all."

"That is why. Where's my credibility after I admit publicly that I let myself be taken in by the oldest con in the book?" And that's what still got to him.

What prevented him from sleeping on the plane back to Boston late Saturday night and again in his own bed last evening. How had he misread Amber so completely? Her sincere gaze, her genuine excitement, that *connection*.

"I have to talk to her again first." Because things just didn't add up. He was a cop who acted on gut instinct and he was seldom wrong.

"Ego." Derek finished his soda and signaled for a refill. "You can't admit she conned you, so you're going to let her get away with it?"

"I'm going back to Vegas first chance I get. I'm going to find her, and then get some answers, and a divorce."

"Don't forget to press charges," Derek said. "Now I have another question for you."

"Shoot."

"To quote Jay Leno to Hugh Grant, 'What the hell were you thinking?'"

He hadn't been thinking. He'd been feeling and everything he'd felt had been so damn good. Which only made him feel more like a fool in the cold light of day.

"Never mind. Let me know when you plan to go back. I'll go along and help you out," Derek said.

"I appreciate it." But Mike probably wouldn't call his cousin.

Next time he faced Amber, he wanted to be alone.

A little while later, Mike left Derek and headed to the station to finish up some paperwork before starting his shift tomorrow. He'd taken today off in case court ran long, so he might as well make productive use of the rest of his day.

By the time he headed home, jet lag and plain old exhaustion beat at him. He let himself into his apartment and was immediately on alert. The dead bolt wasn't flipped shut. He'd been tired this morning, but he couldn't have been too tired to lock up.

Hand on his holstered weapon, he stepped inside. Everything seemed normal. He walked through the entry, gave a cursory glance into the kitchen, passed the empty den, entered his bedroom and nearly keeled over.

Amber lay in his bed wearing nothing but one of his collared shirts. She was a vision. The shirt was buttoned low, showing off a generous hint of cleavage, making his mouth water. Her long, bare legs peeked from beneath the hem of the too-big shirt. Her red-painted toenails teased him from beneath his navy blanket. And those riotous blond curls fell over her shoulders in gorgeous disarray, making him forget everything but his body's immediate and obvious reaction.

He blinked, certain she was nothing more than a mirage, but when he opened his eyes, the vision remained. That was when he noticed the rest.

She lay on his bed surrounded by cold hard cash.

"Amber?"

He still didn't believe she was real, even as every emotion imaginable rushed through him, from desire to relief, shock to gratitude, curiosity back to desire again.

Until she spoke. "Hi, honey, I'm home." She waved at him.

Anger, the emotion he should have felt first, finally emerged. "What the hell is going on?"

"I know you're angry and you have every right to be, but before you say another word, look around me. Money. Granted, it isn't all of it, in fact it's half. Less cab money and airline fare, but I can explain—"

"Get dressed." He stepped forward and began collecting the clothes she'd left scattered at the foot of the bed, tossing them at her. "I'll meet you in the other room."

He couldn't think clearly when she was stark naked beneath his shirt, lying seductively in his bed. Memories of making love to her came at him from all sides and he needed his head on straight to deal with her rationally like the sober cop he was now, not the guy who'd rescued her in Vegas and then let her sucker him.

IT COULD HAVE GONE WORSE, Amber thought. She'd seen a flicker of desire in Mike's gaze before he'd banked it in favor of his anger.

She could work with that flicker. Amber had one goal and one only—she wanted to get back to having a real life, one similar to her life before her father had grown ill. Mike and this sudden marriage offered her possibilities she wanted to explore more fully. And she wanted that chance.

Before he could let his emotions overcome him and refuse to deal with her at all, she slipped on her shoes and headed for the other room.

She found him, arms crossed, staring out the window onto the street below. Her heels clicked on the wood floor and he turned at the sound of her approach.

"I thought I told you to get dressed."

She glanced down at her sandal-clad feet and the shirt that covered as much as any skirt and top would. "I *am* dressed."

"That's not what I meant." He exhaled a frustrated sound. "Never mind." He shifted his hands to his hips. "Go on. Explain."

She followed his movement with her gaze and paused. "Would you mind taking off your gun first?"

He rolled his eyes and removed his gun, muttering under his breath the entire time. "It's not like I'd shoot you," he said finally.

"You look pretty upset, not that I blame you."

He held up one hand. "Start at the beginning. It was a scam, right?"

"Wrong!" she said, wanting him to understand that from the beginning. "Everything that happened between us was as much of a surprise to me as it was to you. And just as real. I had every intention of being there when you woke up. I'd made coffee and everything, but then I got a call on my cell phone—"

"From who?"

She met his gaze. "Marshall."

"Your ex-partner. The one who was manhandling you."

She nodded. "He wasn't happy you ran him off. All day long I'd had the feeling I was being followed," she admitted.

"Yet you didn't say anything."

"You'd already confronted Marshall. I didn't want you to have to deal with J.R., too. He's Marshall's right-hand man. I thought I saw him and so I ducked into the wedding chapel to get away."

He exhaled a rough breath. "Go on."

"Anyway, like I said, that morning, Marshall called my cell. He knew about the money you'd won, and our marriage. He said he'd taken my father from the nursing home and the only way I could get him back was to meet him and hand over the cash or else. I didn't believe him at first so I hung up and called the home. They said Marshall signed my father out. I wanted my father back and I had no other option but to do as he said."

He held out his hand. "Give me your cell phone."

She narrowed her gaze. "It's in the other room."

She ran back to his bedroom and returned with her phone, handing it to him. "Here. Why?"

"To verify your story." He turned on her phone and played with some of the buttons. "Incoming at the right time, outgoing immediately after…" He hit another button and placed the phone to his ear.

"What now, Officer?"

"Detective. I'm calling your friend Marshall." He made a frustrated face and handed her back her cell phone. "It's disconnected. But at least I can see you aren't lying, for whatever that's worth. What did Marshall want the money for?"

"To buy into a poker game. He needed to make some big cash to pay off a guy he owed. He promised he'd win back what I took so I could pay you back in full."

Mike couldn't believe the idiocy coming from her lips. "Exactly what guarantee did Marshall have that he'd win at cards? Isn't that why it's called gambling? The outcome is uncertain?"

"Unless you know how to count. Look, he's good at what he does, but something went wrong. He only won back half of what I owe you. But if you remember, you said if you won, half was mine, so technically you're paid back in full—less the taxi and airline ticket, which I'll pay back. But I never intended to take any of your money, so I promise I'll pay you back every cent of the other half, too. Somehow." She smiled and fluttered her lashes at him, trying to make light of the mess she'd gotten herself into.

"Damn right you'll pay me back," he muttered.

"The first thing I did afterward was to come back to your hotel room, but you were gone," she pleaded, wide-eyed and rushed, obviously hoping he'd buy her story.

"Should I have waited around for *my wife* to return with the stolen cash?"

She winced. "I'm sorry. I really am."

"You could have woken me. I stepped in with Marshall once. I would have helped you again."

She drew a deep breath. "My life is complicated. I wanted to get settled here and make things work with you. I even hoped to eventually move my father here if our relationship was strong enough."

"But we'll never know because you didn't trust me with the first big thing that came up." And that, Mike thought, hurt more than it should have.

So did the wounded look in her eyes at his bluntly spoken words.

"It's got nothing to do with trust. It's habit. I've been on my own for so long. I never had my mother, and my father was loving and fun, but he wasn't always around. Look, I'm not used to turning to anyone. Marshall had my father and it was up to me to save him. But I came back. And I'm here now…"

It wasn't enough that she distracted him with her long, bare legs and flashing cleavage, but he was drawn to her plea of understanding, to her words. She expected him to buy her crazy story. Crazy enough to be at least partially believable because she had come all the way east to find him.

Still, she was obviously omitting plenty and this woman was trouble. So why was he still so damn attracted to everything about her, including her fantastical tale?

His phone rang, interrupting his thoughts. He walked to the portable and picked up the receiver. "Hello?"

"Mike, it's Derek. You've got to come deal with your father. In person."

Damn. "What's he done now?"

Amber watched him, curiosity all over her expressive face.

"He strung cats around our front porch," Derek said.

Mike shut his eyes and groaned. "Live cats?" Mike asked, his stomach in knots. "Or dead ones?" He crossed his fingers as he waited for an answer.

"Stuffed ones, but that's not the point. Dammit, Mike, Gabrielle's going to have a heart attack wondering what he'll string up next!"

Mike ran his hand through his hair. "I hear you. I'll be there in an hour."

He glanced at Amber and knew he had no choice. He wasn't letting her out of his sight again until he could decide what happened next.

"Get dressed. For real this time," he said.

"Where are we going?" she asked, wide-eyed.

"To meet your father-in-law."

"NOBODY CONS King Bobby!" King Bobby Boyd bellowed into his cell phone, yelling at one of the men who worked for him in Texas. He had enough connections in the underworld to do his dirty work, but there was a lady involved and King Bobby didn't like to hurt the fairer sex. For now, he'd just use those connections to get himself some answers. Now, if she didn't cooperate, then he'd have to come up with another way to convince her. And that would be a pity.

But for now he'd take things slow. "Listen to the information I got and write it down. Got a pad and pen?"

He waited for the yahoo on the phone to get something to write with and puffed on his cigar.

"Calm yourself down or you'll have another heart attack," Emmy Lou said from the bed. "It's bad enough the doctor told you to cut out cigars and you don't listen—"

"You ready now, you redneck simpleton?" Bobby ignored his wife's yammering, waiting for the man on the other end to return to the phone. "Good. Listen up. Blond hair. Curly. Pretty gal. First name's Amber. Used to work as a concierge at one of the bigger hotels in Beverly Hills. Start with that and see what you can turn up." He flipped his cell phone closed and took another puff.

"I really don't think Amber had anything to do with you losing," Emmy Lou said. "She seemed like a nice girl, not the kind who'd distract men so her partner man could fleece a table." She shifted the V-neck top to even out her ample bosom.

"Maybe not, but she's the only lead I got. You can't con a con and that weasel she was with stunk to high hell. I knew he was no good."

"You mean he outconned the King and you don't like it."

"Damn straight. And then he ran away fast like the pansy-ass I pegged him for. Didn't give me a fair shot to win my money back." Take it back was more like it.

King Bobby had been counting cards since he was a kid on his father's knee and the only way he'd get beat was by another con.

"You don't need the money. You're the richest man in all of King's County," Emmy Lou cooed at him.

"It's a matter of pride, woman! I'm gonna get me my money back and that little lady named Amber's my key."

CHAPTER FIVE

MIKE DROVE to his father's place, lost in thought, and Amber didn't intrude. She wanted him to think about everything she'd told him, but most important she wanted him to realize what it meant that she'd returned. Let him remember how special their wedding night had been and what awaited him if he agreed to give her a second chance again.

Besides, she wasn't going anywhere. First, she couldn't return to Vegas until King Bobby was gone and no longer looking for her. And to know that, she needed to track down Marshall. Amber couldn't shake the memory of Caroline's comment about King Bobby being "connected." She couldn't grow up in Vegas, hanging around the men her father ran with, and not know about the darker side of a gambler's life. And she couldn't risk the chance King Bobby had just been bluffing. She'd have to stay hidden.

But there was more to her being in Boston than simply her fear of King Bobby. She *wanted* to stay with Mike and convince him she wasn't the kind of person he now thought she was. He needed to accept that his first impression, the gut feeling that allowed him to bond with her in the first place, was the correct one.

She wanted to get to know her husband. She hadn't been able to put him out of her mind and not just because she had betrayed him and owed him, both an explanation and money. He was as sexy as she remembered, with a day's worth of razor stubble and the sport jacket he'd worn to court giving him an edgy appeal. But gone were the easy smiles and relaxed aura he wore in Vegas. In their place was a wary man who'd been betrayed.

She gnawed on the inside of her cheek and glanced out the window. The cityscape had long ago been replaced by green grass, trees and open fields, so different from the dry desert of Nevada or the smog of L.A.

She could get used to the fresh new scenery. She definitely liked Boston, at least what she'd seen of it, and starting tomorrow, she'd explore more. It might be a great place to start over. And with luck, she could find a job at one of the big hotels here.

Her grandparents had passed away a few years ago and all she had left of family was her father. She could move him out here, too, so she could spend whatever time he had left with him without Marshall nearby to cause trouble. And she could know, for sure, if this marriage had any possibility of lasting. Not just because she wanted Mike to see she was a good person, but because *she* needed closure for herself.

She wasn't a quitter. She'd entered into this marriage; she was going to do her best to make it work out.

Based on the hard expression on Mike's face and the set of his jaw, Amber knew she was getting way ahead of herself, but that's how she operated in life. Gung ho and full steam ahead, using her charm and photographic memory to their best advantage. That's how she'd carved out a job as one of the best concierges in Beverly Hills.

Brad Pitt himself had requested her services, as did the rest of his pals. The only drawback to her life in L.A. was the fact that she couldn't get her father on her health insurance plan. It had been the only thing that had drawn her back to Vegas and into Sam's world of underground high-stakes poker.

But it had also inadvertently led her to Mike Corwin. The man was real. Her day with Mike had shown her what had been missing from her life in Beverly Hills. It wasn't just that she'd been too busy for a social life of her own. Her job had consumed her and at the time, that had been fine with her. But the fear of losing her father, combined with her unforgettable day—and night—with Mike had shown her that she needed someone to come home to at night. Someone to talk to. Someone who could make her feel as alive as Mike had in the twenty-four hours she'd spent with him.

She just wanted a chance to see if he was the one she was meant for. And she intended to get that chance in the same way she did everything else in her life.

She'd earn it.

"What's wrong?" Mike asked, breaking the long silence.

"Nothing. Why?"

"You sighed."

"I didn't realize I had."

"Listen, about my father..." He trailed off.

"You mentioned that he's...*off*, I think is what you said."

He nodded. "He's reclusive and eccentric," Mike said, choosing his words carefully. There were none to really prepare Amber for what she was about to encounter, but he might as well try.

No doubt Edward would scare her off, either by his crotchety attitude, the way he lived or the fact that once his father realized there was something between Amber and Mike, Edward would do his damnedest to run her off before the curse kicked in.

Mike shook his head and groaned. "You'll see what I mean soon enough." They were almost at the exit leading to Stewart, where his father lived in an old house on the edge of town.

"What about your mother?" Amber asked. "Does she live there, too?"

He shook his head. "They're divorced. Have been for ten years. She's remarried. She and my stepfather live about an hour from Boston, too, in the opposite direction from here."

"I'm glad you're talking to me again." She curled her jeans-clad leg beneath her and turned toward him, obviously settling in for more "get to know you" talk.

"I just want you to be prepared when you meet my father."

"My father-in-law," she said too cheerfully.

"About that—" Without insulting her or getting into too much detail about the *family curse,* he needed to figure out how to ask her not to bring up their marriage to his father.

If she'd never stolen the money and bolted, he supposed he'd have brought her back and dealt with his father's insanity. But she'd betrayed him. He couldn't trust her, and he really didn't even know her. And she wouldn't be around much longer so there was no reason to upset Edward and get him started on the damn curse.

"Listen, I'd rather you not tell my father we're—"

"Skunk!" Amber shrieked, pointing straight in front of them.

Mike slammed on his brakes, narrowly missing

the animal in the middle of the old country road leading to his father's house.

"Are you okay?" he asked Amber.

She nodded. "Close call."

He agreed. He was about to drive around the skunk when he caught sight of his father, walking in front of the car.

Mike closed his eyes and muttered a curse. He shifted the car into Park and opened the window. "Dad, what the hell are you doing? It's a skunk. Get in the car before it sprays us all!"

But to Mike's surprise, his father bent down and grabbed the animal by the tail.

"What's he doing?" Amber asked, wide-eyed with shock.

"It looks like he's bringing it over."

Before Mike could find the button to shut the window, Edward leaned over and said, "Michael, meet my new pet, Stinky Pete."

"For the love of… Get that thing out of here."

"He's descented. But don't tell that to anyone in town. It keeps people away."

"They don't come around anymore anyway," Mike said, wondering how his father had allowed himself to descend so far into his own world.

Edward Corwin looked like a modern-day mountain man. His black hair, wiry and sprinkled with gray, hadn't seen scissors in ages; neither had his beard. He wore khaki shorts, old shirts and beat-up sandals, but they were stylish enough for Mike to know his father still made trips to town from time to time.

The house he lived in had been built back when Edward and his brothers owned their own construction business, in the days before their generation of Corwin men had suffered from the curse, when the brothers had been on speaking terms and life had been as close to normal as Mike suspected his father had ever known it to be.

After the feud over Mike's aunt Sara Jean, the business had gone bankrupt, the partnership ended and the brothers made their own living doing handiwork. Edward had worked as a plumber, at least until he'd became so strange. Now, no one wanted him in their homes.

But by that point, Mike had been making a decent living and deposited money monthly into his father's bank account. By silent agreement the men never discussed it, although Mike knew his father used the money for necessities like food and clothing. If he was also bankrolling the odd purchase of voodoo paraphernalia or other items, Mike preferred not to know about it.

"Get in the car. I'll drive you back to the house," he said to his father. He didn't look at Amber, afraid to see the horror in her gaze.

For some reason he didn't want to own up to yet, he cared what she thought of his father.

Edward opened the back door and climbed into the seat.

"He's descented, huh?" Amber asked.

"Who's she?" Edward asked Mike.

"I'm Amber. Does he bite?" she asked.

Mike shrugged. "Last time I checked, no. But he didn't have a skunk last time I was here, either."

Amber laughed, the light tinkling sound that had enchanted him in Vegas did so again now. "I meant the skunk, not your father. Does Stinky Pete bite?"

Knowing his father wouldn't talk to her, Mike glanced in his rearview mirror. "Dad, does the rodent bite?"

"No."

Against all common sense, at least to Mike's way of thinking, Amber turned around in her seat and faced Edward. "Can I hold him?" she asked.

Any sane woman would have run screaming by now. Any rational human would have insisted they leave immediately.

Amber took the skunk from his father's hands.

And Edward let her.

Then he did the unimaginable. He invited her inside the house.

Nothing inside the old cape-style structure had changed since Mike's mother had moved out except the clutter. Mike was used to it.

Amber excused herself to use the bathroom and Mike jumped on the opportunity to discuss the reason for his visit. "Dad, Derek called and asked me to talk to you. He and Gabrielle appreciate your concern for them, but they'd really like for you to stop..." How did he put it politely? "Stringing crap up over their door and sprinkling fairy dust on their walkway."

"Someone's got to ward off evil spirits. They're tempting fate. So who is she?" Edward waved a hand toward the doorway Amber had gone through.

Mike didn't pretend to misunderstand. "Her name is Amber Rose. I met her in Vegas."

"I thought what happens in Vegas stays in Vegas?" his father said, cracking a joke for the first time in...well, longer than Mike could remember. "Yet you brought her home with you?" Edward's gaze narrowed.

Mike knew there was no way around the truth. Besides, who was he going to tell? "We got married," he muttered.

"Married!" Edward shouted. "Are you out of your mind? The curse is going to get you yet. Unless... You don't love her, do you?"

Mike shook his head. "I don't even know her."

"Well, praise be, there's hope for you yet." Edward raised his hands in the air, then ran to the nearest cabinet and returned with a jar of red dust.

"Don't come near me with that stuff," Mike ordered in his sternest voice.

Edward frowned and placed the jar on a table.

"You aren't in love with her, you barely know her, and you just met her this weekend so you wouldn't know if she was knocked up. That means you married her because she's hot. Sexy hot." Edward nodded, seemingly talking to himself and satisfied with his own answers. "That makes sense at least. No love, no curse. Then again, remember your cousin Derek's first marriage? The curse kicked in there anyway."

Mike rolled his eyes. "Derek was a workaholic and he wasn't in love with his wife. That's a recipe for disaster any way you look at it. There was no curse needed. But back to Derek. Will you promise me you'll leave Derek and Gabrielle alone? Quit trying to protect them from the damn curse."

"What curse are you talking about?"

Mike glanced up to see Amber standing in the entrance to the den, watching them, but staring at Mike intently.

"You didn't tell her about the curse?" Edward's expression turned to one of horror.

"No, and neither will you. Just like you'll mind your own business with Derek and Gabrielle. They choose not to believe in the curse and that's that. Understood?"

"What curse?" Amber asked again.

Mike grabbed her beneath the elbow. "Later," he said to Amber under his breath. "Dad, we've got to go."

"But we'll check on you again tomorrow!"

"No, we won't," Mike said. "I work the day shift," he reminded Edward, in case his father thought Amber had any kind of say in his life.

Because she didn't.

And he had no time to visit his father tomorrow.

"Then can one of you call me tomorrow?" he said to them both. "I want to know more about my daughter-in-law and this quickie marriage."

"We will!" Amber waved goodbye as she let Mike guide her to the door.

Mike scowled at her. She and his father would not be bonding anytime soon.

"Hey, I just want to know more about the curse," Amber said, eyes twinkling.

Mike shut his eyes for a brief second and wondered what rabbit hole he'd fallen into when he'd married Amber Rose. And how he was going to climb out when she seemed intent on burrowing in.

AMBER ALLOWED MIKE the solitude of his thoughts again on the ride home.

More than he probably realized, she understood how he felt when he looked at his father and didn't get the response he desired. Although it wasn't Alzheimer's Mike was dealing with, it was probably mental illness or severe eccentricity. In any case, the resulting frustration was the same that she experienced.

But she'd liked Mike's father. And since he wasn't her parent and the expectations weren't there, she could simply enjoy his company. After all, he was more of a presence than she'd ever have again from her own father. Maybe that was something she could teach Mike. A small gift, a way for him to appreciate what he did have in his parent.

For now, she settled for imparting empathy and understanding. As they pulled out of the driveway, she reached over and put her hand over Mike's.

He glanced at her in surprise. He said nothing, but he didn't pull away, something she took as a positive sign. Not that she believed she'd overcome any real hurdles, but she was glad she could be there for him anyway.

MIKE WAS EXHAUSTED, but his night wasn't over yet. His biggest challenge sat in his favorite recliner, making herself at home in his apartment.

If he didn't have to work tomorrow morning, he'd pour himself a drink.

"I've never held a skunk before," Amber said.

"I bet not."

"Your father's an interesting character."

He raised an eyebrow. "Character's an interesting way to put it."

"So tell me more about the curse that seems to drive everything he says and does."

Mike groaned. "How about you tell me how

you plan to pay me back all that money first." He wasn't mercenary. The money itself meant less to him than the fact that she'd left him and now he couldn't trust her.

She pursed her lips, cocked her head to one side and sighed. "Okay, but you first. What curse?"

He tried not to roll his eyes at something his father, uncles and an entire town took too damn seriously. "Legend says that an ancient witch by the name of Mary Perkins cursed the males in my family. Apparently one of my relatives ran off with a woman who was already engaged to another man, William Perkins. William's mother, Mary, was a witch—keep in mind, this was during the Salem witch trial era—and she cursed the males in the Corwin family line as a way of getting revenge."

Amber leaned forward in her seat, revealing the ample cleavage he'd held in his hand. Tasted in his mouth.

Mike broke into a heated sweat.

"And what was that curse?" she asked, oblivious to his desire, enthralled instead by the story that had haunted his family for generations.

He could repeat it by heart. "Any Corwin male who falls in love will be destined to lose his love and his fortune."

"Nasty curse," Amber said.

"Yeah. Just because I had a horny relative, every

male down the family line has suffered unimaginable pain and misfortune." He shook his head.

"But your cousin Derek is married to a woman he loves now, right?" she asked.

Mike raised an eyebrow. "Just how long *were* you standing there, listening to the conversation I had with my father?"

She waved her hand, dismissing the question. "Are they happily married?"

"So far…but my father's convinced Gabrielle miscarried because of the curse and he's been trying to protect them from future harm with his voodoo and hocus-pocus."

"Then those *were* juju dolls I saw hanging from the trees by the house."

Mike nodded, preferring not to go there. "Gabrielle is a famous author whose research dispels paranormal belief for a living. Ever hear of Gabrielle Donovan?" he asked.

She nodded. "Yes! I've seen her books!"

"She's convinced Derek that all the family misfortune has been a combination of circumstance and coincidence. Frankly, I'm inclined to believe her, too. Now, does that answer all your questions?"

"It does," she said, sounding surprised he'd leveled with her.

"Now, about my money…?"

She made a tsking sound. "You do have a one-track mind, don't you? I'm your wife, remember?

What's mine is yours and what's yours is mine." She held up her hand and the big gaudy diamond flashed at him from across the room.

He hadn't realized she'd kept the ring, let alone continued to wear it.

Seeing it dangle on her finger again brought everything crashing back. The fun, the rush of excitement and most of all the desire he'd felt the moment he'd laid eyes on her. And their wedding night, something he hadn't been able to forget, no matter how angry he'd been.

That same desire had enveloped him from the moment he walked into his apartment and found her nearly naked on his bed, as well as a yearning he'd been tamping down during the visit to his father's, watching her accept Edward as if he and his descented skunk were normal. He'd felt it again as she'd held his hand during the hour-long ride home in silent understanding.

"My wife?" he repeated her words.

She nodded. "Legally."

He started toward her in a deliberately predatory way. "If you're going to insist on calling yourself my wife, I'm going to want something more from this marriage than the aggravation I've had so far."

She met his gaze without backing down. "I think the time we spent in your hotel room was pretty darn good." Her eyes widened. "I'd even call it aggravation free, if you ask me. Don't you agree?"

The memory of consummating their marriage was potent and his body hardened at the reminder. It suddenly didn't matter that she'd betrayed him. He still wanted her as badly as that first time.

Wanting to make sure she understood his intentions, he stood over her chair, grasped the armrests and leaned over her, his lips inches from hers. Her warm, feminine scent tempted him, aroused him, drew him in.

"We have unresolved issues," he said, staring into her beautiful blue eyes. "The money and the marriage."

"I know we do. But you need to know I didn't want to leave you and I came back—"

He didn't let her finish, cutting off her words with his lips. She was his *wife* and she was willing and he kissed her hard and deep, branding her as his.

Amber kissed him back, but let Mike take charge. She wasn't going to pass up the chance to be with him again, to remind him how good they were together. To feel it for herself.

His large hands cupped her face and he tipped her head, giving his tongue better, deeper access to her mouth. He thoroughly claimed her, leaving no place untouched. All she could do was hold on to his shoulders and feel.

His hands slid from her face to her neck, his thumbs caressing her skin, tracing the line of her collarbone, his fingertips moving lower to the swell of her breasts beneath her T-shirt. He teased her with his touch, dipping lower, but not quite touching where she needed it most. The throbbing tips of her nipples pressed harder against her shirt, begging for him, while moisture trickled between her legs, building an empty, aching pressure only he could fill.

She arched her back, silently imploring him to stop teasing her with featherlight strokes of his hands on her breasts.

He raised his head and met her gaze, his eyes dark and intense. "What do you want?" he asked, his voice gruff. "You need to tell me."

She swallowed hard, her heart pounding in her chest, desire swamping her, yet not fulfilling her needs. "You. I want you."

"I want you, too," he said, not sounding at all pleased with he admission.

"And it makes you angry that you do."

A muscle ticked on the side of his face. "That about sums it up."

She knew it would take time for him to believe in her again and that was okay. That he still wanted her was enough. It gave her something to work with.

"One step at a time," she told him, referring to their relationship. "Then you'll see how good things between us can be."

Never breaking eye contact, she took his hand and placed it on her breast. Over her shirt and through her thin bra, his touch burned and aroused her, but she was more concerned with breaking through his self-directed anger. He wanted her and was furious with himself for it.

"One step at a time. Starting here and now," she said, encouraging him.

He curled his hand tighter around her breast. She felt her nipple tighten, turn rigid against his palm. Unable to control her reaction, a low moan of satisfaction rumbled from deep inside her. She watched the fight he waged within himself and she saw the minute he lost the battle.

The angry tension in him eased. He kissed her again, more gently, more accepting, yet still demanding in intensity. She shifted her body and his hips settled around hers, the hard length of him fitting directly between her thighs. The thick, bulging pressure hit her at exactly the right point and she moaned aloud.

His hands cupped and molded her breasts while, attuned to her other needs, he rocked against her, each thrust of his body bringing her higher and closer to a fast-coming climax. She needed to feel him harder against her and bent her knees, seeking more intimate contact.

Without warning, the chair tipped back and

Mike lost his balance, nearly toppling over her and onto the floor.

"Oh my God, that scared me half to death," she said. "Are you okay?"

Mike drew a deep breath, still trying to calm his twisting stomach. "Too damn close to a roller coaster for my peace of mind."

She met his gaze. And laughed.

They'd been both caught off guard and the shock of being jolted back by the recliner interrupted the moment, yet it sent her into a fit of laughter.

He began laughing, too.

He couldn't remember the last time a makeout session had turned into something fun. Amber, her blue eyes dancing, her curls a mess around her face, gave the most normal things a unique spin.

She wiped her eyes with the back of her hand. "Too funny. I thought for sure you were doing a header over the chair."

"With our combined weight, I'm surprised I didn't."

"Mike?" she asked, no longer laughing.

He stood beside her. "Yeah?"

"You left me hanging. You?"

He shook his head and grinned. "Yeah, I'm a little unsatisfied myself." He scooped her into his arms and carried her into the bedroom where he had protection stashed in the back of one of his drawers.

He lowered her to her feet by the side of the bed, which was still—stupidly—covered in cold hard cash. He began to scoop it up and toss it into a bag, trying like hell not remember that she'd walked out on him. At least, not now, while his body still throbbed with need. Finally he finished and placed the bag aside. He'd organize it and take it to the bank first thing in the morning.

He turned back to Amber and discovered she'd undressed. And Amber nude was enough to make him forget all his misgivings.

He couldn't draw his gaze from her rounded curves and incredible beauty. With her damp lips and tousled hair, she looked like sex personified. It took him only an instant to shed his clothes, grab and roll on a condom and meet her in the center of his bed.

He laid back against the pillows and let her take control, which she seemed only too happy to do. She swung one leg over him and while holding his hands and staring into this eyes, she lowered herself over him.

She was dewy and wet, ready for him. Her body accepted him, inch by hot inch. He lay still, letting her set the pace. And though he wanted to take it slow, savor how tight she was around him, he needed to feel more of her and he thrust upward until they were joined together in the deepest possible way.

The sensations quivered throughout his entire body and he let out a low groan. "You feel so damn good."

Her eyes were wide and heavily glazed as she managed a nod. Her hips began to rotate, clenching him tighter in her heat. Her eyelids fluttered closed. As he thrust in and out again, she picked up a familiar rhythm. One that belonged to them alone.

He had a second to realize that sober sex with Amber was a helluva a lot different from the last night they'd spent together. Hotter. More intimate.

And then his body couldn't wait and he began to push upward, inside her, searching, reaching higher. Thought fled. Only feeling mattered.

She matched him thrust for thrust, grinding into him. She moaned and the sexy sound brought him higher, closer. Somehow he held off until she came—her body milking him for all it was worth, her soft cries triggering his release.

But it was the sound of his name on her lips that caused everything inside him to burst open. Taking him up and over with the strongest, sweetest climax he'd ever experienced.

They lay in silence, the only sound his heart pounding in his ears. He rose and headed for the bathroom. When he returned, he climbed back into bed. Amber curled around him as if she'd been sleeping beside him for a lifetime.

"Mike?" she asked sleepily.

"Yeah?"

"Next time you're on top," she said, tossing one leg over his, and immediately falling asleep.

His wife locked him in for the night. In his bed, in his apartment, in his *home*.

What the hell was he going to do with her?

CHAPTER SIX

MIKE AWOKE to the smell of coffee. He knew immediately where he was and what he'd done. A quick glance told him the bag with the money remained in the corner of the room, but was his wife here, too?

If so, they needed to have a talk about their divorce, something he had no choice but to pursue. He couldn't remain with a woman he didn't trust enough to be certain she'd be around in the morning.

He climbed out of bed and pulled on a pair of jeans before walking to the kitchen. The sound of pots and pans clattering told him Amber hadn't bailed on him and sure enough, she padded barefoot around his kitchen, humming as she cracked eggs into a bowl. An overwhelming sense of relief mixed with pleasure as he watched her work in his kitchen, once again wearing nothing but his shirt.

Considering the conclusion he'd come to moments before, he pushed away the fact that he liked having her here, chalking it up to good sex the night before.

Not just good sex. Great sex. His body jolted alive at the memory.

He cleared his throat.

She turned to him with a big smile on her face. "Good morning!"

"You're still here."

The light dimmed in her eyes, but she kept the smile. "I told you I would be. So how do you like your eggs?"

Now that he was sure she was here, he was suddenly in no rush to have the divorce conversation. But the longer he stalled the more difficult it would be. "Surprise me."

"Why don't you go shower," she said, waving a fork in the air as she spoke. "Breakfast will be ready when you're through."

He paused, torn about when to discuss their future. She looked so pleased with herself that he couldn't hurt her again by bringing it up just yet.

"Don't worry. All the silverware will be here when you return," she said, turning away from him. "Now go."

He winced. Still, all through his shower, he reminded himself she was feeling bad because of something *she'd* done, not him. It didn't help his guilt.

A short while later, they shared fluffy Spanish omelets made with ingredients she'd obviously found in his refrigerator and delicious hot coffee.

"You make a mean omelet," he said, complimenting her while shoveling the last of his breakfast into his mouth. "It's delicious."

"Thanks. I used to cook breakfast for my dad when I was growing up. He liked my Spanish omelet so I thought you might, too."

Conversation remained light, topics like Boston weather and what time he had to leave for work flowing easily between them.

Mike waited until they'd finished eating to bring up the discussion he knew they had to have. And when he couldn't stall anymore, he decided it was time. "Amber…"

"Mike…"

He chuckled at their timing. "You first."

She met his gaze. "Well, I came here on the spur of the moment and I didn't pack my things. I don't have a suitcase or clothes…" She studied him with doe eyes, making him feel responsible for her yet again.

And damned if despite it all, he didn't like it. He exhaled a slow groan and weighed the possibilities. He could give her his credit card and be taken for a fool again or he could hand her limited cash and hope she was telling the truth.

"I'll give you some money and you can pick up what you need for a couple of days." He saw the opening for a serious conversation and took it. "As soon as I have some free time, I'm going to look into a quick divorce." That had been to the point, he thought, disgusted with his lack of tact.

He wiped his mouth with a napkin and rose to clear his plates off the table. Maybe if he kept busy, he wouldn't see the hurt in her expression or shock in her eyes. He sure as hell had the bitter taste of the words on his tongue.

Amber wasn't surprised by Mike's declaration, but despite his intentions, she wasn't letting him go that easily. In order for her to see if she and her husband had a future, she needed some time being his wife.

While making breakfast, she'd formulated a plan that would put herself in the center of his life and give him a chance to get to know the real Amber.

With a little Las Vegas luck, by the time she was finished, he wouldn't be able to let her go. "Let me know what you find out," she said, not using the word *divorce*.

"I will."

"Can I borrow your car?" she asked.

He raised an eyebrow. "What for? You're in the middle of the city. You can take a cab or the subway anywhere you want to go."

"Even to visit your father?" she asked. Edward had seemed like a man in need of family or a friend. She understood Mike didn't have the time during the day, but she did.

He shook his head. "Oh, no. There's no reason for you to go stirring up things at home."

"Okay." She let out a forced sigh. She'd comply with his request. For now. "Let me have the keys in case. I'm used to having a car and I don't want to feel trapped." She raised an eyebrow and held out one hand.

It was a test. She only wanted to see how far he'd extend his faith in her. She was perfectly willing to take public transportation wherever she needed to go. She just wanted some little indication of trust between them.

"Fine," he said through gritted teeth, handing her his car keys.

"Thank you!" She jumped up and without thinking, kissed him on the cheek.

The spicy scent of soap from his recent shower and his delicious aftershave seeped into her pores. A warm, fuzzy feeling overcame her and she let her lips linger against his freshly shaven skin.

He didn't move, remaining frozen in place. She heard her heart beating inside her chest and with everything inside her, she wished he'd turn his face so their lips could meet and break the emotional barrier he'd so obviously erected between them.

Not even sex last night, which had been incredible, had thawed him out this morning. He was attracted to her and enjoyed things between them when he let himself, but he was angry at himself because of it. And, of course, he was still furious with her.

She'd been trying hard to ignore the deliberate distance, but now she admitted to herself how much it hurt. How badly she wanted his forgiveness.

Instead of kissing her, he cleared his throat. "I have to call my partner and tell him to pick me up on his way to work." He rose, breaking the connection that had been way too short.

She forced a nod. "Have a good day."

"Thanks."

"And Mike?"

"Yes?" He gripped the back of the chair tight with one hand.

"I *will* be here when you get home."

THE FIRST THING Amber did after Mike left for work was to call Paul and check on her father.

She discovered that Paul had made arrangements to have Sam moved to a new nursing home as soon as a room became available in the place Amber had chosen. In the meantime, he'd taken Marshall's name off the visitors' list. He'd also made certain the staff understood Marshall was no longer allowed to see Sam, and that the older man was not to be taken out of the building without his or Amber's consent.

Amber called the nursing home herself and made certain her father was calm and doing okay after his outing yesterday. The staff had assured her Sam was fine. His condition allowed him the serenity of not worrying about his daughter's predicaments, for which Amber was grateful—at least for the moment, while her life was such a mess.

Her dad might have been a professional cheater, but to Amber, he'd had a heart. He'd also had an understanding of the human condition. He realized the men involved in those high-stakes poker games, men like King Bobby, were, typically, extremely wealthy people who viewed life as Sam did—as a gamble and a risk. Or the competitors were cons like Sam himself. He'd never knowingly stolen from someone who was risking their mortgage payment or child's education. Odd morals, but they existed.

And Amber had based her own beliefs on his. Her father had taught Amber how to recognize a chronic gambler and steer clear. Even at her most desperate, when she'd first needed money for her father's care, she made sure the competition in the poker games she'd played met her father's criteria—filthy rich and stupid, or bored. Easy marks or fellow cheaters.

Which might explain how this last game had gone sour, Amber thought. Maybe King Bobby recognized a fellow cheater in Marshall because he was one himself. Maybe King Bobby was smarter than he appeared. Maybe he really *was* connected with people who could hurt her if he didn't get back the money he'd lost. Amber had always known she could only live the life with people like Marshall for so long before she got bit by her actions.

She trembled before catching herself. She'd made her bed, so to speak. Now she had to fix things, but first she had to understand what exactly was going on. Her next phone call was to check the messages back at her apartment. There was a flurry of normal calls, friends and other things that were part of her life.

And then there was one last unnerving message—another old contact, Robyn Lane, a concierge at the Beverly Wilshire in California, spoke in detail.

Amber hit Replay. She needed to make sure she'd understood her friend correctly. "Hi, Amber, hon, it's Robyn Lane from the Beverly Wilshire. Long time! Hope Vegas is treating you right. I thought you'd want to know three dudes from Texas were asking around here last night for a concierge named Amber. They didn't have a last name, but they described your funky blond curls and paired with your not-so-common first name, I thought they might be looking for you, even though they had the wrong hotel. Of course, I didn't give them any information. Just took their card to pass along to you in case you're interested in contacting them. Gotta go. Call me." A loud beep indicated the end of the call.

Karma was a bitch.

Just ask Earl. But Amber wasn't a TV character. She was real and she just wanted to put her old life behind her. So far King Bobby hadn't found her, but she couldn't afford to go back to Vegas until he was finished looking. But if Mike was successful in his bid for a quick divorce, she'd have nowhere else to go. She'd already determined she had her reasons for wanting to stay with him that had nothing to with avoiding King Bobby. And she planned to do her best to make certain Mike had no time to think about wanting her to leave.

Still, she couldn't discount the possibility that King Bobby would track her via the Crown Chandler Hotels. He was certainly rich enough to buy the information he needed.

She placed a call to the Chandler in Beverly Hills to speak to Sydney London, the day head concierge. Sydney hadn't heard that anyone had been looking for her, but she promised to ask the other employees and get back to Amber as soon as possible.

Her nerves were raw. But the irony was, Amber still didn't know why King Bobby was after her. Did he know she was involved with cheating? Did he just want to use her to get to Marshall? Was he just out to regain his money, which she didn't have? Or equally frightening, did he want plain old revenge?

Amber really liked her legs in one piece and didn't want them broken, something a *connected* man like King Bobby could have done with ease. Drawing a deep breath, she sat down with her cell phone, a pad and pen, and began calling all Marshall's old hangouts to discover if anyone had heard from him in the last twenty-four hours or so. After twenty minutes, she knew that no one who was a friend or acquaintance had seen or spoken to him. Still, she figured he couldn't lay low forever and left messages for him everywhere. She didn't leave her phone number. She just said to tell Marshall to get in touch with her immediately. He knew how. She wasn't going to provide any more of a trail than she had to.

By the time she finished making calls, her hands were shaking and she was no closer to solving her problem than when she'd started. But she'd been as proactive as possible, keeping up that Vegas spirit, that luck combined with hard work would achieve the best results. All she could do now was hope Marshall heard she was looking for him and chose to get in touch.

After a refreshing shower that calmed her down, she redressed in yesterday's clothes, took the money Mike had given her, adding it to the tally of what she already owed him, and headed out shopping.

She filled the morning buying inexpensive but chic outfits to impress her husband and make him drool.

On her travels, she'd passed Mike's police station. She'd noted the address of his precinct from papers in his apartment, and she noticed on the corner by the station was a beautiful restaurant. She wanted to do something nice for Mike, but she didn't want to use his money to do it. The one thing a concierge did was to learn the lay of the land where she'd work— the hotels, restaurants, shops, et cetera. Amber didn't have a job in town—yet—but if she intended to remain here, she might as well start making contacts right away. And with the right schmoozing, she could pull off a surprise for her husband.

The minute Amber stepped inside the exquisitely decorated restaurant and smelled the delicious aroma of Italian food, she formulated an addition to her plan. Once she explained to the owner that by feeding the local police department, he would hopefully increase his lunch and dinner trade, he agreed to send over free lunch. Of course, it helped that she mentioned she was a concierge at the Boston Crown Chandler hotel and she'd return the favor by talking up his restaurant to the hotel clientele. Once day soon, she hoped her words would be true and she'd do as she promised.

Pleased with herself and her plan, Amber headed home. Close to noon, dressed in fresh clothes, she sat down at the old PC in Mike's apartment and booted it up. She printed out maps of the area and took note of the five-star restaurants in the vicinity, and then the smaller cafés. It would take time, but she'd learn the area by doing a little research each day.

Finally, she shut down the computer and stored her papers on what she wanted to consider *her* side of the bed, on *her* nightstand. Then she headed to Mike's precinct in time to view his reaction to the spread of Italian food that arrived out of the blue.

MIKE DEPOSITED the remains of the Vegas winnings in the bank and spent the morning at the station. Although he had no real right to pry, he ran a credit check on Amber Rose and discovered no shady dealings—providing him with another glimmer of hope she wasn't running a scam on him. Though she could be using him to fund her life during a rough patch, at least she wasn't lying to him outright. By omission was another story. The woman was a bundle of contradictions. Savvy enough to make it on her own for years, dealing with a man like Marshall, yet emotional enough to be hurt by

Mike's lingering anger. He couldn't let her big eyes get to him. He had to stick to his divorce plan.

"Hey, man, you've been distracted all morning. Everything okay?" his partner, Dan, asked.

Mike nodded. "Everything's fine. Just jet-lagged, that's all." Mike had no intention of telling Dan about his marriage to Amber or the rest of the drama. The fewer people who knew, the easier it would be to put his wife on a plane and fly her out of his life. Things could go on as usual with nobody any the wiser, Mike thought.

Even his father would see and respect the wisdom in that plan.

His father. Mike had promised Edward he'd call him today, but he didn't want to answer questions about his marriage while he had a bunch of nosy cops sitting within listening distance. He'd just have to call later, from the privacy of his home.

Privacy with Amber there? Now, *that* was a joke. Mike shook his head and tried to focus on the phone calls he'd been making.

"Is there a Mr. Mike Corwin here?" someone with a heavy Italian accent asked.

Mike swiveled in his chair. "I'm Corwin. What can I do for you?"

"Lunchtime," the balding man said as he strode over to Mike's desk.

Behind him, two women followed with bags, and they began to unload containers of delicious-smelling Italian food. "Where can we put this?" one of them asked.

"Wait. I didn't order anything." Mike rose from his seat.

"Not to worry," the man said. "A woman named Amber stopped by my place of business this morning. She's *mutta bella*," he said, beaming. "And smart. She suggested I bring my food to Boston's finest and let you indulge. Then maybe you'll recommend my place around town. *Capice?*"

Dan stood beside him. *"Amber?"* he asked, obviously recognizing the name.

Before Mike could unstick his tongue from the roof of his mouth to answer, Tom, their captain, cleared an old table. "You can put the food right here," he said, grinning. Turning to Mike, he said, "You can explain later. For now, we're all going to enjoy."

Amid murmurs of approval, his colleagues began to filter into the room, waiting for the restaurant staff to finish the setup. They'd even brought plastic plates, forks and knives.

Mike's stomach churned, torn between wanting to kill Amber for infiltrating this part of his life, and gratitude because he and his colleagues rarely had the opportunity to enjoy a decent lunch. Thanks to Amber, they would indulge today. And everyone in the precinct seemed thrilled with the surprise.

Only Dan, who'd met Amber in Vegas, seemed as concerned as Mike himself. "What's going on?" he asked.

Mike spread his hands in front of him.

"Better yet, what kind of a psycho woman follows a man across the country and then proceeds to feed his friends and coworkers?" Dan continued, not giving Mike a chance to reply.

Not that he knew what to say anyway.

"His wife, that's what kind of psycho woman would do something like this," Amber said, suddenly appearing beside them. "Hello, Dan," she said, patting his shoulder. "How's married life treating you?"

"Oh, shit," Mike muttered.

"Wife?" Dan practically shouted. "What the hell did you do in Vegas anyway?"

Silence descended around them, broken soon after by an impromptu round of applause.

Mike could barely process his thoughts as people slapped him on the back, shook Amber's hand and complimented him on bringing back a gem of a wife—a woman who cared not just about his stomach, but his friends' too.

Only Dan watched them warily.

"I'll explain later," Mike promised his partner.

"You bet you will. Natalie will want to have dinner with the two of you." He shook his head. "You. Married." He looked perplexed and confused.

"Yeah, I know how you feel," Mike said. "Go eat." He turned away from Dan and toward Amber. "You. Outside. Now. *We* need to talk."

She raised an eyebrow, but let him grab her hand and pull her onto the street.

"What the hell are you doing?" he asked once they were alone on the sidewalk in front of the station.

Amber blinked at him, all soft eyes and confusion. "I thought you'd be surprised, not mad. What's wrong? You don't like Italian food?" she asked, obviously trying for humor.

Mike clenched his jaw, steeling himself against her appeal. He needed to be strong and make her understand how things should be between them until they returned to Vegas. "I don't like my private life being bandied around. Especially since I didn't plan on telling anyone we were married."

"Oh."

He heard her disappointment and felt it inside him. Once again, her error had left *him* feeling lower than dirt. Despite it all, the last thing he wanted to do was to hurt her.

"Look, this is a complicated situation," he said, meeting her gaze.

"Do I embarrass you?"

He took her in with one glance. From her strappy sandals, simple sundress, to her sunny hair, she was a breath of fresh air. "Hell, no, you don't embarrass me. Those guys inside are probably frothing at the mouth with jealousy." Unable to stop himself, he ran his hand through her soft curls.

She wet her lips and her eyes turned softer with gratitude, and hazy with that damn attraction that was always there between them. Simmering just below the surface.

Daring him to ignore it.

As if he could.

He didn't know who started it, but soon his lips were on hers, seeking her sweetness, apologizing for hurting her, showing her she wasn't an embarrassment, but a woman he desired. His tongue swept through her mouth, feeding off her delicious taste.

"Excuse me," Dan said, clearing his throat when they didn't break apart right away. "But there are people inside waiting for an explanation. And some just want to congratulate you."

Mike stepped back.

Amber's cheeks flushed pink. "I guess we should head back in."

Mike inclined his head and gestured for her to walk ahead of him. Which gave Dan the opportunity to add, "And some of us just want to know if you've lost your damn mind."

But even his partner's concern couldn't stop the grin that spread across Mike's face. Because as

Edward had said, Amber was hot. And she was a challenge—he didn't know what she'd do next.

Still, Mike had to admit she was trying to make things up to him. She treated him like the center of her universe, going out of her way to please him. It was difficult not to remember all the things that had drawn him to her in the first place.

KING BOBBY stared at the phone in the office of his dealership, willing the darn thing to ring.

"A watched pot never boils," Emmy Lou said, peeking into the room.

"Go away, woman! You sound like my momma!" No wonder he had a mistress waiting for him whenever he could escape from the woman's nagging.

As if on cue, the telephone rang and he let out a whoop of glee. "Speak to me!" he demanded.

After listening for a few minutes, he barked to the man on the line, "So someone at the Chandler admits that an Amber once worked there? That's it? If I need to do your thinkin' for ya, I got no need to pay you. Just tell 'em your boss wants to open a hotel and is interested in this old employee of theirs. Throw some money around until you git access to her employment file. I need a last name!" he bellowed, his blood pressure rising.

"Once they get her names they should check the Department of Records," Emmy Lou suggested.

King Bobby hadn't realized she was still there, damn nosy broad.

If he hadn't knocked her up when she was young and she hadn't threatened to take him for all he was worth, he'd be long divorced by now. Emmy Lou liked being King Bobby's queen. Good thing she came in useful once in a while.

"Good idea, sweet cheeks," he said. Then he repeated her words to his guys out in Beverly Hills. "Next time you call me, I want concrete information!" he bellowed so they'd know he meant business.

After hanging up the phone, he pulled out his bankroll and peeled off a number of hundreds, then waved them at Emmy Lou. "Why don't you go shopping. I have work to do."

Emmy Lou smiled, pleased, and snatched the cash from his hand.

"I won't be home for dinner," he said to his wife's retreating back.

She wouldn't care.

Mentally, she was halfway to the mall already. With money in her pocket, she wouldn't be home early tonight, either. She'd call her friends, hit the stores, head to an expensive dinner and come home toasted.

"Whoo-wee!" He picked up the phone and dialed his lady friend.

If his yahoos found that Amber's information, the King would be gettin' lucky tonight. In more ways than one.

CHAPTER SEVEN

AMBER ATE DINNER alone that night, after Mike called to tell her he'd be working late as a last-minute favor for a friend. She was disappointed, but she'd just learned something else about her new husband. She already knew he was a man who cared for his family and now she discovered he was also a good friend. Both were traits she could admire.

Mike was so different from the sleazy characters she'd met on the poker circuit, and he was more settled than most of the guys she'd encountered in Beverly Hills. They'd been aspiring actors or models, men with more love for the face they saw in the mirror than any woman. Not that she'd given any of them a chance.

It wasn't that Amber didn't believe in happily ever after. She did. Her family had a healthy history of love and fidelity. Her grandparents had been happily married for a lifetime and if what she'd heard of her parents' courtship was anything to go by, they'd been deliriously in love. Her mother had given up her career as a showgirl to have Amber and she'd planned to stay at home with her. Only, she'd died while giving birth to her daughter.

Amber shook her head, bringing her thoughts back to the present. To herself and to Mike. In L.A., she'd thought she'd been too busy for a relationship, but she realized now she'd just never met a man who made her want that happily ever after for herself.

Until Mike.

He had longish, dark hair she loved running her fingers through and beautiful blue eyes she could get lost in. And within him, there was a sense of honor and decency she wanted to emulate.

Mike Corwin was the best kind of man. She wanted to be worthy of being part of his life.

This afternoon, she'd loved the chance to do something nice for him, like arranging lunch. And though he'd been upset with her intrusion, the reaction of his fellow cops had helped smooth things over. They'd enjoyed the meal she'd sent over and they'd all eagerly wanted to meet his new bride.

Though Mike had wanted to keep their relationship a dirty little secret, she'd seen the hint of pride in his eyes when they'd referred to her as his wife. It had helped ease her hurt, she admitted to herself. When she'd seen the yearning in his eyes, desire meant for her alone, that hurt had disappeared. And when he'd kissed her, she'd known she was doing the right thing. Now all she had to do was convince him.

A relationship took work and commitment and Amber was willing to give it both. Once Mike understood she'd never betray him again, Amber believed he would give the same.

She'd ordered in a small pizza and had just finished cleaning up and freezing the extra slices when her cell phone rang.

She picked it up from where she'd left it on the counter. "Hello?"

"Amber, it's Sydney."

At the sound of the voice of the concierge from the Crown Chandler hotel, a sick feeling spread through Amber's stomach. "Hey, what's up?"

"I got that information. I'm sorry, but a new employee gave you up. Those Texans waved some bills around and the guy pulled your employment file. I'm not sure what details they have, but they got a long look. I'm sorry," she said again. "He's been fired for violating confidentiality, but that can't undo the damage."

Amber closed her eyes and shook her head. "It's not your fault. I appreciate you getting back to me." At least now she knew where she stood. "Talk to you soon."

"Bye."

Amber disconnected the phone. If nothing else, King Bobby now had her full name. Of course, the

only way he could track her down was if he discovered she was now married.

To do that, he'd have to get information on her at
the city hall where her marriage license had been
filed. If he got Mike's name and address, she was
dead meat.

She bit the inside of her cheek. First thing tomorrow morning, she'd have to find out if anyone
had recently requested information on Amber Rose
at city hall.

If the worst happened, she'd have to come clean
with Mike. She shook her head, fighting frustrated
tears. Just as she was starting to make a little head-
way with him, he'd discover she'd been keeping
things from him. After that, he'd never trust her
again. And she'd never get another chance with
this special man. That possibility scared her more
than anything.

She refused to let that happen. Pulling herself
together, she renewed her search for Marshall, making phone calls with no luck. When her former
partner went underground, he was better than a
gopher, she thought, disgusted.

Well, she'd done all she could for tonight. Instead of worrying, she turned her attention to
Mike's father. She'd promised to call Edward, and
so she looked through Mike's phone book for a
number she could reach him at.

Once she'd made sure Mike's dad was okay,

she'd wait up for her husband to come home and make him a happy, happy man. Before her world crumbled down around her come morning.

IT HADN'T TAKEN LONG. Amber was looking for him already. Marshall tossed his precharged, prepaid, disposable cell phone onto the bed. According to his sources, there hadn't been a single one of his haunts Amber hadn't contacted. Marshall would have been pleased if not for the fact that that his contacts had also informed him that big Texas bag of wind, King Bobby Boyd, was also looking for him and asking questions.

That thought made Marshall break into a cold sweat. He wasn't hiding without reason. King Bobby had enough clout with powerful, dangerous men to put the fear of God into a guy who'd never believed in any higher power except his own good luck.

This mess was stressing him out. He stripped and walked across the bedroom naked, intending to take a long, hot shower in the bathroom of the house he was currently inhabiting. Marshall had all sorts of contacts and this residence belonged to a friend of a friend, who sometimes traveled different gambling circuits when the heat was on in Vegas. This was one of those times, so the house was empty. After paying off the houseboy, Marshall had let himself in and prepared himself to wait this mess out.

They were nice temporary digs except that he was bored. He had too much time on his hands, worrying about whether King Bobby would find him and break his legs—or worse. He knew he could stay underground as long as he needed to without being found. What he wasn't sure of was whether he could trust Amber to keep her mouth shut about their scam if King Bobby managed to track her down first.

Marshall let steam fill the shower stall and thought about Amber. He didn't feel too bad about letting her take the heat. King Bobby was a Southern gentleman. He wouldn't hurt a lady, he'd only bully her into telling him Marshall's whereabouts. Since Amber didn't know where he was, she couldn't reveal a thing.

She could, however, tell King Bobby he was a class-A con, confirm the King's hunch about Marshall cheating that night, and cause him to go on the run. Because King Bobby wouldn't mind calling out his goons to hurt *him*.

Marshall could call Amber back on her cell and warn her, but she was already furious with him. She'd never believe him and she'd sure as hell never tell him where to find her.

So he wouldn't call her.

Yet.

Nor could he look around for her. She had too many contacts. If he asked questions, he was bound to arouse suspicion. Or run into King Bobby, who was on the same path.

But Marshall wasn't stupid and there was a much easier way to find his beautiful Amber. He'd just let King Bobby do all the work. The man was already hot on her trail. All Marshall needed to do was keep an eye on King Bobby without being seen. The Texan would lead Marshall right to Amber.

He'd show up, remind her of how special their bond was, how lucrative their partnership could still be. By the time he located her, she'd be bored with her cop husband and ready to come back to Marshall.

If not, he'd just have to make her see the error of her ways.

MIKE WASN'T AVOIDING AMBER. He wasn't. The fact that he'd volunteered to cover someone's shift tonight when he could have gone home to his wife didn't mean a thing.

Except that by the time he got in around midnight, Amber was fast asleep and he didn't have to talk about her visit to the station today. Instead, he walked into his bathroom, and could only marvel at how quickly she'd made herself at home.

His countertops were now filled with feminine

things—creams, shampoos, conditioners and other assorted items he didn't recognize.

He picked up one bottle, opened it and sniffed, inhaling an unfamiliar, feminine scent. An arousing scent.

As an only child, he'd never had to share his space before and Amber's takeover should have felt like an intrusion. Except it didn't. She'd made herself at home and he didn't mind.

He found an odd sense of peace being part of a couple, even though being alone had never bothered him before. While he and his cousins, Derek and Jason, had had to deal with the stigma of being a Corwin man, the women—like Jason's sisters—had married and thrived in love and life. In Mike's father's mind, that fact had also proven the curse was alive and well, kicking male Corwin butt.

Mike headed back to his bedroom to discover Amber had claimed her night table with a box of tissues, a paperback book, what looked like lip gloss and a stack of papers. He grinned and settled into bed, wearing nothing but boxers. He wasn't about to change his routine for the female sleeping beside him. He propped one arm behind his head and stared into the dark, not at all tired despite the late hour. As he breathed in deep, her scent wrapped around him, awakening him even more.

Go figure. Mike hadn't been determined to remain a bachelor, but until now the lifestyle had suited him fine. So why did he *like* all the feminine touches Amber provided in his apartment?

He punched up his pillow and rolled onto his side, hoping to somehow take the edge off his arousal and fall asleep. Suddenly Amber sighed and wrapped her arm around his waist. From behind, she cushioned him in head-to-toe contact and warmth, snuggling in with another deep sigh.

He shut his eyes, but how could he even think of sleep when he was surrounded by a new female in his bed and his life?

An enigma named Amber, full of surprises and secrets.

MIKE AWOKE with a morning hard-on and Amber's hand on his groin. Helluva wake-up call, he thought. The woman was obviously put on this earth to make him a very happy—but insane—man.

Mike knew he should get some answers from Amber while he had her cornered here, but he couldn't think about anything except the warmth racking his body. He rolled over to find Amber staring at him, sultry heat in her gaze and a smile on her lips.

"Morning," she murmured.

"Morning," he said gruffly.

"How was work last night?"

She wanted him to think, let alone have a coherent conversation while her hand was wrapped around him?

She slid her grasp up and down the length of him and he groaned.

Amber grinned. "I take it you like that?"

He pushed her hair back off her face. Even first thing in the morning, while tousled and sleepy, she was too damn appealing.

"What's not to like?" Encouraged, she picked up the pace, making damn fine use of her palm and her fingers, taking him closer and closer to the edge of climax. He knew it wouldn't take much for him to come.

But he didn't want to fall alone. "Hang on." He reached for his nightstand, opened the drawer and retrieved a condom, making quick work of the foil and sliding it on.

He turned to Amber, who had pulled off her soft negligee and now lay naked and waiting for him. One of the things he found special and refreshing was the honest way she gave herself to him each time they made love. She seemed so open and honest with her body and even her soul. It made the lies and omissions seem out of character. Every time he touched her, he wanted to believe in her again.

Pushing those thoughts aside, he straddled her and looked into her eyes. Warm, welcoming eyes that matched the softness of her body as he slid inside. She was wet and ready, as he knew she would be, accepting all of him quickly, her gaze never leaving his face.

She bent her knees and pulled him in deeper and the sensation was so incredible, he couldn't keep his mind focused on anything except the building friction between their bodies. Heat licked at him like rising flames attacking him from all sides.

He threaded his hands through her hair and began to glide in, then out again, possessing her, taking her faster and faster still.

Amber was lost. Everything inside her was concentrated on the pressure point between her body and Mike's. His every thrust brought her closer. Waves pummeled her, bringing her higher as the feelings inside her tightened, coiling, building with each hard, demanding push.

She matched his rhythm easily now, knew what would make her feel best as she rolled her hips, seeking deeper, more intimate contact until suddenly she was *there*.

Climaxing.

Milking Mike's body so she could prolong the exquisite sensations, never wanting them to end. And they didn't. Her orgasm seemed to go on and on until he collapsed on top of her. Even then, she was able to wring one last wave of pleasure from her body before his breathing evened out.

Finally he rolled off her.

By the time she caught her breath and opened

her eyes, he'd returned from the bathroom and climbed back into bed.

"You're something else," he said, pulling her into his arms.

He no longer seemed to fight their closeness and she snuggled in beside him, wanting this connection as much, if not more, than she'd wanted sex.

"So how *was* your night?" she asked.

"Pretty routine." His hand brushed the back of her hair.

She liked the feeling.

"You never did tell me why you decided to become a cop." Amber was fascinated by this man she'd married.

He shrugged. "I never really thought about why."

Amber laughed. "Liar. I have a feeling you think most things through."

He wondered how she knew him so well. "I wanted a career that made sense, something that had rules, where things were black and white."

Amber swallowed hard. "Why?" she asked, wishing he'd confide in her. Trust her.

For a few painful seconds, silence created a cavern between them. Until he finally spoke. "Because things at home were anything but stable."

Thank you, she said to herself, grateful he'd opened up. "I understand."

He cleared his throat. "You were out cold by the time I got home," he said, changing the subject.

She laughed. "Yeah, I made your life pretty easy. You didn't have to come home and deal with your wife."

"And you made sure I didn't have to deal with you first thing this morning, either."

She glanced at him.

His hot gaze conveyed pure sexual heat, but clear understanding, as well.

Cornered, Amber thought. She'd hoped to distract him with sex. Keep him happy and he wouldn't think about things like divorce.

"Well, I think you dealt with me pretty well," she said coyly. The man did know how to satisfy her.

"Very funny." But his arms around her squeezed tighter.

So far, at least, he wasn't letting her go. "I called to check on your father last night," she said, hoping she wasn't about to destroy the peace between them.

He groaned. "You didn't."

"I did." She rested her head against his shoulder. "He'd asked us to call and I didn't know if you were too busy, so I did. I tried the number in your phone book and it had been disconnected. So I tried the other number you had listed and got his cell. Did you know he disconnected his home phone?"

"I knew. He has some crazy notion about spirits traveling through the phone lines."

Amber disagreed. "Actually I think he's just looking for attention."

"Excuse me?" Mike stiffened at her suggestion and she patted his chest to calm him.

The warmth of his skin nearly distracted her into picking up where she'd started this morning. But she needed to bond with him outside of the bedroom. They needed to talk about things that were important to them both and he'd begun bridging the distance by admitting how hard his childhood had been. She was merely drawing some deeper conclusions, things someone close to the situation wouldn't be able to see as easily.

"Your father has been alone for so long, he thinks that's the way it has to be. But the crazy things he's doing to your cousin Derek and his wife, and cutting off his landline…" Amber drew a deep breath. "It looks like a cry for attention. I don't think he really believes in voodoo."

"And the curse? Are you telling me he suddenly thinks it doesn't exist?"

She let out a sigh. "No, after talking to him, hearing his concern about you not falling in love, I can tell the curse is real to him."

"Just not the other things, like voodoo?"

She shrugged. "I'm not entirely sure. But he kept me on the phone for an hour last night, asking a lot of questions interspersed with long silences that told me he didn't want to hang up or be alone." She paused, then asked, "Did you ever get yourself into a situation you couldn't undo, no matter how much you wanted to?"

"Well…"

She nudged him in the side with her elbow. "I do not mean our marriage. I think you like being with me, no matter how much you're fighting it."

He didn't immediately argue the point, giving her a real flicker of hope.

"I'm talking about backing yourself into a corner like your father has done by isolating himself," Amber clarified.

Mike cleared his throat. "It's more than isolation. My father hasn't spoken to my Uncle Thomas in over thirty years. He blames the curse, but he's willingly retreated behind walls for years."

Amber heard his voice crack. Her heart in her throat, she rolled over and stroked his cheek. "I believe he's lonely. I think he does the crazy things he does because it's the only way people notice him."

"And you know this from a quick meeting and an hour phone call?"

She smiled. "I know this because I'm good at reading people. It's what I do—I mean, what I did for a living for years."

He raised an eyebrow. "Keep talking. I want to know more about you. Like what kind of partner this Marshall was to you, why you ended your association, anything and everything about you," he said.

He was as interested in knowing her as she wanted to understand him, but unlike Amber, Mike's curiosity ran deeper. She'd told him why she'd left him in Vegas, but her answers only scratched the surface. He clearly wanted to understand why she'd associate with Marshall in the first place, why she was being followed, *what she was still hiding from him.*

And she wasn't ready to shine the light of day on those things just yet. So she'd tell him about the areas of her life she was proud of, the parts she enjoyed, those she wanted him to know because he'd get an insight into who Amber Rose…Amber Corwin…really was.

She drew a deep breath and began. "I used to be a concierge in L.A. and I loved it. I worked at the Crown Chandler in Beverly Hills and people skills are my forte. I have a photographic memory and it really helped in my line of work. Remembering names and faces is a crucial part of the job, but it was never a problem for me. I met A-list celebrities and made it a point to accommodate their every wish. I was the master," she said, remembering.

"What happened? You said you *used* to be a concierge. Why not anymore?" he asked.

Clearly he didn't mind her rambling.

"Well, my dad got sick and I had to come back

to Vegas. He didn't have health insurance, so I became his primary caregiver."

"That must've been tough." He pulled her closer, his fingertips stroking her arm.

She appreciated his strength and support, two things she hadn't had enough of lately. She'd thought she was used to being independent. She realized now just because she'd been used to it didn't mean she'd enjoyed it.

She sighed. "It wasn't easy. I took a job at my friend Paul's bar because he would let me leave whenever Dad had an emergency. I'd hoped the progression of his disease would be slow, but it wasn't."

Mike continued to run his fingers over her arm, comforting her. "Do you want to tell me about it?"

"There's nothing to tell really. It's a sad, degenerative thing. I kept him home as long as possible until one day the neighbor who checked on him for me called to say he'd wandered off." The fear Amber had experienced that day washed over her, nearly choking her again now. "We canvassed the neighborhood, all his favorite places."

"Where was he?" Mike asked.

"Wandering downtown on the Strip, looking for an old casino where he'd first met my mother. It was torn down years ago."

"That's awful."

She saw her chance to link her life and experience to his. "It's similar to how your father lives in his own world. Except when you talk to Edward, he's *present*. He's there, in front of you, aware. Does that make sense?"

He nodded. "It does. But let's not talk about Dad right now. What happened once you found your father? And what's his name? I'd like to refer to him as a real person."

She smiled. "His name is Sam, and you would have liked him," she mused aloud. "That night, I brought him back home and the next day, I immediately went in search of a clean, well-run nursing home for him. And that, as they say, is that."

She had to get Mike off this subject before he probed too much deeper.

She'd have to lie or omit information and she just didn't want to do that to him. To them.

She pushed herself upright, holding the sheet against her chest. "Mike, what I'm trying to get at is that with my father, all opportunities to communicate and have a relationship are gone. But you still have that chance with Edward."

He frowned, clearly unhappy with her subject change. "Don't you think I do what I can? But if I want to save my own sanity, I have to limit the time I spend with him. It's too hard, too painful."

She smiled in understanding. "But I'm here now. And I can be the buffer. I can help you and Edward. In fact, I want to." Leaning over, she kissed

Mike full on the lips. "You have to shower and get dressed for work."

He groaned, but tossed the covers off himself and rose. "Don't think this get-to-know-you stuff is finished. There's a lot you didn't tell me," he said in warning.

She grinned, keeping things light. She didn't want him to sense she was deliberately hiding things. "I'll make breakfast while you shower," she told him.

His gaze met hers and lingered. "You'll spoil me if I let you."

"So let me," she said softly.

Without replying, he turned and started for the bathroom. Her gaze followed his strong, firm rear end as he walked until the closed door changed the view.

She stood and pulled on one of Mike's shirts, something she was growing fond of doing, before heading to the kitchen to make breakfast.

She might as well keep busy now. She wouldn't be able to find out if anyone had pulled her marriage certificate from city hall until 9:00 a.m. Las Vegas time.

She whipped up scrambled eggs, orange juice and hot coffee, then waited for Mike to join her. She wanted to give him as many positive memories of them as a couple as possible before she was forced to disillusion him once more.

Amber sighed. She was a survivor. She'd always known how to get by, and if Mike followed through on the divorce, she knew she'd get through that, too. But that didn't mean she wouldn't fight—for herself *and* for him. If the time came, she'd walk away knowing she'd given it her all.

KING BOBBY WAS in a celebratin' mood. "Amber Rose married Michael Corwin this past weekend. Whoo-wee! I got me some information!" He tossed his hat in the air, Texas style. His sources had come through again.

He had a name and an address, though there were no signs of her at her Vegas apartment. He'd have to set his sights on the husband, then. Detective Michael Corwin.

"Dang woman married a cop," King Bobby muttered. Which meant he couldn't head East and show up at the cop's place, guns blazin'.

He'd have to go slow and subtle-like. He picked up the phone in his office and dialed home. "Emmy Lou?" he bellowed. "Book me a flight to Boston!"

Some things a man had to handle for himself.

CHAPTER EIGHT

MIKE AND HIS PARTNER often ate lunch at the deli near the courthouse, one block from the station, and today was no different. Dan was extolling the virtues of married life while Mike remained silent. He didn't have a typical marriage, so why bother joining the discussion? Besides, for the last two days Dan had been happy to provide enough conversation for the both of them, allowing Mike to deflect most inquiries about his personal life.

"So enough about me and Nat. How's Amber?" Dan asked before biting into a French fry.

"Fine," Mike said in a monotone.

"And how's married life treating *you?*"

"Just fine," he said in the same tone.

Dan rolled his eyes. "The hell it is. Not if you're still giving me short nonanswers. Just how long did you think I'd let you off the hook?"

"You want me to gossip like a woman?" Mike asked pointedly.

"Low blow, buddy." Dan paused to pour more

ketchup on his plate. "Seriously. What's the matter? Aren't you getting laid?"

That was so far from the problem, Mike couldn't help but laugh. "I'm just not going to kiss and tell, no matter how many different ways you ask." Mike had yet to come to grips with his wife and her secrets. Sharing how she'd taken off with his cash wasn't something Mike was willing to confide. Not even with his partner.

Dan narrowed his gaze. "You're being protective of your wife. I'll take that as a good sign." Dan held up a fry to make his point before eating it.

Mike tackled his burger, hoping if he continued to ignore his partner, Dan would change the subject.

"Is Amber cooking for you?"

Apparently Dan wouldn't be deterred. "She makes me breakfast, but I haven't been home for dinner. And before you jump to any more brilliant conclusions, remember it's only been a couple of nights."

"What's her specialty? Cold cereal?" Dan asked.

"Eggs. What's wrong with you, asking stupid questions like that?"

Dan shook his head. "What's wrong with *you?* You've got a hot woman at home who's cooking your meals and warming your bed and you're afraid to go home. When I mention married life, you act as if you're on death row. So I ask again. What's wrong with *you?*"

Mike could understand his partner's concern. But he wasn't about to elaborate. "It's not that simple," he said, jaw clenched.

"It could be. You married a stranger in Vegas. She followed you home. Now you're supposed to enjoy the get-to-know-you honeymoon stage. A little backward, but what did you expect?" Dan asked, his voice tinged with a combination of frustration and curiosity.

Mike had expected honesty. He'd wanted Amber to open up to him immediately upon her return. How else could he begin to understand her?

Hell, it wasn't as if he hadn't given her the opportunity to confide in him. Instead, she'd deliberately changed the subject, which told him she was hiding something big. Something she obviously didn't trust him to know.

Because she didn't think he could handle whatever it was?

For all he knew, she was right. He wouldn't know what he could handle until she confessed. And for such a big reveal, *she* needed to trust *him.* Clearly she didn't. Yet, just as obviously, she was trying to make the marriage work. He, on the other hand, had been grumpy and obnoxious outside the bedroom.

He groaned and pushed his plate away from him. He'd been handling her all wrong, he decided.

"How 'bout you cut the lady some slack?" Dan suggested. "You never know. You just might enjoy having her around."

Mike nodded slowly, having just reached the same conclusion. "Anyone ever tell you that you aren't as dumb as you look? Maybe I should give Amber a break." It wasn't as though living with her was torture.

She was beautiful, sweet, and when he let himself forget she'd stolen his money and taken off, he could almost believe she had a heart of gold. Added to that, there were plenty of perks, as Dan had pointed out. If they could find common ground, maybe they could make this thing work.

Unless whatever she was hiding drove an even bigger wedge between them.

AMBER LOVED *Law and Order*. She watched the television show religiously whenever she got the chance and thanks to syndicated reruns, she could always find it on one channel or another. She'd been curled up on the couch, trying to get lost in the crime drama and not think about her own problems, when Mike came home from work.

At the end of the workday, he was adorably disheveled with a day's worth of razor stubble darkening his handsome face. Every time she looked at him, her desire for him renewed, stronger than before.

Since he'd said he'd grab dinner out, she expected him to shower and head to bed, where she'd have to corner him for a serious talk.

Instead, he sat down beside her on the couch. "What are you watching?" he asked.

Surprised, she decided to test his mood with some simple conversation. "*Law and Order.* Do you like the show?"

He inclined his head. "When I let myself forget I'm a cop, it's pretty good. Catch me up?" He pointed to the large screen.

"Okay. The blonde and her boyfriend had a con going and when things went bad, he bailed on her, leaving her to take the fall," she said, her voice dropping as the explanation reminded her forcibly of her own situation with Marshall.

Mike settled in to watch, but Amber couldn't concentrate on the show.

She knew she had to tell him everything. It was only a matter of time before King Bobby tracked her down. But that wasn't her main priority, much as it should be. No, making this marriage work was her biggest concern. She needed to come clean. Mike had tried to push her for answers earlier. She'd wanted more time as a couple before she dropped the bomb on him. She'd been wrong to wait.

"What are the chances of *that* happening?" Mike asked sarcastically, gesturing toward the television.

Amber had missed whatever he was referring to.

"You see? This is why it's hard for me to get too involved in cop shows. They condense the time frame and things happen that frustrate the hell out of me."

She forced herself to meet his gaze. "You prefer real-life drama?" she asked.

"You know I do. Why?" He'd obviously caught her serious tone.

She drew a deep breath and curled one pajama-clad leg beneath her, steeling herself for his reaction. "Because I've got some real-life drama for you."

Mike raised an eyebrow. "*Your* life?" Shock tinged his voice. He probably didn't believe she was ready to come clean.

She could barely believe it herself. "Someone's looking for me," she said before she could chicken out and disappoint him.

"Marshall and his friend," Mike said with certainty and a good amount of disgust.

She winced because the truth was much worse than whatever he obviously imagined. "Not exactly. There's someone else. Remember the poker game I told you about?"

He pinned her with a steady look. "The one you *stole* my money for so Marshall could buy into?"

She forced herself not to look away and make her actions any worse by refusing to own up to them. If she wanted him to believe in her, she had to make sure she showed him she wasn't the horrible human being he thought.

As if such a thing was possible at this point. From his guarded tone, she meant no more to him than any other suspect he questioned.

"That's right." She swallowed hard. "Marshall was sure he'd win by counting cards. And he did. Only apparently, the man he won the money from was a con himself, a 'connected' con. He isn't happy and he's looking for me."

Mike narrowed his gaze and she could see his cop brain at work, attempting to figure out all the angles. "Why is he looking for you and not Marshall?" he asked at last.

"Because the snake's gone underground, that's why," she said, opening and closing her damp palms in frustration. "I've been trying to find him for the last few days. I've called every place and person I can think of and nobody's heard from him," she said, allowing Mike to see her exasperation. "I'm not sitting around doing nothing, but he's disappeared."

"Because he's a pro." Mike's disgust was obvious. "If you can't find him, the guy looking for him won't be able to, either. But that doesn't explain why this guy would be looking for you. It's not like you were the one who cheated."

Here we go, Amber thought, her stomach twisting into tight knots, making her sick.

At her silence, Mike looked at her warily. "Right?" he asked, pushing for the one answer it hurt her to give.

The man was a cop and she was about to tell him she was a cheat. For all the rationalization she'd done for the last few months, she suddenly couldn't face what she'd done.

And yet she had no choice.

"Well?" he snapped at her. "It's a black-and-white question. I said, Marshall was the one cheating, not you." His voice hardened on that one word.

"Not exactly." She wrapped her arms around herself. "There's a lot you don't know about me."

"Not for lack of trying," he reminded her in a biting tone.

"I know." She rose and smoothed the wrinkles in the silky pajama pants she wore, trying to find the words to explain. "Let me start at the beginning. I was born in Vegas and my mom died in childbirth."

"I already know that. Go on." His words held the strength of steel. His patience was obviously wearing thin.

But she had to do this her way. "My dad was a Vegas con. He knew how to count cards and that's how he made a living. I'm not going to say I condone it, but I grew up around him and his friends. Other than the years I lived with my grandparents, that's really all I knew." As she spoke, she felt the prickling of the hair on her arms as it stood up on end.

"So you learned from him," he said, his voice now flat, his expression carefully neutral.

He must have made an extremely good interrogator, Amber thought. She just wished she wasn't his subject. But she was, and everything she stood to lose suddenly loomed in front of her. All the possibilities she'd dreamed of—a second chance in a new place, with a good, decent man. A life away from Vegas and the sin that came with that city. For Amber not to lose those things, she had to reach Mike. But she couldn't begin to read his emotions and her stomach continued to churn.

"I did learn from my father. Don't all children? Of course, it helped that I had a photographic memory," she said lightly. She laughed.

He didn't. "I thought you said you were a concierge in Beverly Hills. Was that a lie?"

As he spoke, deliberately cold, thinking the worst of her, Amber saw a flicker of hope in his blue eyes that told her he wanted to find something to hold on to between them, too.

She grabbed on to that emotion and like a lifeline, she clung to his gaze. "I haven't lied to you," she said, her voice steady and reassuring. "I admit that I left things out, but only because I didn't think you were ready to hear them. But I haven't lied."

Mike exhaled a slow breath, conflicting thoughts filling his head. She hadn't lied. But she had done things he couldn't have begun to imagine.

He reminded himself that he shouldn't be surprised. He'd known she wasn't telling him everything. Giving her the benefit of a doubt, he attempted to look at her life from every angle. A young girl who'd never had a mother with only a con-artist father and older grandparents from whom to learn. A child with a natural affinity for her father's so-called craft.

Unfortunately, any way he viewed the situation, she was a thief, stealing from poker opponents and later, from him.

He and his wife weren't just polar opposites. They diverged on the fundamental concept of honesty and integrity. Those notions defined his life.

The cop and the con. As he looked at her beautiful, imploring face, he couldn't find any middle ground.

"If you didn't lie, then how did card counting fit into your Beverly Hills life?" he asked at last.

"It didn't. Not until my father got sick." She ran her hand through her curls.

He couldn't help noticing her hands shook. This wasn't easy for her, either. But she'd had time to prepare for this conversation. He was hearing it all for the first time.

He forced himself not to think, just to listen.

"I had health insurance through the hotel, but it didn't cover my father. And when I went to look at the nursing homes I could afford, it made me sick. I couldn't put him in one of those places." Her voice cracked as she spoke and her pain affected him, slicing deep.

How could it not? He had a father he loved, too. One who, he admitted to himself, he'd thought of institutionalizing rather than allowing the man to live alone, never knowing what he'd do next. Whether he'd step over the line that defined sanity. Could he have left Edward in one of those places? Mike wondered.

He wanted to reach out to her, to hold her and tell her he understood her pain. But he couldn't. Because as much as he empathized with her emotions, he didn't understand her choices.

In the wake of his silence, Amber drew a shaky breath and continued, "So I contacted Marshall."

"And you became partners," Mike said. He heard the disappointment in his voice as the memory of his first meeting with Amber came back to him in vivid detail.

A lovers' quarrel, Marshall had said.

Ex-partners, Amber had claimed.

The illegalities had never been mentioned.

Mike's blood chilled. If he'd known, he'd never have spent the day with Amber. Never have married her.

She touched him on the shoulder.

A mixture of warmth and hurt flooded him on contact and he jerked away.

"Hey! Don't you judge me until you've been in my shoes!" she said with indignation. "Imagine what you'd do if you couldn't pay for decent care for *your* father." Her eyes flashed with defiance, defending her choice.

"I have thought about it, dammit. While you explained your reasons, it's all I could think about. I'm trying like hell not to judge you, but I'm a cop. Right and wrong is just too clear-cut in my world." He ran a hand through his hair, wondering how she couldn't see the solid barrier her past...hell, her present, placed between them.

"Then consider yourself lucky things are so simple for you," she said coldly.

Once again she was angry at him for something he hadn't caused, he thought, the irony strong. This woman and her damn contradictions, her warped sense of right and wrong.

"Why don't you continue," he said, suddenly exhausted, but knowing she hadn't finished.

Amber let out a sigh. "You know the rest. High-stakes poker games for big money. Every penny went to the home for my father's care. I supported myself with savings and the money I made working at my friend Paul's bar. Look, I'm telling you this because, despite how it all looks, I believe in honesty. I've wanted to tell you all along. I just didn't know how you'd react to the truth."

"Like hell. You're confessing now because you're cornered and you need protection." Did she really think he was an idiot? he thought, frustrated.

"I'm telling you because if King Bobby is coming after me and I'm staying here with you, you need to know what's going on. Again, it's about honesty."

"*King* Bobby? What the hell kind of a name is that?" He couldn't help but laugh.

She tried unsuccessfully to block a grin. "King Bobby, owner of the biggest used-car dealership in all of Texas," she said in a Texas drawl.

"Oh, brother." Mike rolled his eyes. "How do you know for certain he's after you?"

She recounted how she'd seen King Bobby and his wife at the Bellagio after she'd gone looking for Mike. She explained the trail King Bobby had left from Vegas to Beverly Hills, asking about her. "He's a smart guy and chances are, he'll dig up our marriage certificate and track me down here. It's only a matter of time. I don't know what he wants, but I like my body the way it is too much to let him find me."

Mike liked her body, too. That was part of the problem.

"We have two choices. Hang around like a sitting duck for this King Bobby character to find you, or hide out."

"*We* have two choices?"

He shook his head in frustration, not sure if he wanted to strangle her or kiss her senseless and make her problems go away. "Did you really think I'd just abandon you to deal with this guy on your own?"

"Frankly, I didn't know what to expect from you." She sniffed and turned away.

That disappointed him. Hadn't he come through for her before?

"Go pack up your things."

She frowned at his order. "To go where?"

To the only place he could think of where she'd be safe. Where a man named King Bobby from Texas would have a hard time tracking her down. "To my father's place. This King would never guess to look for you at the home of a reclusive old man without a phone." And when Edward *had* had a telephone, his number had been unlisted.

"Are you sure he won't mind us staying there?" Amber asked, obviously surprised at Mike's choice of hideouts.

"Not us. You." Mike bit the inside of his cheek. "I can't get off until this weekend. I'll have Derek head over and prepare my father. You can take my car first thing tomorrow. It's a fairly easy drive."

And since she needed a safe place to hide out, Mike trusted her not to run away again.

Her eyes turned soft and liquid as she stepped toward him. "I really appreciate your help, considering how you feel about me."

She had no idea how he felt about her. Hell, most of the time *he* had no idea how he felt about her. He just knew how he felt about what she'd done.

Not trusting himself with words, he stepped out of her reach and gave her a curt nod.

Mike headed to the bedroom to shower before bed. He needed a good night's sleep so he'd be able to think more clearly tomorrow. Although once Amber climbed into bed beside him, sleep would be the last thing on his mind. She'd end up with her hand—or her mouth—on his body, expressing her thanks.

And as he'd proven more than once, he had no self-control when she touched him. In bed, their differences weren't so obvious. If he was smart, he'd send her to his father's tonight, but he knew his cousin wouldn't brave Edward's house at night, unannounced. And since Mike knew Edward didn't always answer his cell phone, Derek would have to make the trip in person.

In good conscience, Mike couldn't spring Amber's visit on Edward without warning. Tomorrow

would have to be soon enough. He'd have to survive one more night sharing a bed.

Then he'd send his soon-to-be-ex wife to stay
with his father while Mike looked into this King
Bobby character. His father, Amber and Stinky
Pete together under one roof. Mike shuddered at
the thought.

Hopefully, Mike could straighten out the mess
Amber was in and divorce her without too much
trouble. He paused in the doorway and glanced at
the woman standing in the family room, appearing to be contemplating *something*. She twirled her
finger around one lock of hair and looked as if she
was planning her next move.

He had no real idea how her brain worked and
wasn't sure he wanted to find out. She'd be gone
before he knew it and his life would get back to
normal.

Unfortunately, normal had been solitary and
routine, and the notion didn't bring him the comfort it should have.

HE MUST BE A WEAK MAN, Mike decided, because
when Dan picked him up for work he was humming. So was his body, the result of a spectacular
bout of first-thing-in-the-morning sex and a long
thank-you/apology kiss from Amber as she walked
him to the door and said so-long.

"Goodbyes are permanent and I'll be seeing

you on Friday," she'd said, ever optimistic. She totally ignored the fact that he didn't approve of her choices any more this morning than he had last night, something he'd made certain she understood. Just because they'd shared another night of mind-blowing sex, he didn't want her to think anything else had changed.

A divorce was in the cards, Mike thought. A perfect play on words if ever there was one.

He'd given Amber directions to his father's house along with his cousin Derek's home and cell phone. Since Derek's wife Gabrielle had had a stalker issue last year, his cousin understood Mike's concern and had taken a ride out to Edward's this morning. He said Edward had complained nonstop about having his privacy invaded, but he'd also begun rinsing glasses in the sink in preparation. Unusual to say the least.

Could Amber's assessment of Edward be correct? Was he too ingrained in his reclusive life to ask for help, yet looking for a way out? Mike refused to get his hopes up. What could Amber possibly know about the crazy old man Mike called his father?

And yet Mike found himself placing hope in Amber's ability to reach Edward during her stay there. Once again, he found her contradictions maddening. Was she a card-counting cheat or a warm, caring, insightful woman who wanted to help Mike's father? Could she really have had no choice?

No! He crumpled up the paperwork he'd filled out incorrectly because he hadn't been concentrating. They were too different. He couldn't possibly trust her. And she caused complications in his life he just didn't need.

He'd help her, then file for divorce. With *that* settled, he refocused on work.

CHAPTER NINE

AFTER THE MORNING RUSH HOUR, Amber drove to Stewart in Mike's car. She'd had an hour to think about her choices and the things she wished she'd done differently in life. But regret couldn't change the facts. All she could do was go forward and hold on to hope, an attitude she'd learned early in life, each time her father had dropped her at her grandparents' and left for his next "business trip." She'd wait expectantly for him to come back, and he would. In the meantime, she'd made the best of where she was and appreciated the life her grandparents had given her. Until she joined her father for good. At the time, she'd just decided and then moved on. Just like she wanted to move forward now.

The drive to Mike's father's house was an easy one and she took in the scenery, marveling in the differences between the dry desert out West and the lush greenery in the East. She'd heard about fall and winter, but she'd never experienced either season firsthand. She wondered if she'd get the chance this year.

The farther away from Boston and Mike she drove, the more nervous she became about showing up on Edward Corwin's doorstep, and she tightened her grip on the steering wheel.

Sure, she'd liked Mike's father, but he was still a hermit of sorts. And even though she *thought* she understood him, she didn't have a psychology degree. She doubted he'd welcome her with open arms. Still, she was a people person who trusted her instincts and her instincts told her Edward needed a friend. Fate was giving her an opportunity to do some good for Mike and his father and she intended to make use of it.

Maybe a small thank-you gift would help soften her intrusion into his home. She pulled off the highway one exit before Salem for a brief pit stop. According to her directions, Stewart would be the next exit, so she had to find something for Edward here. She checked out the stores in a small strip mall in search of a fitting present for Edward Corwin.

The first store in the row of shops was a boutique with items that seemed too froufrou for a gruff man like Mike's dad. The liquor store was next, but Amber doubted Mike would appreciate her adding alcohol to his worries about his father.

The last store was a New Age shop named Crescent Moon. Intrigued, Amber peeked in the cluttered window. Barely bigger than a walk-in closet, the place oozed eccentricity. It was perfect.

She opened the door and bells tinkled over her head. As she stepped inside, a pleasing scent welcomed her. Incense, she guessed, and she glanced around. Oddities surrounded her, along with more familiar items like silver jewelry, turquoise and other types of stones.

Dreamcatchers hung from the racks and she lightly touched one, wondering what Edward would think of it. Would it trap his evil spirits as well as it supposedly caught bad dreams?

"Welcome to Crescent Moon." A big woman approached her. "I'm the proprietress, Clara Deveaux. Can I help you?"

Her skin was smooth, her hair jet-black, and she possessed an ethereal beauty. Her brightly colored, multipatterned dress floated around her as she moved.

"I'm looking for a gift," Amber said.

"As you can see, I have an abundance of things to choose from." She waved her hand and her many bangle bracelets jingled around her wrist. "For whom are you shopping? The items in my store have very specific uses. To help you, it's best I know all I can about the recipient."

Amber nodded, enjoying the sound of the woman's voice. "It's for a man. My father-in-law, actually. I'm going to stay with him for a few days and I need a thank-you gift."

"Since you're here and not at the gift shop, I assume you don't want to take the traditional route." A mischievous smile twinkled in her eyes.

Amber laughed. "That's right. My father-in-law is…different." She chose her word carefully.

"We're all different." Clara spoke with what seemed like wisdom beyond her years. Amber judged her to be in her mid-fifties, like Edward.

Amber nodded, acknowledging the other woman's point. "He's a loner by choice and he believes in curses. One specific curse to be exact. He's explored voodoo and claims to ward off evil spirits," Amber explained. "I'd like to bring him something that says I respect his beliefs."

What she really wanted was to get closer to Edward and maybe help father and son gain a better understanding of each other while they still had the chance. She knew too well how quickly those you loved could be taken away from you.

"If he fears a curse, he'd be happiest when surrounded by positive energy."

"That makes sense. I'm Amber, by the way." She extended her hand for Clara to take.

They shook in greeting. "Amber. Pretty name."

Amber smiled. "Thank you. My mother chose it," she said wistfully.

"I'm sorry she's passed."

Amber raised an eyebrow in surprise. How did Clara know?

Still, Amber inclined her head. "Thank you."

"What's your full name, Amber?"

"Amber Rose…Corwin." She used her newly married name out loud for the first time. It seemed strange on her lips.

"Corwin as in the Stewart Corwins," Clara said knowingly.

"How do you—"

"You told me your father-in-law is a loner who believes in curses. The Corwin curse is well-known in these parts. Any male with that last name has a rich history of tragedy behind him," Clara said, her gaze warm and unnervingly understanding.

Amber was surprised that the Corwin curse seemed to be common knowledge outside of the Corwin family. Apparently it held power over more people than just Edward. "Do tell. I'm new to the area and to the family."

Somehow, asking Clara about her new relative didn't seem odd. And if she was going to be able to help Edward, she needed to know what she was up against.

Clara nodded. "This will take some time. Let me make us tea first."

A few minutes later, Amber was sitting across from Clara at a small corner table she hadn't noticed earlier.

Over orange-scented tea, Clara explained the legend of the Corwin curse. Her description matched Mike's, but she elaborated more on the way in which the current generations in the town of Perkins, which was a mere two miles from Clara's store, had perpetuated the myth by illegal, as well as immoral means. Both Stewart and Perkins were still recovering from former mayor Mary Perkins's so-called reign of terror.

"Now, I'm not saying the curse is real. And I'm not saying it's not. But Edward Corwin's attempts to ward off bad spirits make sense. He just needs to use more positive forces than negative ones. That's the purpose of my business here. To help people do right by others."

Amber smiled. "Thank you for sharing this with me. I feel a little more prepared now." She enjoyed the other woman's openness and warmth. "This is all fascinating," she offered, spreading her arms wide and gesturing to the store, as well as the story.

"It's Wiccan belief, honey. My mother taught it to me. *'An It Harm None, Do What Ye Will.'* Translated, it means as long as you don't do anything that will hurt anyone, it is allowed." She paused to sip her tea and Amber did the same. "Sounds to me that's what your father-in-law needs. Some good around him."

"Oh, I agree. That and people who care. He's been alone too long."

Clara patted Amber's hand. "You're wise for one so young. If only all people were as accepting and understanding as you, I wouldn't be going out of business."

"Going out of business? Why?" To Amber, the woman's generous spirit was as obvious as the pleasure she took in her beliefs. Why would she close up shop?

Clara sighed. "Lack of interest combined with development. This whole row of stores is slated for demolition," she said sadly.

"I'm so sorry. Are you planning to move the store somewhere else?"

"It's not easy to find a place where people need the kind of help I offer, but I've been looking at rental space in Stewart. With their rich history of curses, I'm thinking people might be receptive to my wares." Her gaze didn't hold Amber's too long and she reached for more tea.

"Sounds like a good plan." Amber knew of at least one person in Stewart who could use Clara's help. "What do you think I should get for Edward Corwin?"

"A dreamcatcher for sure. He always— I mean, he should get use from one. And there are candles and incense that might help. But most of all, that man needs a few good spells cast around him for a change." Clara picked up their empty teacups and placed them in the backroom, on the sink.

Amber wiped down the small table. Then, on impulse, she pulled out the directions and copied Edward's address onto one of Crescent Moon's business cards by the register. She purchased the items Clara had suggested for Edward and waited while the woman wrapped them.

"Thank you. This has been an enlightening morning. I'm so glad I stopped by."

"Me, too. You're a good person, Amber Rose Corwin."

Amber flushed at the compliment. "I wish my husband felt the same way."

Clara studied her for a moment, her stare deep, her expression intense. "He doesn't see the world the same way you do. Just keep on doing good deeds. He'll come around."

Amber hoped the other woman was right. "Speaking of coming around, if you have some free time maybe you could visit me at Edward Corwin's and introduce him to some of those good spells you mentioned earlier."

"That's a tempting offer." Clara's eyes sparkled as she accepted the card and glanced at the address. "It's so busy I'm not sure I can get away," she said, laughing as she gestured around the empty shop.

Amber chuckled, too.

Clara's visit was sure to lighten the tension in the Corwin house during Amber's stay. Besides, anything this Wiccan woman had to offer must be better than voodoo, the jujus and red dust on Edward's doorstep.

In fact, the more Amber thought of it, the more she guessed that Clara might be just what Edward Corwin needed.

As Amber approached Mike's father's house, her nerves took over and her stomach flipped in anticipation. She didn't know what to expect by way of a greeting. She parked in front of the house, beside an SUV that hadn't been here the last time she'd visited. She pulled her purse and the small packed bag from the backseat and walked to the front door. Then, drawing a deep breath, she rang the bell.

To her surprise, Edward didn't answer. A dark-haired man greeted her instead. His good looks weren't as rugged as Mike's, but there was a family resemblance. Amber guessed this man was Mike's cousin.

"Amber?" he asked.

She inclined her head. "Derek?"

"Good guess." He extended his hand and she shook it. "Welcome."

"Thanks. I didn't expect you here." She glanced over his shoulder into the house, but she didn't see Edward.

"I thought I'd smooth things over," he said, gesturing for her to come inside. He took the bag from her hand and placed it by the stairs, then led her into the family room she'd seen the other night.

"It's really nice of you to help me out, but I'm sure you have better things to do than babysit."

"I hardly consider getting to know my cousin's wife babysitting. Why don't you have a seat." He pointed to an old blue velvet sofa and she chose a space in the middle.

Derek sat in a chair across the room and studied her without saying a word.

"Mike told you about us?" Amber asked, breaking the awkward silence. Considering how much he didn't want people to know their official status, she thought maybe Mike had told his cousin she was just a friend who needed help. So she was surprised when Derek had called her Mike's wife. But she cautioned herself against reading too much into it.

Derek raised an eyebrow. "Mike and I are close. We don't lie to each other."

Ouch, Amber thought. Direct hit. Apparently this man knew more than she'd realized. She didn't blame Mike or Derek for their feelings about her past, but she refused to let Derek bait her into a confrontation.

"I'm glad he confided in you. It's good that he has someone he trusts," she said to Derek. She met his gaze without flinching. She'd done what she'd done, but she refused to let her past define who she was—and who she wanted to be.

The crunching sound of a car driving up the gravel distracted her, but not Derek.

He leaned forward, his hands clasped in front of him. "Look, you must realize a quickie marriage in Vegas isn't exactly the best way to start a lasting relationship."

He was blunt and Amber respected that. And he obviously didn't know what to make of her, not that she blamed him. If the situation were reversed, she'd look out for her family, too. A family she didn't have. Both her parents had been only children, leaving Amber without siblings or cousins. She envied Mike his relationships, she realized for the first time.

It was another void she hadn't let herself acknowledge until now. And another good reason to create a lasting future here—if she and Mike were meant to be.

The front door opened and a beautiful woman with auburn hair hanging past her shoulders walked inside. Derek's surprised gaze slid the other woman's way for a moment before turning back to Amber.

Amber leaned toward Derek, wanting to end this conversation before their visitor heard. "I'm not going to hurt Mike," she assured him.

"What do you call deserting him the morning after the wedding?" Derek pinned her with his gaze, cutting her no slack, not dropping the subject as she'd hoped.

"Back off, Derek," the woman said, her high heels clicking against the floor with every step. "Everyone has a past, everyone makes bad choices now and then. You ought to know. It's what they do with the present and future that counts. I'm Derek's wife, Gabrielle, by the way," she said, striding over to where Amber sat.

Amber smiled at the other woman, grateful for her show of support. She rose. "I'm Amber. It's nice to meet you."

Derek pushed himself up from the chair. "I thought we agreed you were going to stay home today?" Derek asked.

Clearly he hadn't wanted her to meet his cousin's ne'er-do-well, *temporary* wife. But despite the censure in his tone, love and pleasure shone in his face, softening his features. These two shared the real thing, Amber thought, and a whisper of jealousy flushed through her.

Envy.

She wanted what they shared. More than she'd even realized.

Gabrielle shook her head and her glossy hair fell over one shoulder. "I said I'd stay home and work— I'm a writer," she explained to Amber. "But then I realized that Amber could probably use some help getting settled, not to mention some company. It's not like Edward's going to give her any."

"Where is he, anyway?" Amber asked. There'd been no sign of her host since she'd arrived.

Derek shrugged his shoulders. "He said he was going out. That could mean any number of things."

"How did he take the news that I'd be staying here?"

Derek paused, probably trying to find a nice way to express his uncle's words.

"Never mind," Amber said. "I can only imagine. Where's the skunk?"

"The what?" Gabrielle asked, glancing nervously around the room.

Amber laughed. "Stinky Pete. He's Edward's descented skunk. Edward doesn't like to advertise Pete's lack of odor though. He thinks Pete will keep visitors away."

Derek pinched the bridge of his nose. "What the hell will he think of next?"

Gabrielle shuddered. "I think it's safer not to ask."

Derek's cell phone rang and he answered. "Hi, Dad." He paused. "You ran into him where?" Derek listened, then, "Yes, I know why he's buying extra food and things. I'll explain later." Again, Derek paused. "No, don't get him riled up. I'll talk to you when I get home." He flipped the phone closed.

"What is it?" Gabrielle asked, placing a hand on her husband's shoulder.

Derek shoved the phone back into his pants' pocket. "My father saw Edward at the supermarket in town, talking to himself and buying more food than one man needs." He shot a glance at Amber. "Don't worry. People won't automatically think he has company just because he's stocking up. They'll assume he wants to avoid coming back to town for a while. But I'd move your car around back to be safe."

"I will." She paused. "If you don't mind my asking, why would your father wonder about Edward's shopping habits? Wouldn't he make the same assumption everyone does?"

"My father knows his brother pretty well, but their relationship is strained. Hank, my father, lives with my uncle Thomas," Derek said.

"You see, Thomas and Edward fought over a woman," Gabrielle continued. "She married Thomas, and Edward stopped speaking to his brother. He blamed the curse, moved to the far side of town, and when his marriage to Mike's mother didn't work out, he became a recluse," Gabrielle finished helpfully.

Derek shot his wife an annoyed glance. "She didn't need so much detail."

"Relax," Gabrielle told him. "I'm sure Mike already told Amber about it. While she's living here, she should understand what she's dealing with."

"He did. I just didn't know everything, so thank you."

"Maybe that's because your husband didn't think you'd be around long enough to worry about it."

"Derek! That's just rude." Gabrielle shook her head in frustration. "Go to work. Go buy things for Holly's visit. Holly's his daughter," she told Amber. "Go do anything but stay here. Come back when you can be more friendly." She pushed him toward the door and he allowed her to take control, probably happy to be rid of the burden Mike had placed on him.

"He's loyal to his cousin," Amber said, understanding Derek's attitude toward her. "I can't say I blame him, but I'm hoping he'll give me a chance to prove he's wrong for distrusting me." Amber sensed she needed this man on her side if she wanted to reach Mike.

"He will," Gabrielle said pointedly. "He has better manners than he's shown you so far. Give her a chance," she called to her husband, who was still standing by the door.

Derek groaned. "Oh, hell. If Gabrielle wants to get to know you, then so will I. Who knows? Maybe you'll be good for my cousin after all."

"That's the spirit. True love conquers all," Gabrielle said, smiling.

"Who said anything about love?" Derek asked. "Besides, that's the last word you should be using around here. You'll send Edward into a frenzy."

Gabrielle walked over and patted her husband's cheek. "Just go," she said lovingly before kissing him on the lips.

"Come home soon," he said.

"I will."

Derek turned to Amber. "Welcome to the family," he said slowly and maybe a little reluctantly.

He took Amber by surprise. "I appreciate your support," she said. "Or at least the chance to earn it."

"Just don't make me regret extending the welcome mat."

Amber crossed her heart. "I won't."

Suddenly an old car engine banged and rattled outside. "Sounds like Edward's home."

"I brought him a gift," Amber said. "It's still in the car. I'll just—"

Before she could finish her thought, the front door swung open and Edward walked inside. Derek quickly moved Gabrielle out of the way of the man pushing an old shopping cart in front of him.

If Amber hadn't met Mike's father once before, she'd have thought she was looking at a homeless person. His pants were baggy and old, his shirt torn, and he muttered under his breath.

"A man's house ain't his castle if he's gotta share

it. I got you fresh milk and some fruit. Gonna take up room in my fridge, though. I picked up some dry cereal for you. Don't complain if you don't like the brand."

"Thank you," Amber murmured.

She shot Gabrielle a questioning glance. Once Derek left, she'd question the other woman, a writer with insight, about her feelings regarding Edward's eccentricity, behavior and loneliness.

For now, though, she focused on Edward. "That's so thoughtful of you. I appreciate you letting me stay here. Can I put those things away for you?" Amber asked.

"I can do it myself." Without meeting her gaze, the older man walked past her to the kitchen.

Derek sighed. "Look, I think this is as good as its going to get. The fact that he bought food at all is a near miracle. Mike said he gave you some cash, so if you need anything, you can pick it up in town. Or better yet, call me and I'll grab it for you. There's no reason to advertise that there's someone new in town, let alone a woman staying with Edward, the loner."

Gabrielle nodded in agreement. "Especially since you want to keep a low profile."

"You're right. Thank you," she said, grateful she had these people looking out for her.

But how long would their generosity—or her luck—hold out?

KING BOBBY HATED IT in the East. He missed the Texas air and wide-open spaces. Worse, there was no sign of the pretty lady in sight. She wasn't comin' or goin' from the tiny apartment building Mike Corwin, the cop she'd married, listed as his place of residence. And it was tiny. What kinda man lived in a matchbox like that?

He got claustrophobic just looking at it. In fact, he'd even started to feel like *he* was bein' followed. But it had to be his imagination. He didn't know anyone who'd be lookin' for him.

Not that it mattered. Because he wasn't leavin' here until he found Mrs. Amber Rose Corwin *and* his money.

CHAPTER TEN

MIKE TOSSED HIS KEYS on the counter and headed directly to his bedroom. After a long day at work, he wanted nothing more than to get some sleep, wake up, work tomorrow and then drive to Stewart. Dan had let Mike borrow his car since the newlyweds still had Natalie's. Mike appreciated the loaner. He didn't want Amber with him any longer than necessary.

He was worried about his family bonding with Amber. It was easy enough to do, Mike knew. And if that happened, the divorce and life *after* Amber would be twice as difficult. But Mike was probably worrying about nothing. Edward was a loner, through and through. Besides, he wouldn't bond with any woman he thought his son might fall in love with. He'd push her away—and fast. Amber's beauty itself gave Edward cause to worry about his son falling hard.

As for Mike, he knew what Edward didn't: he *couldn't* fall for her. Not with what she'd done, what she'd kept from him. But damn, he did miss her vibrant personality and her laughter.

And if, by slim chance, Edward got soft, then Amber still had to get by his cousin Derek, who wasn't at all happy with Mike marrying a stranger in Vegas, let alone allowing her back into his life after she'd stolen from him.

No, he didn't have to worry about any of his family members being taken in by Amber. There would be no new ties being created back home that would make a divorce any more difficult when this was over.

Only Amber herself.

She'd been in his apartment for a few days and yet he was forced to admit the place felt empty without her. And in the same way he'd avoided coming home to her the two nights she'd been here, he'd made the decision *not* to come home to the quiet apartment tonight. Not until it was late and all he'd have time to do was sleep, he thought, glancing at the empty, perfectly made bed.

He normally left it rumpled and ready to climb back into, but Amber had made the bed when she'd been here. The crisp bedding looked fresh and inviting.

And lonely.

Gone, too, were the items she'd placed on the nightstand, the feminine clutter, evidence of a shared life. Mike shook his head hard.

Was he really bemoaning the loss of a woman whom he'd classified as a liar by omission, a cheat by admission?

Yeah, he thought. He was.

Damn.

The phone rang and, grateful for the distraction, he answered on the first ring. "Hello?"

"When are you getting your woman out of my hair?" his father blurted, not bothering to say hello first.

Mike realized he should be more worried about Edward driving Amber crazy than Edward softening toward her.

"I'm working on it," he said.

And he was. He'd started by digging into King Bobby Boyd's background. Earlier today he'd called the small downtown Texas police department where King Bobby Boyd's Used-Car Dealership was located. Thanks to professional courtesy, he'd gotten some basic information, which hadn't been the least bit helpful.

No police record, not even a driving infraction. The man was squeaky clean and, according to the chief, full of hot air. Mike would have been relieved, except that the chief also mentioned that King Bobby was as dirty as his used cars, only no one had been able to pin anything on him. And he didn't only deal in stolen cars. It was common knowledge that the man had big-time criminal connections. But again, the man couldn't be arrested for the company he kept, and nobody had ever managed to pin anything on King Bobby Boyd. Even the Texas chief had used the stupid moniker of King.

Without a rap sheet, Mike had turned to a P.I. the police chief had recommended. It wasn't a direction Mike had wanted to go in, but he had no choice. If he couldn't catch the King for being involved in illegal dealings, he'd just find another vice. In Mike's experience, guys who liked the rush of high-stakes poker games always came with other failings.

Mike planned to uncover King Bobby's skeletons and use them in exchange for the man's agreement to leave Amber alone. Mike wouldn't call it bribery, it was more of a quid pro quo. In any case, he now knew King Bobby was a legitimate threat.

"Hey, these minutes are costin' me money. Are you listening?" Edward bellowed into the phone line.

Technically they were costing Mike money, but he didn't correct his father. "Sorry, Dad, can you repeat that? I didn't hear you."

"I said I feel like I'm livin' in a zoo. With your wife stayin' here and your cousin Derek and *his* wife coming and going like they own the place, a man can't get any privacy."

"I'm sorry," Mike said, trying to figure out what

was so odd about his father's complaints. "At least they're keeping you company."

"Have I ever asked for company? And did I mention Amber's makin' herself at home? She's cleaning. I don't need a woman keepin' house for me. I can see my kitchen counters. I dang near forgot they were white. The shelves in the family room are dust free and I can't find Stinky Pete's favorite toy. He's moping around here like he lost his manhood again."

"His *what?* Never mind," Mike said before his father could answer.

Just then it dawned on him what was bothering him about Edward. His father *said* the words of complaint, but he didn't really *sound* as though he meant them. Could he be enjoying the company? Once again, Mike had to wonder if Amber understood his father better than Mike did.

"I may have to go back to town tomorrow to get Stinky Pete another toy," Edward said.

Mike also opted not to ask what Stinky Pete's toy was, figuring it was another thing he was better off not knowing. "Go back to town?" Mike asked instead. "You were there already today?" His father rarely went to town. To do so twice in one day was unheard of.

"Had to get milk and cereal for my guest."

Mike couldn't suppress a grin. His father, who

lived alone and kept to himself, had ventured to town to make Amber's stay more pleasant.

And again Mike had the sense Edward was simply filling Mike in on his day, not moaning about it the way he pretended to. He *was* enjoying the company.

"I'll be damned," Mike said aloud.

"The hell you will. I got enough jujus around here to spare one for you. I'll give one to ya when you come to get your wife. When did you say that would be again?"

Mike swallowed a chuckle. "I didn't. But I'll be there tomorrow after work to see how things are going."

"I'm coming!" Edward yelled. "Damn woman made me some bedtime tea. I used to know someone once who selled newfangled tea and she was no good. It's a bad sign, I tell ya."

Mike didn't reply.

And Edward kept talking. "Your wife also brought me a New Age dreamcatcher. Another bad omen. She says it'll help me keep the curse away, but last time I owned one it brought more bad luck. What do you have to say to that?" his father asked.

What the hell was a dreamcatcher and where had Amber found one? His father's ramblings were beginning to give Mike a headache.

"It all sounds harmless, Dad. And look, it's better than stringing up fake cats." Or live ones. Mike left that thought unsaid.

"I gotta go drink my tea. Amber says it'll help bring good dreams, not bad. See you tomorrow." Edward disconnected the call, leaving Mike staring at the dead phone line.

Mike's head spun with the information his father had given him. Amber had shown up and taken over. She was caring for his father in a way nobody had in years. It had been just a few short hours and the change in Edward was noticeable.

Mike was in shock. And he suddenly realized he had to figure out what his father really needed from other people in his life, and then to be sure he received it from now on.

He stripped off his clothes and climbed into bed. Though he tried to sleep, his mind was too full.

Of Amber.

He owed her for opening his eyes to his father's needs.

He missed her in his bed, her soft body curled against him, her hands making him ache while he slept.

He yawned and forced his mind back to what he could handle. He owed her. And he could repay her by fixing the mess she was in with King Bobby Boyd so she could return to Las Vegas and to her own father.

Leaving Mike alone to handle his.

AMBER AWOKE to a hammering sound coming from outside her bedroom window. She immediately remembered she was at Edward's house, but she couldn't imagine what was causing the noise. She'd slept in her pajama pants and top, so she pulled on a hooded sweatshirt and headed to check out the source.

Once she set foot in the family room, she saw Edward peering out the window through a pulled-back curtain.

"What's going on?" she asked. "Who's banging out there?"

"That son of a bitch Harry Winters is selling his house. The realtor putting up a For Sale sign is the one making all the racket," Edward said.

"Who's Harry Winters? Your neighbor?" Amber asked.

"Best damn neighbor a man could have. Want to know why? He lives alone and never bothers me. He never has company, and he's got no family to come visit. Everything around here stays quiet. That's why," Edward rambled.

Amber watched his agitated state with concern. He paced back and forth, periodically glancing out at the window facing the only house nearby.

"I wouldn't worry about it." She tried to think of something to calm him down. "The market's pretty slow right now. The chances of him selling quickly aren't that good."

He shot her a wild-eyed look. "But people will come to look at the house. They'll look at me. They'll talk. And then the curse will come up. I don't want to be a freak show for people to gawk at."

Amber lowered herself into a chair near the window, hoping to calm him down. "If you take down the jujus and the totem poles, nobody would know there's anything here to talk about."

"And leave myself unprotected? Have you lost your mind?" His voice rose. "Do you want to know what happens to Corwin men who aren't careful?"

"What happens?" she asked quietly. She didn't know if her soothing tone would relax him, but it was worth a shot.

"Same thing that happens in the end to every Corwin man. Take my grandfather. He was in love with his wife. Only he caught her in the act with the neighbor, him buck naked, them going at it like rabbits, to hear him tell it. My grandfather shot the bastard and my grandmother had a heart attack right then and there. He was never the same." He placed his hand over his heart, which had to be beating rapidly. She could tell by Edward's flushed face that his blood pressure was off the charts.

"Sounds like something out of a soap opera," Amber said, the pain in this family tree unfathomable. Poor Edward.

"Well, it's real life. Then there was my folks.

Had us three boys and they were happy. Thought they'd beaten the curse and then they got careless. A huge nor'easter hit the coast and wiped out most of the town, including my father's blacksmith business. Tools, equipment, building, all gone." Edward swiped the air with his hand.

Amber reached for rational thought on this one. "Aren't hurricanes common on the East Coast though?" she asked gently, so as not to further upset him.

"Yeah, I heard that explanation more than once. Gabrielle likes to spout that nonsense, too. An act of God, nobody's fault, there's no such thing as a curse," he said, mimicking phrases he'd obviously heard. "The storm hit late in the day and we were all home from school. Only, my father was at his shop. Mom was worried about Dad, so she left us with my grandmother to go look for him. She never came home. A flash flood hit hard and she drowned." Edward turned away from Amber.

But not before she caught the burst of pain and fear in the older man's eyes. She now understood why he believed so strongly in the curse. A weaker man would allow his tragic past, not to mention the awful things he'd gone through in his own life, to drive him insane. For Edward Corwin, it wasn't just his own life that carved out his reality, but the lives of his ancestors, too.

"Every Corwin male who ignored the curse has

lived to pay the price. Myself included. Stayin' here alone on the edge of town has been my salvation." Edward nodded his head, emphasizing his point.

Amber was tempted to mention that it had also been his downfall, but she realized he wasn't in any frame of mind to hear those words, let alone understand them. "Why don't I go outside and talk to the Realtor. See what his plans actually are," she offered.

Before Edward could answer, Gabrielle's little black Lexus convertible pulled to a stop in front of the house. She headed up the unpaved walkway and Amber opened the door before she had to ring the bell.

"Uncle Edward, you need to pave the driveway or I'm going to break an ankle," Gabrielle said, grabbing on to the doorframe for balance before she stepped inside.

"I ain't your uncle," he muttered.

Gabrielle glanced at Amber and grinned. "Yes, you are. You're my uncle by marriage. When are you going to stop arguing with me?"

He made a frustrated sound and returned to peering out the window.

"What's going on?" Gabrielle asked.

"The house next door just went up for sale," Amber explained. She looked from her pajamas to Gabrielle's pretty skirt and sleeveless top.

Somehow the other woman managed to look like

a model even at 9:00 a.m. A pale model, but maybe it was the precarious trek across the gravel that had shaken her, Amber thought.

"Harry Winters is moving?" Gabrielle asked, obviously surprised. "I thought he liked being alone as much as you do," she said to Edward.

"Yeah, well, after you got Mayor Mary Perkins arrested last year, Harry wasn't afraid to go out anymore. He met a lady friend at the Wave not long after it was rebuilt from the fire."

Gabrielle raised her eyebrows. "And just how would you know all this?"

Amber wondered that herself. For a man who rarely left the house and didn't talk to anyone when he did, Edward sure knew a lot.

Edward glanced away, refusing to meet their gaze. "Harry and me talk sometimes. Don't look at me like I'm crazy. Neighbors do that," he muttered, a mass of contradictions. "Now, would you two go away and give me some privacy?"

"I really should jump in the shower first," Amber said.

"And I brought my laptop to work down by the lake." Gabrielle gestured out back.

"I got my own work to do," Edward muttered and walked out of the family room, planning to do who knows what, who knew where.

"Difficult old coot," Gabrielle said, but there was obvious affection in her tone.

The women parted ways, agreeing to meet up later.

Amber showered and pulled herself together for the day. She picked up a book from Edward's shelves and a towel to sit on, then headed out back, settling herself beneath a tree for shade. Beside her, Gabrielle clicked away at her computer.

A warm breeze blew through the moist air. "This humidity is awful." Amber ran her hand through her hair.

"I've done book tours out West and I think the dry heat can kill you. But I'm sure the humidity takes some getting used to," Gabrielle said with a laugh.

"How would you know, with your perfect hair that falls so straight?" Amber eyed the other woman's glossy tresses with envy only another woman could understand.

"We always want what we don't have."

"Amen," Amber said.

"Right now, I'm growing out a short bob. I'd kill for long curls like yours," Gabrielle said.

In her concierge days, Amber had opted for the sleek and sophisticated look. A flatiron and lack of humidity had helped her accomplish that goal. But on take-it-easy days like today, she let it dry naturally.

She stretched her feet out and looked over the

lake. "Is that Edward fishing?" She pointed to a place far away from where they sat.

Gabrielle glanced over. "Mmm-hmm."

"He looks peaceful." So different from the stressed-out man he'd been earlier. "Fishing must relax him," Amber said.

"There are no fish." Gabrielle perched her sunglasses on top of her head. "But at least he seems calmer."

Amber nodded. "Did you ever notice how he teeters on the edge, between sanity and mania, and back again?"

Gabrielle nodded. "The whole family notices. It's easier to just leave him alone as much as possible. Trust me, you don't want his attention focused on you. I should know." She ran her hands up and down her arms, glancing out across the lake. "I lost a baby six months ago," she said softly, obviously confiding her deepest secret.

Amber was touched Gabrielle had chosen to tell her. "I'm sorry."

"Thank you. The reason I wanted you to know this now is because of Edward. His reaction was crazy. He took the miscarriage as a sign the curse is at work. Ever since, he's been making me crazy and that's pretty hard to do." Gabrielle forced a laugh.

"I've seen your books in stores. Based on the subject matter you write about, I'd bet it's difficult to spook you."

Gabrielle inclined her head. "Exactly. But when Edward gets in one of *those* moods, like he is today, all rational thought flies out the window. Even I get nervous."

"I can understand that. So the curse is pretty well known around here?"

Gabrielle nodded. "The stuff of town lore," she said, a frown on her face.

"What about Mike? Where does he fall on the curse-believing scale?" Amber asked.

"Well, he's never acted as if he feared it, not the way Derek has. Then again, he's never been serious about a woman, either. Coincidence or intent?" Gabrielle shrugged, but she studied Amber with her astute gaze. "I couldn't tell you. But he's married to you now…"

"But he isn't in love. *We* aren't in love. No love, no curse. So maybe I was just a safety net for him." Even as Amber asked the question, the thought hurt her.

She'd married Mike on a whim, but she'd taken those vows seriously. She'd begun to care about his family and she *knew* she cared about him. Enough to want him to care about her in return.

Gabrielle shook her head. "Don't read too much into it," she said, as if knowing Amber's thoughts. "Every situation in the world has been played out in Corwin male history. If they want to find a way to say the curse exists, they will. If they want to overcome it badly enough, they can do that, too. As for Mike, I'd say his biggest problem is across the pond."

"I agree. Edward's like one of those people in the medication ads who suffer extreme highs and lows."

"Now, that's a good point. I wonder if he's ever been to a doctor? A psychiatrist? I don't know. But you should ask your husband," Gabrielle said.

Her husband. The words felt so good, so ripe with possibilities.

"What do you know about our marriage?" Gabrielle had talked Derek into giving Amber a chance, which had made Amber like Gabrielle immediately. And she desperately needed someone to talk to about Mike and her current situation. She needed a friend.

"I know a lot," Gabrielle said, then summarized Amber and Mike's relationship.

"So you pretty much know the whole sordid story." Amber tried not to show her embarrassment because deep down, she was grateful the other woman was well informed. "At least I don't have to retell it. Knowing all that, do you really think Mike will take any advice about his father from me?"

Gabrielle shrugged. "If he doesn't, he should. It's obvious to me how much you care about Mike. He'll be here later today, right?"

Amber nodded. "He's coming straight from work."

"You can find out more then. But I can promise you this. I'm on your side."

One Corwin more than she'd had yesterday, Amber thought, pleased. "Where is Derek?" she asked, changing the subject.

"At work. He's a financial planner. He wants to get as much accomplished as possible before his daughter, Holly, comes to visit for the summer."

"How old is she?"

"Turning thirteen this August. She's a great kid."

Amber recalled what she'd learned of Derek's first marriage. She knew he adored his daughter, but Amber was glad he and Gabrielle had gotten a second chance.

Gabrielle suddenly grabbed her purse and looked through it. "Damn, I forgot them," she muttered, before glancing at Amber. "Do you know if there are any saltines in the kitchen?"

"I don't think so. There are corn flakes, though."

Gabrielle wrinkled her nose and groaned, low and deep. "No, it has to be saltines. I think I'll take a ride into town," she said, shutting her laptop and gathering her things.

Amber narrowed her gaze. "You looked a little pale earlier." And now she was asking for saltine crackers. "Are you feeling okay?"

Gabrielle clutched her laptop against her chest.

"I'm pregnant," she whispered, although nobody else was around to hear.

"That's wonderful!" Amber squealed. "I mean, that's wonderful," she repeated, whispering this time.

"Thank you." Gabrielle's eyes sparkled with excitement despite the morning sickness she was obviously suffering from. "It feels so good to tell someone. I took an early home-pregnancy test this morning after Derek left for work. Once I knew, I couldn't just sit home alone, you know? But you can't tell anyone yet. I want to get past the point I was at last time before I tell anyone else. I don't want Derek to get overly protective."

"I understand. I do. But won't he be upset you kept it from him?" Amber knew the consequences of keeping secrets from her husband firsthand.

Gabrielle shook her head. "He'll understand. Besides, if I tell him, he'll take my shoes away and insist I wear sensible flats. He'll drive me crazy!"

Amber laughed. "Well, we can't have that!" In just two meetings, Amber had already pegged Gabrielle as a woman with incredible fashion sense and taste, especially in designer shoes.

"Besides, Derek loves you," Amber continued. "That's obvious even to someone who's only seen you together once." Just thinking of the way husband and wife had looked at one another left Amber feeling wistful and sad.

She wanted that for herself. Love, caring, family.

Speaking of family, she checked her watch. It was noon Eastern time, 9:00 a.m. in Vegas. She normally called the nursing home around ten, after her father had eaten and been bathed and dressed. That way the staff could tell her what kind of day he was having. She had an hour to kill before she could check in.

"Do you want me to go to town and pick up some crackers and ginger ale for you?" Amber asked.

Gabrielle shook her head. "Thanks. I'll go. I could use a break from this story. Anything I can get for you?"

"Actually, if you don't mind, I'll give you a small list." Edward's idea of food and Amber's were light-years apart.

She walked Gabrielle back to the house and they chatted like old friends. Amber was thrilled to be the keeper of her new sister-in-law's secret and hoped for a smooth pregnancy this time around.

Gabrielle drove off and Amber headed back inside, her thoughts on Gabrielle and the family she was building with Derek. The more Gabrielle had talked about the baby she was expecting, the more the yearning in Amber's chest grew to one day have those same things for herself. She still didn't know where Mike fit into her future, but she did know she missed him.

She'd slept by herself her entire life and yet she'd had a hard time falling asleep alone last night. She'd missed snuggling into Mike's warm body. Even more, she'd missed waking up to his sexy morning smile, his gruff hello and the eager way he'd thrust inside her once he allowed himself to let go. Even if he was upset with her, in bed they were one hundred percent compatible. How many married couples could say the same?

Mike was different from other men. No man in her past had ever filled the space inside her the way he did. None had left an aching emptiness when they were gone. He *could* be her family, her future—if he'd put the same effort into the relationship she intended to.

Because she already knew how easily she could fall for him.

CHAPTER ELEVEN

MIKE LEFT the station and drove directly to his father's house, looking forward to seeing Amber more than was prudent. But prudence had never played a role in this impulsive relationship, which, he admitted, was what had him so on guard, off-kilter—and exhilarated all at the same time.

His cell phone rang. A quick glance told him Dan was calling and he pushed the speaker button to keep it hands free. "Talk to me," Mike said.

"You had a phone call at the station. A P.I. in Texas," his partner said.

Elvin Rogers, the man Mike had hired to investigate King Bobby Boyd, Mike thought, and his heart rate kicked up a notch. Maybe he'd finally get the information he needed on the stupidly named man so Amber could feel safe.

"Thanks for letting me know," he said to his partner.

"No problem. What case are you working in Texas that I don't know about? Are you holding out on me?" Dan asked.

Mike laughed. Sometimes his partner could be such a baby, constantly needing reassurance. "It's not a case, it's personal."

"And you're not going to fill me in," Dan said.

Mike heard the rebuke in the other man's voice. "Maybe someday." When he could look at himself in the mirror and not feel like such a tool. "I've got to go," Mike said.

"Fine. Just remember what we talked about the other day. Enjoy your wife the way I'm enjoying mine," Dan said.

"Thanks for the advice, Dear Abby. Talk to you later."

Mike hung up and called the P.I., only to get his answering machine informing callers *Elvin Rogers, private investigator extraordinaire was on the case.*

Mike groaned. What was with these Texas yahoos giving themselves nicknames and pats on the back? He left a message for the other man to call him as soon as possible and once again left his cell phone number, which Elvin hadn't bothered to use.

As Mike settled in for the rest of the drive to Stewart, it wasn't thoughts of King Bobby that filled his mind, but his partner's words. *Enjoy your wife,* echoed in Mike's head. It wasn't the first time his partner had given Mike that advice. The last time, Mike had gone home intending to do just that. Then her *news* destroyed his intent and ruined his mood.

Not Amber's. She'd been able to put their argument behind her and make love not war. She easily seduced him into doing the same. As he eagerly drove to see her, he had to ask himself, *why was he fighting it?*

He already knew they were incompatible long-term, but when they were together, they were almost combustible. They both knew he'd succumb to her charm anyway, so why not *enjoy* the time he had with her?

He couldn't think of one good reason. His mind made up, and his mood lightened, Mike allowed himself to look forward to seeing his wife.

MIKE ARRIVED at his father's house to find Amber had parked his car around back, a smart move for which he credited his cousin. Outside was quiet and the front door unlocked, something he'd have to discuss with his father, at least for as long as Amber stayed here. When Edward was alone, Mike figured nobody had the nerve to bother him.

Mike let himself inside. "Hello?" he called.

No answer.

He figured his father was down by the lake. As for Amber... With a shrug, he headed down the short hall to the guest bedroom. It had been Mike's room when he was a child, but when his mother moved out, and Edward showed no interest in re-decorating, Mike had renovated it. This way he could stay over if the need arose, in a queen-size bedroom with a decent TV.

Amber's voice carried into the hall. She was on her cell phone, he realized as he stopped in the doorway. He was about to turn around and walk away, giving her privacy, when her gaze caught his.

A wide smile brightened her face and she waved him inside.

She was glad to see him, and like a teenager who hadn't seen his girlfriend in too long, his gut churned and his heart kicked into high gear.

He settled beside her on the bed and waited for her to finish her conversation.

"I understand, Nanette. I know he had a rough morning, but I'd hoped he'd feel better this after-noon." She gripped the receiver tighter in her hand.

Obviously she was talking to someone at the nursing home and her father wasn't doing well.

"Thanks. I'll call in the morning," she said, then hit the off button, placing the phone on the night-stand.

"Your father?" Mike asked.

Amber nodded. "He's more out of it today than usual. The good news is he doesn't know I'm not around to visit him." Her voice cracked with the admission.

Her pain touched him and he reached out to pull

her close. "He can't tell you, but somewhere deep inside your father, he knows that you love him, that you're caring for him the best way you can," he said gruffly.

She tilted her head back and studied him. "Do *you* believe that?" she asked, her eyes wide and hopeful.

Mike knew she was asking far more than whether her father, in his Alzheimer's-induced state, sensed her caring. What she wanted to know was whether Mike now believed she had done the best, the *only* thing she could do back in Vegas for her only parent.

Mike cupped her cheek in one hand and stroked her cheek. "I believe you *thought* you were doing the best thing you could."

She let out a tremulous breath and treated him to a sweet smile. "Well, that's a start."

He didn't reply. He couldn't. Her skin was soft, her hair curling gently around her face, and he was entranced. Then, when she moistened her lips with her delicate tongue, his body went up in flames.

"I missed you last night," she said. Her fingers idly stroked the bed, making him realize how badly he needed her to stroke him.

It had been like this from first sight, Mike thought, this unique yearning for her.

Only her.

"I missed you, too." The admission cost him a chunk of pride, yet he didn't care.

"What did you say?" She cocked her head to the side, a twinkle in her eyes. "Are you really admitting that you missed me?" she asked, obviously pleased. Her genuine pleasure at their connection was a tangible thing.

He'd made her happy and he was glad. But she didn't need to know he'd lost his inner battle. It was up to him to come to terms with wanting her despite their differences, and with accepting what she offered, only for as long as she was his wife. Those were his burdens to bear.

He pushed those thoughts out of his mind and turned his attention to the woman in front of him. "Yes, I missed you. I admit it. I hope now that you've gotten what you wanted out of me, you're not complaining?" He shifted his touch from her face and ran his hand along the back of her hair, savoring the feel of the long strands against his skin.

Amber shook her head and grinned. "Far from it. Want to know just how glad?"

He nodded and she looped her arms around his neck, pulling him close until his lips closed over hers. He kissed her with all the longing and pent-up desire that had been building ever since she'd left Boston. Kissed her with the same passion she exhibited and then some.

He eased her backward until she lay on the

bed, their mouths never breaking the sensual connection. He pulled her shirt up and slid his hand beneath the soft cotton, moving upward until he reached her breast, covered by a sheer slip of a bra. Ignoring the material, he cupped her in his palm and moved his hand in deliberate circles until her nipple peaked against him. Then he moved to the other breast, arousing her the same way.

Beneath him, her hips rotated in a rhythm that begged him for so much more than he was giving her, and he reveled in her soft whimpers. He slid his mouth from her lips, across her cheek, and began nibbling on her earlobe. His tongue trailed a path down her neck, pausing only in places he knew would make her writhe in need.

Ignoring his own desires in favor of hers wasn't easy. He wanted nothing more than to bury himself in her soft heat and slake the yearning, if only for a little while. Because with Amber, the need for her always returned, fast and with more intensity than before.

She reached for him, obviously intending to lift his shirt, but he held her hands at her sides. "Your turn first," he whispered in her ear.

He reached for her, about to lift the hem of her shirt, wanting to replace his hands with his mouth and give her even more pleasure.

The sound of yelling suddenly intruded on

their desire-filled haze. His father's yelling. From outside.

Mike closed his eyes, wanting to push reality away, but he couldn't.

Amber shot backward against the pillows, re-adjusting her clothes as she moved. "Something's wrong!"

He rose and shifted the waistband on his jeans. His body still hadn't absorbed that *it* wasn't going to happen and he tried to find some comfort before heading outside to see what had upset his father.

Amber stood.

"Are you okay?" He touched her pink, flushed cheek.

"No," she said shakily. "But it doesn't matter. Let's go see what's going on."

He nodded. The immediate connection had been broken, but the heat they'd generated left the promise of more to come.

Together they ran, heading out the front door.

"What's wrong?" Mike asked, running up to his father.

"Some stranger's takin' my jujus off the trees out front!" Edward yelled, storming up to the house.

A car slowly pulled up the graveled driveway, seeming to follow him. Mike didn't recognize the automobile and from the way Amber perched her hands on her hips, and squinted as she glanced over, neither did she.

"Where were you?" Mike asked his father.

"Out doing my daily check of the property. Once in the morning, once in the evening. And it's a good thing I stick to routine because I found a trespasser!"

Mike ran a hand through his hair. "This has to stop," he muttered, glancing at his agitated father.

Amber placed a calming hand on Mike's back. She couldn't talk to him now, but Gabrielle was right. They did need to discuss Edward's mental health and the possibility of having the older man see a doctor.

The car came to a stop and to Amber's surprise, Clara Deveaux stepped out from the driver's seat, Edward's beloved jujus in her hand. Between her own father's health and Mike's return, Amber had forgotten all about Clara's possible visit.

The other woman made an impressive sight as she strode up the driveway, her long, flowered dress flowing around her as she moved.

"Who is that?" Mike asked.

"What is *she* doing here?" Edward yelled.

Before Amber could reply, Clara spoke to Amber. "It's a good thing you asked me to come. This man needs saving worse than I thought if he's relying on black magic to help him keep the curse away." Clara waved the juju in the air.

"*You* invited her here?" Edward turned toward

Amber, his face beet-red, his eyes deep and accusing.

"Who is she?" Mike asked once more.

Amber's invitation, which had seemed like an answer to Edward's troubles, suddenly seemed ill-advised. Not that she knew why.

But Edward glared at her with a look of betrayal in his eyes. Like father like son. His expression reminded Amber of Mike's the night she'd confessed.

Lord help her, Amber thought, her stomach clenching because she didn't know what kind of trouble she might have caused by bringing Clara here. Mike, who stood beside her, was as confused as Amber by his father's reaction.

She opted for the simple truth. "I met Clara when I was buying your gifts," she said to Edward. "The dreamcatcher, the tea and candles. You liked them, remember? Clara's lovely, which you'd see if you just give her a chance."

"I knew those things reminded me of *her!*" Edward yelled before darting around Amber, and running for the house.

He returned minutes later, armed. "Git going! Leave!" he shouted at Clara. "I don't need your help!" He dangled Stinky Pete in front of the woman, like a loaded gun.

"Dad!" Mike shouted. "Put that thing away."

It was like a scene out of some bizarre comedy. Amber expected Clara to run away screaming.

Instead, the other woman strode up to Edward, getting in his face as if she had the right. "Give me that poor animal. A descented skunk?"

"How did you know it's descented?" Amber couldn't begin to imagine.

"It's obvious." Clara shook her head as if surprised Amber even had to ask. "Even a crazy man isn't going to live with that kind of odor around him."

"Excuse me, but did you just call my father *crazy?*" Mike stepped forward to defend his parent.

"Pot and kettle," Edward muttered.

"Just how do you know this woman?" Mike asked.

"Ask *her,*" Edward said.

Amber turned to Clara. "Well?"

"I'll explain in a moment," she said to Mike and Amber. She glanced at Edward. "Now, what in the name of the Goddess were you thinking, making that animal your pet, you crazy old coot!" Clara asked him. "You're nuttier than you were seven years ago!"

"And you're bossier," Edward snapped.

"Age will do that to you."

Watching the byplay, Amber shook her head in dismay. Clara hadn't mentioned knowing Edward before. And worse, the mild-mannered Clara Deveaux Amber had met in her shop had been replaced by a strong, take-charge woman with an agenda, leaving Amber feeling betrayed.

"How could you have deceived me that way?" Amber asked Clara. "I invited you here to help him and you used me to…to what?" She splayed her arms in front of her, frustrated and annoyed.

She couldn't bring herself to look at Mike. Beyond his confusion, Amber was sure there was anger simmering below the surface. Anger at Amber for bringing this woman into his father's already off-kilter world, creating more chaos and causing him obvious pain.

"I should have told you…" Clara stepped toward Amber.

"That's right, you should have," Amber said.

Beside her, Amber felt Mike's curious stare, but he remained quiet. Obviously, he was content to observe and find out just what kind of trouble Amber had caused him now.

"Honey, when you first came into the shop, you were just another customer." Clara touched Amber's shoulder.

"And when you realized I was talking about *the Corwins?*" Chilled, Amber ran her hands up and down her arms, shocked she'd been taken in by this woman.

"You were talking about us to this stranger?" Mike asked, his voice hard.

"I was looking to buy a gift for my father-in-law.

I said he believed in curses and I wanted something to show him I respected his beliefs, something that would help him," Amber said. "She drew the conclusion after I gave her my full name."

Mike nodded slowly, seeming to accept that explanation, and Amber's guilt eased a little.

"Edward and I knew each other a lifetime ago—" Clara's stare drifted toward Edward and lingered, softening.

"One I wish I'd never lived!" the other man shouted at her.

"Oh, be quiet, I'm talking to Amber." Clara waved a hand, causing her bangles to clink together the way Amber remembered.

Mike blinked. "They're bickering like some old…couple," he said to Amber under his breath.

She nodded, having caught those same undercurrents. Shocked, Amber merely glanced at Edward, expecting him to balk at being told what to do, but to her surprise, Edward crossed his arms over his chest and heeded Clara's words. He shut up.

Though Clara spoke to Edward in a no-nonsense tone he understood and respected, there was no mistaking how her whole expression changed, grew softer and more caring when her gaze fell on him.

"I don't know what to say," Mike said.

"Beats me," Amber said. But realizing Clara had genuine feelings for Edward allowed Amber's feelings of betrayal to let up. But she was still upset she'd been played for a fool.

Much the way Mike must have felt when he realized Amber had lied to him. For the first time, Amber not only knew what she'd done to him, she was able to empathize and feel his pain. She owed him an apology, not just for the omissions, but for getting angry when he hadn't understood her so-called justification.

For now though, she turned her attention back to Edward and Clara.

"Honey, once you invited me to visit you here, I realized the Goddess had a larger plan at work for me. She'd sent you to my shop for a reason. We had a past—" she gestured between herself and Edward "—and I never lived up to my end of things. You were offering me another chance to right an old wrong," Clara explained.

"Why didn't you just tell me you knew Edward after I'd invited you?"

"I was afraid you'd take back the invitation and I'd lose this second chance at our relationship." Her eyes grew damp and misty at the prospect.

Amber's heart clenched as she finally accepted the other woman's reasons.

"We ain't got no relationship!" Edward insisted before Amber could forgive her.

"We shared a past," Clara said firmly.

Amber wasn't sure she wanted to know what kind of past.

"I promised to help you once, Eddie, and I mean to do it now!"

"Eddie?" Amber repeated numbly.

"Eddie?" Mike echoed. "Somebody's going to have to tell me what exactly went on between you two and when."

Edward shook his head. "I ain't telling you nothing about my personal life," he said before storming off and heading back toward the lake.

"I didn't know he'd ever had a personal life," Mike said, confusion and a whole lot more in his expression.

"Why don't we go inside and I'll make us some tea," Amber suggested.

Amber needed to hear Clara's explanation. And she definitely had to discuss Edward's mental health with Mike. It was going to be a long night.

MIKE SAT in his father's kitchen, watching as Amber made herself at home. He'd grown up here, but his childhood memories weren't the best. He'd lived in an armed camp before his mother had moved out, and the kitchen had never been a place of refuge.

Until now, because Amber was here. Mike didn't know what had gone on between his father and Clara Deveaux, but clearly something important had transpired. He was glad Amber would be beside him when he found out what.

Amber made tea for Clara and herself, and without asking, she poured Mike a cola, his preferred choice in soft drinks. She knew better than to offer him herbal tea. And though he could use something stronger than soda, he always made sure there was no alcohol in his father's house. He had a healthy fear of the possibility of alcohol abuse in addition to his father's other issues. Thank goodness, to his knowledge that had never been a problem. Mike intended to keep it that way.

Once they were all seated, Amber met Clara's gaze. "I didn't know about your relationship with Edward when I asked you here. That makes his distress my fault."

Oddly, Mike didn't blame Amber for trying to help Edward. But he did need to know everything. "Why don't we start at the beginning," Mike said to Clara. "How do you know my father, and what happened between the two of you?" he asked.

Clara sighed. "It was seven years ago. I'd just opened my shop and Edward walked in. He was scruffy and a little grumpy, everything I shouldn't be attracted to—and yet I was drawn to him." Clara met Amber's gaze, probably searching for female understanding.

And maybe forgiveness, Mike realized. After

all, as Amber said, she'd met and invited Clara here without knowing about the other woman's agenda.

"Did Edward...um...look different seven years ago?" Amber asked.

Mike tried not to laugh. He could understand why she'd wonder about Clara's attraction to the wild-looking man Mike called his father.

Clara smiled. "He looked the same. He's an attractive man and all that bluster covers a wounded nature."

Clearly she saw something in Edward that the rest of the world, even his own son, couldn't. A part of Mike always feared digging too deep because really understanding Edward meant that maybe, Mike wasn't too far from the madness himself.

Clara took a sip of tea, then said, "Edward came to my shop the first time because he wanted to find ways to ward off the curse, but after a while, he came back just to see me."

"Edward pursued you?" Amber asked, surprised.

Mike was glad she was asking the questions. For a cop who specialized in interrogation, he couldn't bring himself to verbalize anything that might lead to more intimate knowledge of his father.

"He didn't pursue me directly. But a woman knows when a man is interested. When he cares."

Amber nodded. "I agree. A woman knows." Her

soft gaze slid to Mike's and an uncomfortable lump formed in his throat.

"Edward and I had much in common and I promised to help him overcome his fears," Clara continued. "But he came into my life at a tough time. My father had just arrived in the States from Jamaica. My mother is American and raised me here, but my father arrived with a friend of his, planning to marry me off."

"You were how old?" Amber asked.

"Forty. Too old to be told what to do. But we're never too old to want our parents' approval, now, are we?"

Another telling comment, Mike thought.

"I suppose not," Amber replied. "So what happened?"

"I did as my father asked and went on a date with this man, but I had no intention of marrying him, so I kept it from Edward." Clara glanced down.

Mike stiffened. If his father had come out of his shell, extended himself enough to reach out to her and she'd hurt him… He tensed, waiting. "What happened?" he asked, his voice harsh.

"The next morning, the gentleman brought flowers to my shop."

"And Edward was there," Amber guessed, shaking her head in disappointment.

Clara nodded. "My father was there, as well, making vocal assumptions about my future."

A knot formed in Mike's stomach as he pictured his father's reaction. Just as he'd taken the first steps to letting go of the curse, fate had knocked him down once more.

"Damn," Mike muttered.

Amber covered his hand with hers. "Do you remember this time in your father's life?"

He thought back. His parents had divorced ten years ago. "Seven years ago? I was twenty years old and in college. I didn't come home often and when I did, I rarely came to Dad's house," he admitted, looking away.

Amber squeezed his hand tighter. Mike tried not to blame himself for not wanting to be around his father, but when something like this happened, he felt the kick of guilt strongly. Eventually he'd grown up and accepted his father, failings and all, along with his responsibilities as an only child. He loved Edward and didn't blame him for not being there for him as a real father.

But clearly, if this woman had broken Edward's heart, he would have become bitter and angry and even more entrenched in his negative beliefs. And Mike hadn't been there to help him through it.

"How did Edward handle the situation?" Amber asked, continuing the conversation.

Clara expelled a long breath. "He didn't say a word. Just walked out and took my heart with him."

"Did you go after him?" Amber asked.

"I cleared things up with the other gentleman and my father, but then yes, of course I went after him. But he wouldn't listen. I called. He changed and unlisted his number. I wrote. The letters were returned unanswered."

"That I remember." Mike took his first sip of soda, his mouth dry. "My mother wanted to reach him, to tell him about her remarrying, but he'd changed his number. She was upset that she had to drive out here to tell him in person."

"You need to know, I didn't give up right away. I gave him some time and dropped by a few times, but he always refused to answer the door. There was no talking to the man." Clara spread her hands in front of her, expressing her useless feelings.

Amber wasn't surprised. "So seven years passed."

Clara nodded. "I never met another man who affected me the same way. And then you walked into my shop and I took it as a sign. It was time."

Amber pinched the bridge of her nose. This story had been heart-wrenching, on so many levels, she thought, glancing at Mike, who was sitting beside her, learning about the reasons for his father's mental deterioration firsthand.

"You decided it was time to what?" Amber asked Clara.

"I had to right the wrong I did Edward all those

years ago. I had to know if we could possibly have a future."

Her words echoed inside Amber, rendering her unable to stay angry. Suddenly Amber viewed herself and Clara as kindred spirits, two women who wanted the same basic thing from life.

Amber sighed. "I wish you'd told me the truth so I could have prepared him." Or at least prepared herself. She bit the inside of her cheek before speaking what was on her mind, too aware of the hurt man sitting beside her. "But since I've kept a few secrets of my own lately, I can't hold it against you," she told Clara.

Without warning, Mike rose from his seat. "I appreciate the explanation. Now, if you'll excuse me, I need to go find my father."

Heart in her throat, Amber watched him go. She glanced at Clara and forced a smile. She and this woman had more in common than she'd first thought. From lies and omissions, to hoping for a future with a good man, to the Corwin men and therefore their curse, Amber and Clara shared a bond.

Time would tell which, if either of them, would triumph.

CHAPTER TWELVE

EDWARD REFUSED to come into the house or talk to Mike about *that woman*. Mike didn't know what surprised him more, that his father had at one time stepped out of his self-imposed isolation and reached out to Clara Deveaux or the fact that the woman so obviously still had an impact on Edward now. At a loss over how to handle his father, Mike retreated inside the house where he and Amber ate dinner together, a meal she'd cooked for them by herself.

They shared comfortable conversation, Amber catching Mike up with what had gone on since she'd arrived in Stewart, and Mike filling her in about work and his partner's wedded bliss. A sense of normalcy settled over him and he realized he enjoyed the companionship, something he'd never really had before.

Every time he looked at Amber or inhaled her unique scent, the sexual attraction kicked him hard and he couldn't ignore it. Especially now that he'd given himself permission to indulge.

Today she wore a loose pink T-shirt with a low scoop neck and a pair of dark denim jeans. Barefoot, her red-painted toenails peeked out from beneath the hem of her pants. And her curls flowed around her shoulders, sexy and disheveled. She looked more delicious than the meal and he had a hard time keeping his mind on the food and conversation—instead of the *dessert* he hoped they'd share later on in bed.

When they finished eating, she filled a plate for Edward, covered it with tinfoil, and left it for him on the counter. "Maybe he'll eat when he comes inside."

Mike doubted it. "I'm sure he'll appreciate it," he said to Amber, not wanting to put a damper on her good intentions.

"Not that we'll ever know for sure." Amber laughed. Obviously she already had his father's number.

Edward would never admit to appreciating anything. But Mike had noticed Amber's caring nature and surely his father would, too.

Together they brought the dishes over to the sink. She quickly rinsed and put them in the dishwasher while he cleaned the table.

When she finished, she leaned against the counter, looking like a woman with something on her mind.

He wasn't in the mood for deep conversation. He'd had enough of that today.

"Are you upset with me for inviting Clara here?" she asked.

"Am I acting like I'm mad?" he asked.

Because he wasn't. Surprisingly, he didn't blame Amber for Clara's intrusion. After all, Amber had been duped into believing Clara was a stranger.

And Amber had forgiven Clara because, as Amber had so rightly pointed out earlier, she'd done her share of duping.

"No, but I sure stirred things up around here," Amber said, her eyes growing soft. "I wouldn't blame you if you were angry."

"Stirring things up seems to be something you do well." He couldn't hold back a grin. "Maybe I'm getting used to it."

Her eyes lit up in obvious shock and more than a hint of pleasure. "Michael Corwin, are you *teasing* me?" she asked.

He thought for a minute then said, "Yeah, I guess I am."

"Can I ask what caused the change?"

He shook his head, adamant about not getting into anything that could lead to an argument. "How about you just accept it and enjoy, instead?"

Her lips turned up in a smile. "I can do that." In one smooth motion, she looped her arms around his neck and placed a long, lingering kiss on his lips.

He liked her like this, compliant and willing, soft and easy in his arms. While he had her, he wasn't about to let her go. He slanted his mouth over hers, deepening the kiss, while tangling his fingers in her hair and tugging lightly.

She responded with a sweet moan, arching her back and pressing her chest against his. The softness of her body contrasted with the hard pucker of her nipples beneath her shirt and he could swear steam rose between them.

"Let's move this to the bedroom," he suggested, unwilling to wait another minute.

At the sound of Mike's voice, Amber stepped back and suddenly realized where she was—in Edward Corwin's kitchen. "The bedroom sounds good," she murmured.

He agreed with a low rumble from deep in his throat.

Her body agreed, too. More than anything, she wanted to satisfy the need he always created inside her. "But we can't continue what we started."

The words didn't come easily and the startled look on his face would have been priceless if it didn't hurt so badly.

And Mike wasn't laughing. "Why not?"

She gripped the counter behind her. "Because we're in your father's house. It's disrespectful, for one thing."

His eyes opened wide. "You were willing earlier! And we're *married,* for heaven's sake!"

"I know." More and more, she was beginning to think she wanted to stay that way, for more reasons than just the physical. That was why she'd changed her mind about sleeping with him now. She wanted to be smart about every move she made. "I just wouldn't be comfortable doing…it…here."

Throughout the day, she'd come to some conclusions she hoped would prove valuable in the long run. Mike had no problem with her in bed. Sexually they were one hundred percent compatible. But it was the other areas of their marriage that needed strengthening. She couldn't work on those if she succumbed to his charm in bed while allowing him to erect barriers everywhere else.

A muscle ticked in his jaw and he folded his arms across his chest. "Tell me you don't plan on sleeping in separate rooms while we're here?"

She shook her head, glad he sounded so frustrated at the notion. "Of course not. We'll sleep in the same room, in the same bed. We just won't have sex," she said, lowering her voice on the last word. "Relationships are about more than the physical."

He grit his teeth, clearly disagreeing. "And how do you think we'll get through the night?" He reached out and stroked her cheek, his voice tense with suppressed sexual tension.

Tension she felt, as well. But as much as she

desired him, a short-term fix wouldn't help her in the long run.

"We'll talk," she whispered in his ear, seductive yet deliberately playful. "We'll share intimate secrets and get to know each other better." She brushed her lips across his to silence any objection.

Then, taking his hand, she led her husband to bed.

IN THE BEDROOM, Mike found himself caught in a trap of his own making. He had taken the weekend off from work, a spur-of-the-moment decision he'd made after seeing his father's reaction to Clara Deveaux. He'd sensed a storm was brewing and he wanted to be there to help his father weather it.

But once again, irony bit him in the ass. Here he was, with his wife, having made the decision to sleep with her now and worry about leaving her when the time came. Didn't it figure that she'd decide to hold back?

She wanted them to get to know each other, he thought, frustrated in more ways than one.

Maybe if he fell asleep—or pretended to—before Amber came out of the bathroom, he could avoid what was sure to be a drawn-out conversation, not to mention the ache of being constantly turned on as he lay beside her. Unable to act on the need that had been eating him alive since their encounter in the kitchen.

And though he'd like to think she'd purposely led him on, to tease him in a minx sort of way, what he'd glimpsed in her eyes prevented him from thinking so little of her. She wasn't flirting only to make him suffer. She was as drawn to him as he was to her. As carried away as he'd been. Only she'd come to her senses, out of respect for his father.

Which would have impressed him if not coupled with her need to *talk*. The female term for bonding emotionally.

He punched his pillow and rolled over, away from the door, a minute before he sensed her presence in the doorway. He knew she was there before she said a word. The fresh scent from her shower permeated the air around him and the light padding of her bare feet had sounded against the floor. His already-strung-tight body hardened even more... though he knew he wouldn't be getting any tonight.

She slid into bed beside him, the ripple of sheets and heat of her body alerting his senses even more.

"Are you awake?" she asked, placing her hand on his shoulder.

He couldn't get away with faking sleep. With a groan, he propped himself up against the pillows, resigned to conversation. "I am now."

She shook her head and laughed. "You were before. I heard you muttering to yourself as I walked inside."

He hadn't realized he'd spoken out loud. She had him so distracted he couldn't think. Now he couldn't tear his gaze away from her V-neck sleep shirt that gave him too small a peek into her cleavage.

"Focus, Mike. I want to talk," she said, obviously holding back laughter.

How could he, when a stray piece of hair curled around her cheek, tempting him?

"What is it about this conversation you're trying to avoid?" she asked knowingly.

"What is it about this conversation that's so important to you?" he asked, turning the question back on her.

She snuggled closer. "I want to talk about your father."

Her answer took him by surprise. "You don't want to talk about *us?*"

"Not this time."

Her light laughter should have relaxed him, but the subject didn't. He wasn't any more comfortable discussing Edward than he was talking about *them*.

Still, he eased back against the pillows. Since she wasn't going to accept no for an answer, Edward as a topic was the lesser of two evils. "What about him?"

Amber curled her body against his. Mike grit his teeth, fighting the pleasurable sensations that wouldn't be eased any time soon.

"I was wondering if your father has ever seen a doctor?" Amber asked.

"For a physical?"

She shook her head, the soft curls splaying across his chest. He wrapped his arm around her and accepted the situation, hoping by the time she was finished talking, she'd be as aroused as he was and more willing to finish what they'd started in the kitchen.

"A mental-health professional."

Unprepared, Mike stiffened and bit back the first words that came to mind—*What the hell for?*—knowing how absurd they would sound.

"Relax." She squeezed his tense biceps. "I'm not criticizing, I'm trying to help. So, has he seen anyone?"

"No."

"Why not? You admitted yourself that his behavior is *off.* I've seen it for myself."

"He's been driven to the brink by a goddamn curse that's hovered over this family like a black cloud for centuries. What can a shrink do about that?"

She propped herself up so she could meet his gaze. "What if it's more than that? What if Edward's mood swings and instability are the symptoms of something that can be controlled? Not the result of a so-called curse." Amber spoke slowly. She obviously chose her words carefully.

But Mike couldn't answer her question. To take Edward to a psychiatrist meant learning for certain whether or not his father was insane. And that would bring to light Mike's biggest, unexpressed fear. If Edward was crazy…genetically, clinically crazy and not just driven there by the Corwin curse, could Mike be far behind?

"Mike?" she asked quietly. "Isn't it worth it to find out? Maybe something can be done for your dad."

He exhaled hard. He wanted nothing more than to help his father, his own fears be damned. But he was embarrassed he'd never thought of psychiatric help before. Nobody had.

Until Amber. "I'll look into it," he said at last, before reaching over and shutting the lamp, then rolling away from her. Trying to block the desire and the emotional bonding she'd effortlessly achieved.

Undeterred, she curled around him, wrapping her arm around his waist, claiming her place beside him. "I only want to help you and your family," she said into the darkness.

Nobody had ever wanted to help them before. Make fun of them? The kids had lined up. Whisper about them in town? Even the adults had been game.

"Why?" he asked her.

"Because I'm your wife." She hugged him tighter. "And because I care."

BECAUSE I CARE.

Amber's words were the first thing on Mike's mind the next morning. As he showered, he couldn't stop thinking of what she'd said. Was there help for his father? If so, it was worth facing his own fears about the insanity in his family in order to find out.

Last night, Amber had reached out in a way nobody ever had before. She wasn't just beautiful, she was smart and caring and he and his family were currently benefiting from those two attributes. He already knew he couldn't resist her sexually. Now he was having trouble resisting the pull her sweet, caring nature had on him—and the loneliness he hadn't realized he suffered from until she entered his life.

He had no choice but to put her life as a con on the back burner, and focus on letting her help his father. Which would lead to her becoming more intimately involved with his family.

And with Mike.

Before heading to breakfast, he checked his voice mail, but there were no calls from the P.I. in Texas. It was two hours earlier there, so he left another message at the man's office.

After the effort Amber was putting into helping Edward, he owed her. He needed to take care of King Bobby. Before King Bobby took care of Amber.

AMBER COOKED BREAKFAST for the men in the Corwin house, basic pancakes from boxed batter mix and orange juice. All the while, she thought about Mike's reaction to her suggestion about taking Edward to a doctor. He'd been agreeable and yet reticent.

Clearly she'd touched a nerve. Amber wondered if Mike was annoyed that his "temporary wife" was butting into family matters, or if there was something more at stake. What, she didn't know.

But she intended to find out.

Once she'd placed the pancakes on a platter in the center of the table, she called for Mike and Edward to come and eat. Before either of them made their way into the kitchen, the doorbell rang.

Amber heard Mike's footsteps, then his voice in greeting. "Gabrielle! What are you doing here so early?" he asked.

"I heard there's been a lot of excitement in this house. I wanted to see for myself," Gabrielle said. "You're looking good, Mike. I'd have to say marriage agrees with you."

Amber winced and headed out of the kitchen to head any matchmaking attempts off at the pass.

"You'll have to try another tactic if you want to

know anything," Mike said, laughing as he kissed her cheek. "I'm not talking."

"Well, you should be. You're a lucky guy to find a woman like Amber."

"Thanks." Amber stepped forward, alerting them to her presence. "But I think Mike can make up his own mind about me." She smiled at the other woman, whom she'd come to like a lot in such a short time.

Gabrielle raised her hands in the air. "Okay, I'll back off. No more meddling. So tell me, where is she?" Gabrielle glanced around, obviously looking for someone.

"Where is who?" Mike asked.

"Clara Deveaux. The Wiccan woman who has Edward so worked up."

"News travels fast," Amber said, surprised.

Mike groaned. "That's because I told Derek."

"Which is the equivalent of telling me." Gabrielle grinned. "So…?"

"It's not like she lives here," Mike muttered.

Over his shoulder, Amber met Gabrielle's gaze, without words that Mike didn't appreciate Clara Deveaux's presence in Edward's life.

"She left yesterday. But she said she'd be back," Amber added, daring a glance at Mike.

He merely nodded. "If you're here for the show, I'm afraid you're too early. But based on yesterday's performance, I'd say chances are good for a repeat."

"Edward took one look at her and lost it. And Clara showed no signs of backing down." She glanced toward the table. "Listen, why don't you come and have breakfast with us," Amber suggested, changing the subject.

Gabrielle took the hint and dropped the subject. Instead, they shared breakfast and conversation— without Edward, who had somehow managed to sneak into the kitchen, take his pancakes and leave the way he came, probably through the back-porch door.

Mike finished eating first and anxiously shifted in his seat. "Would you ladies mind if I headed outside to talk to my father?" he asked at last.

"Go ahead," Gabrielle said.

Amber shook her head and waved him away.

He left through the back door and it banged shut behind him.

"He seems uptight," Gabrielle said, staring after him. "Is it that Clara woman?"

"It's probably a combination of things. Me, Clara, his father...."

"Family stress," she said, nodding. "Speaking of family, tell me a little about yours," Gabrielle said.

Amber filled the other woman in on her father's situation. "If things work out with Mike, I'd like to move my dad to a nursing home near here." She missed being able to visit her dad whenever she wanted, missed talking to him, even now when she didn't know whether he understood.

A knock sounded at the back door. "It really is busy around here. All the commotion must be killing Edward," Gabrielle said.

Amber turned as Clara opened the door and stepped inside. "Edward's son told me to let myself in. He said I'd find you here."

"Of course." Amber gestured for Clara to join them. "Clara, this is Gabrielle...Donovan or Corwin?" Amber asked her sister-in-law.

"Corwin. I only use Donovan in business because that's how people already know me." She rose to her feet, her excitement to meet the infamous Wiccan woman tangible.

"Gabrielle, this is Clara Deveaux."

Clara eased by Amber and stood in front of Gabrielle. "I'm thrilled to meet you. I carry your books in my store."

"Even though I specialize in explaining paranormal phenomena?" Gabrielle asked, surprised. "I'd think that was something of a conflict of interest for you."

"I'm a businesswoman and your books sell. Besides, everyone is entitled to their own beliefs and opinions, yes?" Clara asked.

Gabrielle nodded, her smile warm. "Of course."

Clara extended her bracelette-laden hand and Gabrielle took it, returning the gesture. "Anyone who can stir up Edward's world instead of the other way around is welcome here anytime," Gabrielle said, laughing. "I love your dress and your jewelry." Her eyes sparkled as she looked over Clara's bold-colored outfit.

"Her ensemble matches your shoes," Amber said, taking note of Gabrielle's fashionable choice for today.

"I'd love to wear something like that, but I'm not used to having so much fabric flowing around me," Gabrielle said. "But it looks beautiful on you."

"Thank you," Clara said. She stared at Gabrielle intently, her wise gaze traveling from Gabrielle's eyes to her flat stomach. "You're going to be wearing more material soon though, aren't you?"

Gabrielle narrowed her gaze. "I'm not sure I know what you mean."

"You're with child."

Obviously surprised, Gabrielle stepped back. "What makes you say that?" she asked warily.

Gabrielle might be surprised by Clara's insight, but Amber wasn't. Nor did she need to dig too deep for an explanation. Amber had sensed something unique about Clara from the beginning. Now, she was more than willing to just *believe*.

"The special glow in your cheeks is a giveaway to one who knows what to look for. Besides, I sense these things." Clara paused and studied Gabrielle intently. "I'm right, aren't I?"

Gabrielle nodded slowly.

Amber could tell Gabrielle didn't know what to make of Clara's pronouncement. Was it psychic intuition or a lucky guess?

But she quickly became more concerned with making sure nobody else had overheard their conversation. "I haven't told my husband yet," she said to Clara, glancing warily around the kitchen.

"And your secret is safe with me." Clara touched Gabrielle lightly on the shoulder. "Do not be put off by me. I only do good by people."

Before Gabrielle could reply, the sound of Edward's shouting distracted them.

"What is that old coot up to now?" Clara asked and took off running outside, leaving Amber and Gabrielle to follow.

MIKE SEARCHED OUTSIDE for Edward for a full fifteen minutes before finding him. He'd checked around the perimeter and down by the lake, finally locating his father behind the boathouse he shared with his neighbor, Harry Winters. Derek located Edward almost the same time, and together Mike and his cousin tried to get Edward to talk about Clara Deveaux. But the mere mention of the woman's name sent the older man into a frenzy of pacing and muttering to himself.

Mike decided not to tell his father that Clara was inside the house. To Mike's way of thinking,

Edward must have cared for Clara, or his reaction wouldn't be so strong now.

Edward had only one coherent comment about Clara and he'd said it over and over. "I don't need to be worrying about Clara Deveaux and neither do you boys. The curse will take care of that woman. You wait and see."

Another reason Mike thought his father's heart had been—and maybe still was—involved. Edward wouldn't be mentioning the damn curse otherwise.

Edward had disappeared into the boathouse to do heaven knew what, and Mike knew when he'd lost a battle. "How about we see what the women are doing?"

Derek nodded. "It's not like we're making any progress with him."

"He'll keep himself busy for hours in there." Mike gestured toward the old building where his father organized tools and things that didn't need organization.

They walked across the back lawn until Mike broke the silence. "Do you think he's insane?" he asked, voicing his greatest fear.

Derek paused and turned to face him. "Is that a serious question?"

Mike grinned. "Strangely enough, yeah. Like, insane as in should he see a psychiatrist?"

"Do you think he would?" Derek asked.

"No, but that's not what I'm asking. Do you think he *should?*"

Derek scratched his head. "Probably. Now that you mention it."

"So you haven't thought about it, either."

Derek shook his head, a sheepish expression crossing his face. "Maybe one of us should have, but no, it never crossed my mind."

Mike exhaled hard. At least he wasn't alone. That made Mike feel better.

"What made you think about it now?" his cousin asked.

Mike shrugged. "Amber mentioned it and I'm thinking she's got a point. But so do you, when you asked if he'd even go. Getting him there won't be easy."

A loud crash sounded from the small boathouse followed by a shout. "I caught an intruder!" Edward yelled.

Mike and Derek did an about-face from the house and ran to see what kind of trouble Edward was causing now. They approached to find that Edward stood outside the boathouse door, gesturing wildly with one hand. In the other, he held his skunk, which was never far away.

Mike's heart pounded in his chest. "Dad, put that animal away and tell us what's wrong." Mike tried to get a look into the storage area, but Edward blocked the way.

"Someone's inside. I didn't get a good look, but I'm gonna get him now." He turned and picked up a large stick. "I'm going in."

Mike put a hand on his father's shoulder. "Let me take a look inside first," he said, easing Edward out of the way.

Derek held Edward back as Mike slipped into the boathouse. It looked like it was going to be another one of those days....

CHAPTER THIRTEEN

AT FIRST GLANCE, Mike didn't see anything unusual inside the old boathouse. And he sure as hell didn't see anyone.

"Hello?" Mike called.

"Mike? Is that you?" a familiar voice asked.

His cousin Jason.

"Thank God you're here," Jason said. "I came around back looking for your father. I couldn't find him, so I went into the boathouse to see if he was in there. I tried to talk to him, but he pulled a goddamn skunk out on me like a weapon. I've been hiding in here so I wouldn't get sprayed." Jason rose to his full height from the corner of the room.

Mike swore under his breath. "It's safe now," he said. "It'd have been safe anyway. The skunk has been descented."

"What the hell?" Jason stepped forward.

"Don't ask," Mike muttered.

Amber was right about Edward needing help. This kind of behavior couldn't continue.

For now, though, he was worried about his

cousin. "What are you doing here back in the States? Aren't you supposed to be overseas training or qualifying or something?" His cousin was a United States snowboarding champion, headed to the next Olympics and destined for gold.

"I take it you haven't heard the news?" Jason asked.

"Apparently not. What's going on?"

Jason groaned and ran a hand through his long hair. "I tested positive for steroids at the World Championships. I probably won't even be eligible to qualify for next year's Olympics."

Mike stared at his cousin, certain he'd heard wrong. "You don't do drugs. How did this happen?"

"Thank you!" He swung his arm in the air in victory. "If only everyone else had trusted me the same way, we wouldn't be having this conversation *here*." He pointed to the dirt floor.

"What's going on in there?" Edward called, interrupting.

"Everything's fine. I'll be out in a second," Mike yelled back and turned to Jason again. "Go on."

"I got suckered by a woman I thought I could trust. I was set up." His voice held all the exasperation he must be feeling.

"You fell in love, didn't you?" Edward leaped in front of them, seemingly out of nowhere. "Didn't you learn nothing from me? Your father? Your uncle? No, you let the curse get the best of you, too." He asked and answered his own question in the voice of a raving man.

"You're still sneaking up on people, I see. Hello, Uncle Edward. Where's your pet skunk?" Jason asked, ignoring the subject of the curse like all good Corwin men.

"Outside with that crazy woman," Edward said.

"What crazy woman?" Jason asked.

Mike inhaled, the musty scent of his surroundings suddenly becoming more than he could take. "Let's move this outside."

"Can we go into the house?" Jason asked. "I've got the press stalking me. My father's home is the first place they'll look. So I thought I'd stay with Uncle Edward. Nobody would think to look for me here."

Apparently Jason had come up with the same solution Mike had for Amber, which in Mike's opinion, made this place a less appealing hideout for both of them.

"I've got more company than I know what to do with. All uninvited, I might add," Edward piped in. Mike didn't need to see his father's face to know he scowled as he spoke.

Jason cleared his throat, an unspoken request for an explanation.

"It's a long story," Mike told his cousin. "And when you walk out the door you're going to meet those visitors. But don't worry. We'll keep your presence under wraps."

Mike's cell phone vibrated in his back pocket. A quick check told him it was a Texas number.

The P.I.

The man's timing sucked, Mike thought. He let the message go to voice mail, planning to deal with it as soon as possible.

As they stepped into the sunlight, a scene of chaos unfolded. Clara held the skunk and chided Edward, while Amber and Gabrielle surrounded Mike and Jason, demanding answers and introductions. Derek, arms folded across his chest, could only watch in horrified fascination.

"Quiet!" Mike finally yelled, silencing everyone.

All eyes locked on him.

"We need to take this inside. Now." His voice was a command and everyone followed him up the grass, through the back door.

But there was no escaping the fact that something needed to change. His father's once-quiet house had turned into a refuge for people running from their troubles. Edward couldn't handle it and since Mike had helped cause the problems, it was up to him to find to find a way out of this mess. God help him.

As Amber watched Mike handle his family, she learned more about her husband. Like her, he was a people person. He knew what made each person tick and how to give them what they needed to calm them down.

He started by sending his father to the garage, instructing him to clean up the boxes and make room for Amber's car inside. She knew it was busy-work, but it kept the older man away from the people and chatter inside, which clearly overwhelmed him. Before Clara could join Edward, Mike asked her to make tea for all the guests, sending her to the kitchen, far from the garage. Clara enjoyed taking care of people and hurried to please Edward's son. Gabrielle, clearly fascinated by the other woman, offered to help.

And though Amber preferred to stay with the men and find out what had happened to Mike's famous snowboarding cousin, she didn't think Mike would want her intruding. "I'll help Clara and Gabrielle in the kitchen," she said, turning to leave the Corwin men alone to deal with their family issues.

"Amber, wait."

At the sound of Mike's voice, her heart picked up rhythm. "Yes?" She glanced back over her shoulder, meeting his gaze.

"Would you mind sticking around?" He gestured to the family room where his cousins had settled into their own seats. "You've got a clear head and I think you might be able to help."

His words caught her by surprise. "Of course I'll stay."

"Thank you. I figure that as a concierge, you've dealt with situations and people that were harder than this," he said, winking at her.

They both knew that as a cop, he could handle people and situations as well as she could.

He *wanted* her by his side, she realized, warmth filling her as she walked over to him.

"Jason, how big an issue do you figure the press will be?" Mike asked.

"If they find me? Pretty big," he said, clearly unhappy with the prospect. "I literally paid someone to sneak me out of the place I was staying, took a flight without prebooking…anything to stay under the radar." He kicked back in his seat, propping his feet on the ottoman in front of him.

"Our cousin is like a rock star," Derek told Amber, teasing Jason.

Like his cousin, Jason had the Corwin good looks with his blue eyes and brown hair. But he distinguished himself with a scruffy beard and longer hair. Yep, Amber could understand the rockstar comparison.

"Don't listen to him. Snowboarding isn't a sport that gets all that much media attention, but the countdown to the Olympics has already started. When the positive drug test is released, all hell is going to break loose," Jason said.

Mike groaned and ran a hand through his hair. "Okay. But hiding out here may not be the best idea." He went on to explain about Amber's situation, and the reasons they couldn't afford media scrutiny.

"Mind if I ask why you'd bring her to Edward's when he hates visitors? Even I'm going to be an intrusion and I'm family." He glanced at Amber. "No disrespect intended."

"None taken," she said.

They all knew how Edward's mind worked.

Mike grit his teeth, realizing his cousin didn't know everything. He drew a deep breath. "Because Amber is my wife."

Jason's gaze traveled from Mike to Amber and back again in obvious surprise. "You're *married?*"

Amber remained silent and glanced at Mike, waiting for him to reply.

"We got hitched in Vegas. It's a long story. Let's just get back to your problem. I think I have a solution."

Jason frowned. "Okay, but I want details later."

Derek, who'd been quiet until now, snorted.

"What was that for?" Mike asked.

Derek glanced at Jason. "That was a snort of disbelief. As in good luck getting anything out of him." He tilted his head to Mike. "He's not saying much."

Amber shifted from one foot to the other. "Can

we *not* talk about me later, when I'm not in the room?" she asked wryly.

Jason laughed. "Sorry, sweetheart. That was rude of me. I'm just jet-lagged and shocked by my cousin's news. I'll make a better impression next time."

Mike rolled his eyes. "Can we get down to business? Jason, I suggest we sneak you out of here. You can stay at my apartment in Boston. Nobody will look for you there."

"That's brilliant!" Amber squeezed his hand only to find both Jason's and Derek's eyes on her.

Watching Mike for his reaction. True to form, there was none.

Amber sighed. "Okay, I'm leaving you men alone. You can catch up while I go see if I have enough to pull dinner together for the whole family before you take Jason to Boston."

"Sounds like a plan—" Before he could say anything more, the doorbell rang.

"Good God, what now?" Mike muttered.

"I'll handle it," Amber said, wanting to ease his stress.

Mike raised an eyebrow. "No, you will not. You're supposed to be in hiding."

She didn't think the person at the door would be looking for her, but she didn't want to add to the tension. "Okay, then I'll make myself scarce. I'll be in the kitchen."

"I'm going, too." Jason rose to his feet. "But not into the kitchen, in case whoever's at the door ends up in there. I really don't want another living, breathing soul seeing me here. This is way more than I bargained for. Come keep me company," he said to Amber.

"Okay, the kitchen can wait."

He walked to where she stood. "Let's go get better acquainted." He placed his hand on the small of her back in a gentlemanly gesture. "After you," he said.

With a shrug, she nodded.

As they headed down the hall, Mike's voice traveled after them. "Hey, cousin, keep your hands to yourself."

Jealousy, Amber thought to herself, surprised. She bit the inside of her cheek and grinned, enjoying the ray of hope that little gesture implied.

WHEN MIKE ANSWERED the doorbell, he found Jason's father, Thomas, and Derek's father, Hank, on the other side.

Uncle Hank was ornery and full of bluster and dressed casually without much care.

Not Thomas. Of all the brothers, he was the most rational when it came to the curse and also the one who cared most about appearances. His khakis were always clean and pressed, his white collared shirt starched.

Both men stood at Edward's door. Neither had been welcome in decades. At least not according to Edward.

"Uncle Thomas, Uncle Hank, come on in!" Join the party, Mike thought wryly.

The men stepped inside, waited until Mike shut the door behind him. "Where's my son?" Thomas asked.

Mike raised an eyebrow.

"Come on, Michael. I know he's here. He told me himself. I drove in circles to make sure nobody followed me. My car's around back."

"I just want to see the ladies," Hank said. "Gotta make sure they're behaving and keeping their men happy."

Mike merely shook his head. "They're in the kitchen, Uncle Hank. Uncle Thomas, follow me." He led his uncle back toward the bedrooms.

The sound of Amber's laughter told him which room they'd chosen. His. His and Amber's. A bolt of jealousy hit him in the stomach hard.

He was jealous of his own cousin. Again. For no rational reason other than he wanted to know he had Amber all to himself. Which he did, thanks to a marriage license he wanted to invalidate. Mike's stomach churned. He wasn't rebelling against the notion, he was hungry. Right.

Uncle Thomas stepped through the bedroom doorway with Mike right behind him.

"Jason!" the older man said, pulling his son into a bear hug.

"Hey, Dad." Jason patted his father on the back. "I'm so sorry—"

"Do not apologize. We both know you didn't do anything wrong and you'll prove it."

"Not in time to compete next year, I don't think," Jason said, his voice hollow.

"Then in four more."

"No." Jason shook his head definitively.

Mike caught the look in his eyes, a look Mike had seen many times growing up. When Jason made a decision, he stuck to it. He'd had to have that stubborn personality in order to be successful in his sport.

"Why the hell not? This is your dream. It's everything you've worked for." Thomas sounded as devastated as Jason had to feel.

Amber eased herself around the two men to sneak out of the room. Mike caught her hand and joined her.

"Why did you follow me? Don't you want to be in there?" she asked, gesturing to the bedroom.

He shook his head. "They need some privacy." And he appreciated that she'd picked up on that fact, too.

She nodded. "Are you okay?"

He leaned one shoulder against the wall and met her gaze. "Why wouldn't I be?"

"Well, to start with, it's crazy around here. And now, you've learned your cousin's lifelong dream has gone up in smoke. I imagine you're hurting for him," she said softly.

"It'll be fine. Jason will figure something out."

She tipped her head to one side. "He seems like a strong man. I'm sure he'll pull through this. It will just take some time."

"I wonder what he'll do once this blows over."

"Whatever it is, I'm sure you'll be there to help him decide. That's what family is for." Amber nodded in certainty. "Speaking of family, I really need to call the nursing home and check on my father."

At the mention of *Amber's* life, Mike's brain, which had been solely focused on himself and his family, kicked back into working mode. "And I have a voice mail that came in while I was out back, dealing with my father's outburst. It was a P.I. in Texas. With all the commotion, I forgot to tell you I'd hired him." He pulled out his cell phone and dialed his voice mail.

Amber stood beside him, waiting, her eyes wide and hopeful. "Maybe you'll have something on King Bobby and we can settle this misunderstanding once and for all."

Mike frowned at her. "You stole from him. I wouldn't call it a misunderstanding," he said, his voice suddenly harsh, thanks to the reminder of who she was and what she'd done.

For a while, he'd allowed himself to forget. He had to admit she handled his nutty father and the family chaos like a trooper. He could probably attribute it to the people skills she'd acquired in her former job, but he sensed there was more to it than that.

When Mike was in high school, he'd never brought girlfriends—or friends, for that matter— to his father's home, for obvious reasons. And as an adult, it hadn't been an issue. He'd never been serious enough about any female to subject them or himself to *this*. He hadn't trusted that any woman, after meeting with his father, would want to stay with him afterward, Mike realized for the first time.

As he stood in the hallway and looked at the woman he'd married, a stranger at first, one he was coming to know better, he realized that she was the one woman he *could* entrust with his family...and his heart.

Pushing aside the unsettling thought, he dialed 1 and his voice mail began to play the lone message. "Hey, there, pardner, it's your P.I. pal in Texas. Got that info on King Bobby, but I seem to keep missin' you. I'll give you a hint in one word. *Mistress.* Call me back for details."

Mike glanced at Amber, his mind still on his earlier thoughts. Yeah, she was the one woman he could trust...if only she were different.

Reality was a bitch, Mike thought.

"What did he say?" Amber asked eagerly, unaware of his inner turmoil.

Mike shook his head. No good would come of rehashing her past here and now. Or ever, since nothing could change it.

"The P.I.'s got something I can use to convince King Bobby to leave you alone."

Her beautiful blue eyes lit up with excitement. "What is it?"

"He said something about the man having a mistress, but I don't know anything definite right now. I'll let you know once I do."

She nodded her understanding. "I can't tell you how much I appreciate you doing this. For Marshall to go so far underground that I can't get any information from the people we both know, he has to be running scared. And that makes me scared." Her voice cracked and she rubbed her hands up and down over her forearms.

Her vulnerability got to him and he reached out, pulling her close. "It'll be okay," he said gruffly. "I'm not going to let him hurt you."

Protective instincts, as well as baser ones, kicked in as he held her against him. Her soft hair, warm body and fragrant scent tempted and aroused him. Unable to help himself, he bent to kiss her forehead, but she tilted her head and his lips caught hers.

She tasted warm and sweet, but her kiss was

anything but innocent, and filled with much more than gratitude. He needed this, needed her, and soon her back was pressed against the wall, his hands braced on her shoulders. All the while, his mouth devoured hers and she returned the kiss with equal fervor.

Until Edward's shouting penetrated the fog of desire between them. As Mike's mind cleared, he heard his father's words more clearly. "I recognize my brother's car. That woman-stealing rat bastard better not be inside my house!"

Mike stepped back, Amber pulled in a deep breath and the bedroom door opened, as Jason and Uncle Thomas came to see what the commotion was all about. Although it was pretty obvious.

"Why don't you let me deal with my father," Mike said to his uncle. Mike could take him into the kitchen to calm him while his uncles slipped out the front door.

"I think it's time your father and I talked." Thomas barreled straight past Jason, Mike and Amber, heading directly for the family room. "Edward? Are you looking for me?"

Mike groaned.

"Let's go make sure they don't kill each other," Jason said needlessly, since they were already following Thomas.

"How could any of you let him into my house?"

Edward yelled, the skunk in his hand. "Doesn't anybody have respect for my authority round here?"

Mike's stomach churned, not wanting his father to go completely off the deep end. A psychiatrist was no longer optional, it was mandatory, he thought.

Uncle Thomas met his brother in the center of the room. "It's time we end this ridiculous feud, once and for all."

"You stole my woman," Edward yelled, his face beet red.

"She chose me," Thomas said. "And in case you've been too caught up in your own insanity to notice, my life was no bed of roses—" He turned to Jason. "No insult, son. You know what I mean."

"And he knows why your life sucked eggs. It's the damn curse at work," Edward yelled.

Jason nodded, humoring him. The cousins all knew the Corwin-curse saga. They could repeat it in their sleep. Whether they believed it or not was another matter entirely.

Amber suddenly, quietly stepped up beside Edward. "If you think the curse caused it all, then why are you blaming your brother?"

"He could have controlled himself!" Edward still yelled loudly.

"It was over thirty years ago," Thomas countered. *"Get over it already!"*

"Over my dead body," Edward said. "Or better yet, over yours."

"Edward Corwin, there is no need for invoking evil, and against your own family, no less." Clara Deveaux burst in from the kitchen.

Gabrielle rushed out after her along with Derek and Mike's uncle Hank.

Clara strode through to the center of the room, her brightly colored, flowing dress almost a bigger distraction than the woman herself.

"God, this is really going to set my father off," Mike muttered, intending to pull Edward away from the confrontations.

Amber's hand on his arm stopped him. "Wait. Let her try to get through to him first."

"Why not just end this now?" Mike asked, speaking so only she could hear.

"Because I trust her." Amber met his gaze, her eyes pleading. "And because I think they have something special."

Mike wasn't so sure, but he couldn't say no.

"Who is this woman?" Uncle Thomas asked.

Nobody answered. Everyone was too busy watching Clara as she walked up to Edward, whisper something in his ear, take his hand and lead him out of the room, away from the chaos.

"Well, I'll be damned," Mike muttered, staring at Amber in disbelief. He couldn't help but be startled by Clara's hypnotic effect on his father.

"What the hell was that all about?" Jason asked.

"Simple. He trusts her." Amber smiled, obviously pleased with herself and the outcome.

Uncle Thomas cleared his throat. "Would one of you please tell me who that glorious woman was?" The older man stared after Clara, obviously entranced.

"Just an old friend of Edward's," Amber said in a clipped tone. One Mike had never heard from her before.

"I've never seen anyone like her," Thomas said in an odd tone.

It was almost…love-struck?

That's when Mike realized what had Amber's guard up. A feeling of déjà vu swept through him, even though he hadn't lived through the brothers' rivalry over a woman the first time.

"I must formally meet her." Thomas took one step toward the front door Edward and Clara had left through seconds before.

"Two morons about to repeat the past," Hank said more to himself than anyone in particular.

"Shut up, Dad," Derek said to his father.

Mike glanced at Jason, shooting his cousin a stern glare. A silent push to intercept his father. But before Jason could act, Amber jumped in front of Thomas.

"Oh, no. You will *not* go near that woman. Don't look at her, don't introduce yourself, steer clear," she ordered, hands on her hips in clear defense of Edward.

Mike stared at her, warmth in his chest, appreciation filling him.

"Young lady, you can't possibly mean to tell me what to do," Thomas said, sounding appalled.

"Oh, yes, she can, Uncle Thomas," Mike said, backing up Amber.

Jason stepped forward. "Dad, you heard the family."

"Family? She's not—"

Mike groaned. "You didn't tell him?" he asked his cousin.

Derek shook his head. "I didn't tell either of them. Figured it was simpler to keep Amber here and out of trouble that way."

"Tell us what?" Hank asked.

"Amber's my wife," Mike said. "And before either of you say one word about her, the curse, or anything else, remember, we're discussing *your* stupidity," he said, glaring at his uncle Thomas. "Not mine."

"Gee, thanks!" Amber said.

Mike glanced her way, surprised to find her laughing.

"Enough is enough!" Jason stepped forward to confront his dad. "Either you want peace with your brother or you don't. But if you go after that woman or any other that Uncle Edward is interested in, I won't be around to see the mess you make of your life," Jason said, obviously meaning every word.

Uncle Thomas blinked. "Of course, you're right." He ran a hand through his neat hair, his face turning red.

"Come on. The whole family is in one place for the first time in years. Let's try to salvage what we can," Derek suggested. He wrapped his arm around Gabrielle.

Mike paused in thought. The family *was* all together. That in itself was a miracle.

"You're right. I don't know what came over me, acting like that." Suddenly unsteady, Thomas lowered himself into the nearest chair, looking older and shaken.

"Maybe it was the curse," Mike joked to diffuse the situation and ease the tension.

Nobody named Corwin laughed.

KING BOBBY WAS HALFWAY through a bottle of whiskey when the private investigator he kept on retainer called him with a report. King Bobby had asked the man to dig up some dirt on Detective Michael Corwin.

"Give me something I can use, Clint, or else I'm gonna serve *you* at my next barbecue," King Bobby barked into the phone. He couldn't take Boston a day longer. He *had* to get back to the ranch.

But he wasn't leavin' without his money.

His high-priced P.I. rambled on about how the detective Amber Rose married had a clean record, on and off the job, and King Bobby's frustration grew. "That's useless to me. I don't pay you for shit I can't use."

And from what Clint had reported so far, it'd be damn hard for even a man of King Bobby's persuasive skills to get the detective to turn on his pretty lady.

"What else ya got?" King Bobby asked, pulling on a long sip of whiskey. The liquid burned, firing up his belly as much as his anger.

"Not much 'cept some background. Detective Corwin's got family in a small coastal town. A place called Stewart," Clint said.

"You don't say…" King Bobby grabbed a pen and made notes. "Tell me more."

He listened to Clint's irritating whine and scrawled the name of the town on the paper. He'd look the place up on a map and see if he could drive there. "Gimme an address."

Clint hemmed and hawed.

"Spit it out, boy!"

"Corwin's father's address is unlisted."

"Shit!"

"Yes, sir, but I'm working on finding it out," Clint said, rushing to assure him. "Don't you worry, I'm on it," the other man assured him.

"Quit kissin' my ass and find me that information!" King Bobby snapped his phone shut, then began slamming through drawers in the hotel room looking for a map, but all he found was a Bible. "I don't want to pray," he muttered.

King Bobby downed the rest of his drink. "Maybe the concierge can git me a map or directions. Concierges are good at getting their hands on things." Ripping the sheet of paper with the name off the pad, he folded it and slipped it into his pocket.

That yahoo Clint could keep digging until he found the lady or the cop's father, but King Bobby didn't have the patience to wait. "I'm gettin' closer. I can feel it." With a little luck, by the time Clint uncovered anything, King Bobby would already have the pretty lady in his sights.

CHAPTER FOURTEEN

SUNDAY MORNING DAWNED bright and early. Mike woke surprisingly rested, considering the events of last night—which ended as quickly as they began. Shaken by his behavior, Uncle Thomas headed home, leaving Jason at his brother's house, something they all agreed would be okay for one night. Derek and Gabrielle took off. And Clara left after assuring Mike and Amber that Edward, though he refused to leave the boathouse, was calm and safe.

In the end, Mike and Amber ate a quick dinner alone and fell into bed exhausted, sleeping wrapped together until Mike's alarm went off at 6:00 a.m.

He didn't linger in bed, regardless of how much he wanted to. Instead, he showered and dressed then went downstairs to have a coffee with his cousin. Half an hour later, he went back up to wake Amber.

"Hey, sleepyhead." He stroked her cheek and she stirred, her eyes fluttering open.

"It's time already?" she asked, pushing herself up against the pillows. The motion shifted her shirt, leaving one ripe breast visible to Mike's hungry gaze.

He groaned and raised the material, covering her before he succumbed to the urge to place his mouth on her sweet skin. "Yeah, it's time. Jason's waiting for me in the kitchen."

"And you're sure sharing your apartment with him in Boston is a good idea?" she asked. Poor Jason would get the couch.

Mike nodded. "Nobody will think to look for him there. It's a big city, not a small town. There's been so much unusual traffic here at my father's, Jason isn't comfortable staying here.

"I'm not surprised."

Mike nodded. "I watched the national news this morning. The fact that he's tested positive is making headlines." Mike frowned, recalling how much his normally carefree, happy-go-lucky cousin had withdrawn into himself as he'd watched the scandal retold over and over as they'd had coffee this morning.

"Poor Jason." Amber swept her hair out of her eyes.

"Poor Jason can inadvertently lead King Bobby here to you if he makes the right connections. That's what worries me," Mike said.

She shook her head, dismissing the notion. "You didn't meet the King. He's not that swift."

"He isn't that stupid or he wouldn't have tracked you as far as L.A. Be smart," Mike warned her.

"Okay, but I don't think it's me you need to worry about. I'm sure Thomas is already fending off the press this morning."

Mike nodded. "But Thomas can handle himself. At least he can when he isn't dumbstruck by a woman," he muttered. "I never thought I'd say this, but it's a damn good thing Edward disconnected his telephone line."

Amber nodded. "I know. Nobody can call and bother him. Don't worry. I'll take good care of him," she promised.

He couldn't stop the smile that pulled at his mouth. "I've seen you in action. I'm not worried about my father while you're around to protect him." Mike grinned, recalling Amber's fierce expression when she'd forbidden his uncle Thomas from going near Clara Deveaux.

Her eyes lit up. "I think that's one of the nicest things you've ever said to me."

"Well, you earned it." Before he could get all emotional, Mike cleared his throat. "Now, remind me of the rules we set up for once I'm gone."

Amber folded her arms across her chest. "I'll be fine. I know not to talk to strangers," she said wryly, meaning the press, if they somehow showed up here.

"Okay, then." Mike glanced at his watch. "I need to go, so humor me and recite the rules."

She rolled her eyes. "Lay low. Don't go outside unless it's absolutely necessary. If it becomes necessary, don't go out without looking out the windows first and make sure nobody's lurking or watching the house," she said, mimicking the instructions he'd given her more than once last night.

"Good. And if the press does show up?"

"Call the local police and then call you. You'll make sure the cops take me seriously." She exhaled a frustrated breath at being treated like a child.

"I'm a cop. That's my job." He leaned forward and placed a quick kiss on her pouting lips before rising. "Be safe," he told her.

She smiled. "You, too."

He inclined his head. "I'll call you," he said and with a wave, he walked out the bedroom door.

AMBER REMAINED in bed long after Mike left with Jason.

I'm a cop. That's my job, he'd said. The problem was, she wanted to be more to him than another person in need of protection. More than some poor woman he was helping so he could get her out of his life that much more quickly.

And despite how protective he was being now, she just couldn't be sure his actions weren't motivated by anything more than simply wanting to

look after her. After all, she hadn't missed the way
he closed down whenever he remembered her Las
Vegas past.

No matter how much she helped him or his family, she was beginning to doubt whether anything
would be enough to overcome his feelings about
her being a con and a cheat.

The rest of the day passed slowly, leaving Amber
depressed, bored and feeling both useless and
angry at herself for indulging in self-pity. She was a
woman accustomed to being strong and working. A
phone call to Paul earlier hadn't helped her mood,
either. He'd been forced to hire a part-time college
student to replace Amber, something she understood, considering she'd left him in the lurch when
she'd run from Vegas and King Bobby. And if that
guilt wasn't enough, Paul had reassured her that
he'd been visiting her father daily in her place. She
owed her friend more than she could ever repay.

She slept fitfully and when Monday morning
dawned, the sky was as gray as Amber's mood.
She'd already cleaned and straightened as much of
Edward's house as he'd allow. Now she made herself busy wiping down the counters in the kitchen
from the mess she'd created while making sand-
wiches for lunch. Amber stared out the window
toward the lake, a place she'd come to love for its
peace and serenity, elusive concepts where Edward
Corwin was concerned.

Clara had shown up early this morning, refusing to leave at Edward's demand. Instead, she'd followed him from chore to chore, telling him about her life over the past years. She'd left her only other employee tending the shop she loved, and she wanted Edward to help her look for new space for Crescent Moon. She said she planned to keep returning until Edward agreed.

"Good luck," Amber said aloud.

But she admired Clara's persistence in going after the man she wanted.

Unlike Amber, who was herself in limbo, unable to move forward the way she dreamed, or even live in the present with Mike. Until King Bobby's threat was neutralized or one of Amber's contacts called back with information on Marshall, she was stuck here.

Now a little stir-crazy, she was even tempted to help Clara find store space herself. According to the older woman, the press had invaded Stewart in search of Jason Corwin, disgraced Olympic hopeful, or looking for quotes from people in his family and his past. With so many strangers in town, she figured nobody would give her a second look.

MIKE WORKED the early shift Monday and returned to his apartment to find his cousin crashed out cold on the couch. As company, Mike didn't mind Jason staying as long as he needed. But as a substitute for

Amber, Jason Corwin came up short. Taking his cue from his cousin, Mike headed for bed, falling into a dreamless sleep.

He woke up the next morning to the loud sound of the TV blaring from the next room and immediately reassessed how he felt about his cousin's visit.

Mike padded barefoot into the room, picked up the remote and hit the off button.

"Hey!" Jason grumbled, annoyed.

"Keep it down, will you?" Mike asked.

"Sorry," the other man muttered as he leaned back against the sofa, hands locked behind his head.

"I know. Anything new?" Mike asked, realizing he'd overreacted. He was antsy without Amber here, something he hated to admit.

Jason shook his head. "Not in my life. I'm just waiting for the reporters to lose interest. According to my father, they're out in full force. God knows what dirt they'll dig up if they ask the right questions." He rubbed his palms against his eyes.

Mike couldn't imagine the pain his cousin must be feeling. "Everyone in town supports you. They aren't going to give the press anything negative to print."

"Except the Corwin curse," Jason muttered.

"There is that," Mike agreed.

Silence followed that pronouncement until Jason spoke first. "I feel awful leaving Dad to take the heat." Jason ran a hand through his hair and rose from the couch. "I should just go back and face the music."

Certain Jason wasn't going anywhere, Mike sank into a chair. "I'd support that notion if your father wasn't such a strong man. He can handle himself and you know that or you wouldn't have gone into hiding in the first place. So just tell me one thing."

Jason glanced over. "Name it."

"Why *aren't* you out there facing the press?" Jason was the risk-taking cousin. The rebel who didn't give a damn what anyone thought. Or he had been.

"Because I want answers first. I need to know why the hell I tested positive. I have a hunch, but no proof. And since the Olympic committee is pretty strict when it comes to drugs, I don't have a hope in hell of qualifying." He slashed his hand through the air and sent a tall candlestick Mike's mother had bought him onto the floor. "Oh, man, I'm sorry," Jason said as he rushed to pick up the piece.

"Forget it." Mike took the candlestick from his cousin's hand and set it back on the table. "Look, anything you need, background checks of competitors, whatever, I'm here."

Jason shot him a look of gratitude. "I know that. I just need time to process the fact that it's probably over for me. And *you* need time with your new wife. Speaking of Amber..." He let out a wolf whistle. "She's one hot babe."

Mike bristled at the crass description. "Lay off," he warned his cousin.

Jason merely laughed, which didn't help Mike's mood. "Since I've sworn off the opposite sex, you have nothing to worry about from me. All I'm doing is admiring my cousin's taste in women. And from what I could see, the rest of the family agrees." Jason slapped Mike on the back the way he used to when he and Mike were kids. "The only one who doesn't seem happy about your marriage is you."

Mike scowled, disliking the reminder. "Didn't I tell you how we met? Why she's running from a goon named King Bobby?"

Jason grinned. "Yeah, you did. But aren't I proof that circumstances and people aren't always what they seem?" Jason asked, his smile fading.

"That's different," Mike said.

"Because you want it to be different." His cousin eyed him intently. "Maybe you should be asking yourself why."

Mike's cell phone rang, saving him from unwanted introspection. He answered the call, identifying the P.I. from Texas on the other end.

Five minutes later, Mike had all the sordid information he needed on the very married, very cheating King Bobby Boyd.

"You look like you got good news," Jason said.

Mike nodded, acknowledging the rush of knowing he'd found what he needed to keep Amber safe.

"Does that mean you're going back to your wife?" Jason asked hopefully.

"Just when did you or any other Corwin become advocates for love and marriage?" The minute the words escaped, Mike wished he could take them back.

Love?

Whoa.

Who'd said anything about love? He had, obviously, but it wasn't what he'd *meant*. And though Jason looked at him funny, he wisely remained silent, leaving well enough alone.

"Earth to Mike," the other man said at last. "I asked if you'd be leaving for Stewart soon?"

Mike shook his head. "Nope. There's no reason. Right now Amber is in good hands and I have to work." And *not* put himself in temptation's path.

Jason snorted. "Yeah, you're right. Uncle Edward is more than capable of taking care of Amber if this King Bobby character shows up. Unless you already know where to find him?" he pointedly asked.

Rhetorical question, Mike thought.

Short of an APB, he had no choice but to wait for the man to rear his large cowboy hat. Mike glanced at his cousin. "You said the press is already in town?" he asked.

"'Fraid so. Asking questions about the *Corwin* clan."

"Which ups the chances of the Texan showing up in Stewart rather than Boston," Mike said.

"Where, with a few targeted questions, he'll end up at Uncle Edward's at some point." Jason shot him a regretful glance. "I was just buying myself some time. I'm sorry, man," Jason said.

Mike groaned, picked up the phone and bargained for more personal time, promising his superior his firstborn, should he ever have one, in exchange for this being the last—if open-ended—time off for a long, long time.

Then, with Jason's laughter and "I told you so" ringing in his ears, Mike headed back to Stewart and his hot babe of a wife.

MIKE ARRIVED at his father's house feeling out of breath, though he'd had an hour in the car to unwind. But once he let himself think about the press swarming his hometown, he'd had an uneasy feeling that things were about to blow up.

"Dad!" Mike yelled as he stormed into the house.

"We're in here," Edward called.

Mike exhaled a long breath. Relieved, he took the steps two at a time—to find his father and

Clara in the kitchen. "I thought…" Mike trailed off. "Where's Amber?" he asked instead.

"Haven't seen her. Not that I've had time to do anything more than listen to this woman's yammering on about the past. Like I still care."

A smile spread over Clara's face. "Did you hear that? He admitted he once cared!"

"Ms. Deveaux, have you seen Amber?" Mike asked.

"This morning, when I arrived and then again during lunch. But not since, now that you mention it." Clara's brows furrowed.

"She's not in the garage or the boathouse. I just came from there," Edward said.

Clara walked to the sink and poured Edward water, though he hadn't asked for any.

He accepted it and took a sip.

Mike shook his head. The connection between these two was the strangest thing he'd ever seen.

"Amber knows better than to wander off until her trouble's resolved, doesn't she?" Clara asked.

Mike sure as hell hoped so, considering he'd clearly instructed her to stay put.

"Amber told you about King Bobby?" Mike asked Clara.

He was surprised Amber would confide in a stranger about her problems, but then, she probably no longer considered Clara a stranger. Amber had an uncanny knack for bonding with people she'd just met. Like him, Mike thought, recalling their initial meeting in Vegas. The memory of that black dress and her curls hanging down her back set his body on fire all over again. When he got his hands on her...

Clara shook her head. "No, Amber didn't say anything." She waved her arm through the air. The tinkling sound of her bracelets followed. "I just sense there's evil somewhere around her."

"Just swell," Mike muttered. "I can't believe I'm asking this, but...general evil? Or evil right now?" Mike had no idea where Amber had gone and if Clara's insight, whatever it was based on, could help him find her, he wasn't too proud to ask.

"When I first said evil, I meant recent, but now that you're asking, there may be more." Without another word, Clara rose and headed out of the kitchen.

Mike followed her to Amber's room. Edward followed and surprisingly for his father, he remained quiet. So Mike did the same. He waited, anxious and uneasy, but willing to give Clara the benefit of the doubt.

"Yes, I can feel her better in here," the older woman said. "I wasn't paying much attention to her needs earlier," Clara admitted. "I was too happy to be here with Eddie again."

Mike's father stiffened, but before he could interrupt Clara, Mike clapped his hand over his father's forearm. "Please. Wait."

To Mike's surprise, Edward relaxed enough to assure Mike he wouldn't throw one of his tantrums.

"But I know she's been bored and feeling useless. She mentioned as much at lunch," Clara said.

"Useless? The house is spotless! I still can't find Stinky's favorite toy—"

"Hush!" Clara said. "A woman needs to be in charge of her life or else she feels powerless. That's what Amber's feeling." She met Mike's gaze. "I'm sorry. I should have listened more carefully for the hidden meaning. It didn't come to me until now."

"That's okay. Anything she said that you can remember will be helpful."

Because if she ran away or went to take care of King Bobby or Marshall by herself he'd throttle her.

Clara sat down on the bed and ran her hand over the comforter and a chill rushed through Mike. "The only thing we talked about was how I wanted Eddie to help me look for a new place for my shop. He's being a stubborn cuss, but I'll win yet. Amber also mentioned wishing she could go into town and check things out for herself…"

"That's it! Thank you!" Mike hugged the other woman. "She went to town to clear the cobwebs from her head." It was the most logical assumption.

Because Mike's gut told him she hadn't run off

on him again. Why did he trust in her that way? he wondered.

He didn't have time to figure it out.

"If she calls, find out where she is and tell her to stay put," Mike told his father and Clara.

"She can't call," they both said at the same time.

Mike closed his eyes and counted to ten. "Dad, we are turning the landline back on," he said as he ran for the door, ignoring Edward's bellowing about evildoers finding him.

Paranoia, Mike thought to himself. A *psychiatric* symptom, he thought, giving Amber credit.

He'd find her. Then he'd give her hell for taking such a risk with reporters roaming around town. At first he'd only worried about them exposing her, but now he was worried in general. Because after the chill Mike had experienced at Clara's words, there was every likelihood King Bobby Boyd was here, too.

And as a cop, Mike's gut had been too reliable to ignore.

WITH ONE OF MIKE's old baseball caps on her head and dark sunglasses, Amber strode through town. She'd even found an old camera in the garage that she'd hung around her neck, hoping to look like one of the media searching for information on Jason Corwin. Her disguise had worked.

She'd purchased a cup of coffee at Dunkin' Donuts and wandered around the local streets, appreciating the fresh air and change of scenery. She'd noticed one or two For Sale and For Rent signs on side streets and she'd taken notes to pass along to Clara later.

The only close call she'd had occurred when she'd caught sight of Derek walking out of the law firm Englebert and Rowe. She'd forgotten that he rented office space from them. Luckily for her, he'd headed to his truck and driven away instead of sticking around. She toyed with the idea of going into the Diner on Main Street, and having a meal she hadn't had to cook herself.

She walked past the front windows, planning to check the menu hanging there, when she caught sight of a large cowboy hat. Reflex and panic kicked in together and she backed against the brick siding, out of view.

"Anyone could be wearing a cowboy hat," Amber muttered as she ordered her breathing to slow. But she couldn't control the rapid-fire beating of her heart or the trickle of sweat working its way down the front of her shirt.

She edged closer to the window, hoping to get a better look at the face beneath the large brim. Between her dark glasses, which she refused to remove, and the glare of the sun, the man's face wasn't clear. But his huge size was.

"King Bobby, in the flesh." Amber quickly backed against the wall once more.

Somehow he'd tracked her here, leaving Amber with a choice. She'd been faced with many potentially life-changing decisions in her time. She'd remained with the father she loved but the lifestyle she hated rather than live with a sense of normalcy at her grandparents'. She'd trusted in Mike, a man she'd just met instead of walking away from the most sizzling attraction she'd ever experienced.

Amber had taken a gamble on Mike and she couldn't regret how that choice had turned out. And yet for the last week or so, she'd been hiding out from King Bobby, unable to find Marshall, living in limbo. Worse, she'd been unable to move forward with her husband, assuming he'd want her when this was over.

Well, no more. Her father hadn't raised her to be a coward. She was going to face King Bobby Boyd and reclaim her life. Once and for all.

IF KING BOBBY HAD HATED Boston, he hated this little dinky town of Stewart even more. Everything was small and scrunched together. Hell, even the service in the only diner in town wasn't up to the King's standards. Nobody came over to take his order and his choice of beer on the menu consisted of piss water.

"Hey, little lady, bring me a rack of your best

ribs," he called to a plump waitress rushing between tables.

She gave him a nod, then disappeared through the swinging kitchen doors.

So far his mission here was a bust. He'd tried asking questions about Amber or Detective Michael Corwin, but people in town weren't talking. They'd clammed up, thanks to the hometown athlete who'd been caught cheating. Numbnuts, King Bobby thought, without bothering to learn the man's name. If he was going to cheat, he should have had the brains not to get caught.

About the only thing this town did have going for it was its loyalty to its own. Nobody was talking to strangers, and King Bobby, with his ten-gallon hat, didn't look like a local. He didn't *sound* like one, either. These darn people had a stupid-sounding accent, he thought.

But if he was going to locate Detective Corwin's family, he had to find someone willing to talk. Since the locals were keeping mum, he'd just start asking the reporters if they'd heard of the Corwins.

"Here you go." The waitress interrupted his planning as she set down his meal.

He glanced at the plate and spoke the first thing that came to mind. "What in the name of Texas barbecue is *this*?" he asked, staring at the tiny baby backs slathered in sauce. Looked like little peckers, they did. "They're *wet*," he added.

The woman scowled at him. He'd hate to be the poor sap she came home to at night. Women like her were the reason men got themselves mistresses.

"Well, of course they're wet. They have barbecue sauce on them," she said. As if he was dumb. And blind.

"In Texas, the only thing wet in a barbecue is our whistle after we drink beer." Another sore subject, given his choices in this joint. "Barbecue is dry rub, honey. And the ribs look like they were ripped off a prize hog, not off some pet piglet in a tutu." He laughed at his joke.

She didn't. "Hey, Mel, there's a problem with the ribs!" she called into the kitchen before turning back to King Bobby. "And I'm not your honey."

"Don't I know that," he muttered.

She started to grab his plate, but he stopped her.

"Never mind. This is obviously as good as it gets around here."

"Never mind," she screamed back to the so-called chef.

"Honey—I mean, little lady, can you bring me whatever's on tap?" He tried for a little more respect.

"Damn out-of-towners," she muttered under her breath as she went to get his beer.

He tucked his paper napkin into his shirt, ready to pick up the poor excuse for a rib, when a female voice interrupted him.

"Mind if I join you?"

He glanced up. And into the eyes of the woman he'd been chasing halfway cross the country. "Well, well, well, if it isn't Amber Corwin, the Little Lady Thief."

CHAPTER FIFTEEN

AMBER'S HEART POUNDED in her chest as King Bobby Boyd looked her over like meat hanging on a rack. She didn't know if he was going to slice her, dice her or spit her back out.

"Isn't this a coincidence," he said in his lazy Texas drawl. "Have yourself a seat."

Acting unfazed wasn't easy, but Amber did as he said, easing herself slowly into the booth across from him. "Hey, King Bobby, long time no see."

He raised an eyebrow, or at least she thought he did. It was tough to see beneath his hat.

"You've given me quite a run for my money."

She forced a casual shrug. "Not really. You just have to know where to look. Obviously you did or you wouldn't be here now. So, why in the world have you been trying to track down little old *me?*" Putting on her best Texas accent, she pointed to herself with her thumb.

He let out a hearty laugh. "I like you, Amber Rose, I really do. Or I did, till I realized you'd associate with someone who'd con King Bobby out of his hard-earned cash!"

Amber narrowed her gaze. So he didn't realize her role in helping Marshall? Or was he trying to trick her into an admission? "What makes you think Marshall didn't win fair and square?" she asked him.

"Because he ran faster than the Road Runner once that guy at the table pegged you for someone he'd met in L.A." Propping both elbows on the table, he leaned forward. "I'm many things, little lady, but I ain't stupid. Once I put all the pieces together, I knew that game stunk to hell 'n' back."

Amber swallowed hard, still not willing to concede anything. "You don't have proof."

"I got two people who went underground, that's proof enough for me," he said, his voice rising, probably along with his blood pressure.

"Calm down before you give yourself a stroke," Amber said to the red-faced man. "What do you want from me?" she asked him.

"Well, now, that's more like it. I want your friend Marshall. Or is he your lover and that's why you're protectin' him?"

Ew, Amber thought. "No! He's not my lover! He's my—" She was about to say business partner, but caught herself before she admitted too much to King Bobby. He could guess all he wanted, but she refused to give him any ammunition. "He's my friend and an old friend of my father's. Anyway, that's beside the point."

"Not really. I saw how he looked at you. The man was interested in more than poker."

Because they'd put on a convincing act for the table, Amber thought. Just not convincing enough or King Bobby wouldn't be sitting in front of her now, guessing their con all too accurately.

Instead of replying to King Bobby, she remained silent.

"Just tell me where he is. Or better yet, tell me where my money is and we'll call it even."

Amber exhaled slowly. She didn't like Marshall much these days, but she couldn't turn him over to this man. Besides, as much as she hated to admit it, they were guilty of the same crime when it came to fleecing King Bobby. It didn't matter that she'd justified her reasons as more moral or altruistic than Marshall's.

Which was exactly why Mike couldn't forgive her, she suddenly realized. Nausea swept over her at the painful conclusion.

"I don't know where Marshall is. Or your money." Her share of the winnings were in Mike's bank where they belonged.

King Bobby cleared his throat. "I can make your life pretty uncomfortable, missy. I got friends in places a lady like you knows nothin' about. But since you're so dang pretty, I might have to settle on takin' things out on your man. Somethin' tells me that law-enforcement hubby of yours won't like a public scandal involvin' his new wife."

Amber reached for the only weapon she had, the one word of ammunition Mike had supplied her with before leaving town. "No, Mike wouldn't like a scandal," Amber agreed. "Anymore than Emmy Lou would like to know about that *mistress* you've been keeping behind her back."

As she grasped at her only straw, Amber broke into a cold sweat, hoping King Bobby would find himself faced with a quid pro quo—that neither he nor Amber could afford public humiliation.

His already-red face turned the color of beets. "How in the tarnation do you know about that? Nobody knows the King's personal business!"

Yes! Amber silently applauded. But instead of outwardly reacting, she waited for him to calm down and make the next move. A trickle of sweat ran down her chest, but she ignored it, knowing she was well on her way out of trouble with this man.

"Damn, I knew you were a smart one," he muttered. "I shoulda just denied it."

Amber shook her head and tried not to laugh. "Thank you," she said.

"Just 'cause I can't touch you, doesn't mean I can't still go after Marshall."

"You'll have to find him first," Amber said, not the least bit sarcastically. She meant it.

"Nothin' stays buried for long," King Bobby said. "Hey, honey," he called to the waitress, "get the little lady here a light beer."

The woman scowled at him, but she headed for the tap.

"I really need to be going," Amber said.

"Not until we toast our mutual agreement to leave our secrets buried. What do you say?" King Bobby asked with a grin.

It wouldn't hurt to do as he asked, she figured. Especially if he left town and she'd never have to see him again. "You've got yourself a deal."

"Good. And while we're at it, we'll toast to me findin' my money another way—and you lettin' me know when you hear from your old boyfriend. Because trust me, he'll be turning up again one day."

Amber raised her brow. Now that she'd made peace with King Bobby, she hoped she'd never hear from Marshall again. But King Bobby didn't need to know that.

As long as The King was happy, Amber was free.

"Bring on the beer," she said, relieved. A few more minutes and this nightmare would all be over.

No sooner had they clinked glasses and toasted than a loud, throat-clearing noise sounded in her ear. "What the hell is going on here?" Mike's voice reached a dull roar.

Amber winced, knowing how bad things must look. "Listen, King Bobby and I—"

Ignoring her, Mike glared at the big man in the booth. "If you've so much as whispered a threat in her ear, I promise you'll answer to me." And if his words weren't enough to send tremors of fear shooting through the big cowboy, his stance was.

Legs parted, arms folded across his chest, muscles bulged beneath his black T-shirt and his thighs appeared rock solid even encased in denim.

A quick glance at King Bobby told her he wasn't impressed, but Amber was. She rose from her seat. "Everything's fine," she assured him.

His gaze narrowed. "You promised to stay put."

"Hey, watch how you talk to the little lady," King Bobby said.

"That's rich, coming from the man who's been stalking her across the country. Which ends *now,* by the way."

"Um, Mike?" Amber interrupted, wanting to tell him she and King Bobby had resolved their issues.

"I can handle this," Mike said to Amber. Then he turned to King Bobby, leaned down and stared into the big man's face. "Listen up. I have enough information on you, your mistress and your little love nest to keep you and your wife tangled up in divorce court for years to come. And something tells me your other associates won't want to deal with someone who's caught up in a scandal. People in your circle prefer to keep a low profile. So if you don't want to keep your sleazy criminal friends and the life you have now, I suggest you leave *my* little lady alone."

Amber couldn't control the squeal that escaped at his use of the word *my*. Warm chills flooded her, at odds with her earlier realization that Mike couldn't possibly understand or forgive her for her past. But she was determined not to walk away from him until she'd bared her soul and heard his response.

Just in case.

King Bobby chuckled. "Y'all are really interestin', that much I'll tell ya. Detective, you need to chill. *Your* little lady and I already traveled this road and reached us an agreement. So why don't you just join us for a beer?"

"No. Thank. You." Mike clenched his jaw. "You said your business is finished?" he asked.

King Bobby nodded. "Until she hears from her pal Marshall, right, honey?"

"Right." She crossed her fingers behind her back.

"And where will you be in the meantime?" Mike asked.

"Where the land is as big as the ribs," King Bobby proclaimed. "I'm gettin' the hell out of the Northeast as soon as I can."

"I'm holding you to that," Mike said.

"King Bobby's a man of his word," the other man said loudly.

Mike treated him to a curt nod, while at the same time clamping his hand around Amber's forearm. Not hard, but not gently, either.

He was furious, Amber knew.

"In that case," Mike said, "we're out of here."

Knowing better than to argue, Amber let Mike lead her out of the diner for what might be their final showdown.

MARSHALL WAS DAMN PROUD, if he did say so himself. Doing an end run around that idiot King Bobby had been a brilliant move. Instead of the King finding Marshall, Marshall had found the King, and the big Texan had done Marshall's work for him, leading him right to Amber.

His gut burned with acid as he thought about what he'd just seen. Amber and King Bobby, sitting there, drinking beer and shooting the shit. *About him?* Marshall's blood fired up at the thought and anger pulsed through him at her betrayal.

There was no other explanation. No other reason why King Bobby would be laughing with Marshall's ex-partner unless Amber had given the King the information he needed to come after Marshall. If Amber had handed over the names of his close friends and associates, it was only a matter of time before someone slipped up and betrayed him.

He couldn't remain out of sight forever. King Bobby would find him eventually.

Damn Amber, anyway. She was *his* partner. *His* woman. They'd belonged together and now she'd turned on him. And why? For that cop husband of hers she'd known for less than one week. Well, he hadn't looked happy finding her with King Bobby, either, but she hadn't protested when the guy put his hands on her and dragged her out of the diner.

Last time Marshall had seen her, Amber Rose had warned him not to touch her ever again. As if he was scum. When he finally got her alone, she'd see the difference between a pansy-ass cop and a real man.

And Marshall would make sure it was a lesson she'd never forget.

Now that Mike had Amber by his side, he vacillated between being furious at her for leaving the house, and being overcome with relief that King Bobby hadn't hurt her.

He didn't say one word on the car ride back to his father's place. He needed to calm down first and, typical of Amber, she understood his anger and remained silent. Unfortunately, by the time he parked the car in front of the house, his tension and frustration hadn't eased.

Once inside, he found a note on the entryway

table from Clara. He read her neat handwriting with Amber glancing over his shoulder, her fragrant, arousing, now-familiar scent seeping into his pores, magnifying every emotion he felt for her, both good and bad.

He was wired.

Tense.

On edge.

The note stated that Clara and Edward had gone to town, looking for store space and for dinner. The craziness of it all didn't escape him. Mike couldn't begin to figure his father out and at the moment, he didn't care to try. He was solely focused on his wife and the fact that *they were alone*.

He slowly turned to face her. Her sunglasses were still perched on her delicate nose, her baseball cap askew on her head, and she stared at him intently with those beautiful, knowing eyes.

"Mike—"

"I came home and you weren't here," he interrupted her. "No one knew where you'd gone." He'd never been so bone-chilling scared in his life.

"I know, and I'm sorry."

"And then I find you breaking bread with the man, forging agreements, making promises—"

She winced at his description. "You have to know that I would never turn Marshall over to King Bobby. I only said that to keep the guy happy. Not that I think I'll ever hear from Marshall again, but I wouldn't give him up to King Bobby." She wrinkled her nose in thought. "Even if he deserves to be taught a lesson. Heaven knows I've learned one," she said quickly.

"Right now, I don't give a damn about what happens to Marshall." But he did understand what she was trying to convey. She was attempting to distance herself from her past and the people in it. She wanted him to believe she'd changed, that she understood the error of her past actions and the type of people she'd associated with.

"Amber, do you realize how lucky you are? The man could have killed you. Or worse," Mike said through clenched teeth.

"What's worse than killing…me… Oh…" Her voice trailed off and she turned pale, the blood draining from her face.

She suddenly understood all the things that had gone through Mike's mind when he realized she left his father's house. Assault, rape, heaven only knew what else. He'd seen a lot in his years on the force.

She swallowed hard. "I'm sorry I didn't listen. That I took off. I didn't mean to blatantly go against you, but I was going stark raving mad doing nothing for days on end. I'm a proactive person, Mike. I've been taking care of myself for years and I've never had anyone to rely on before, nobody else to consider before I acted."

"If he'd gotten you alone—" This time *his* blood chilled at the thought.

She reached out and placed a warm hand on his arm. "He didn't. I knew better. I didn't even know he was in Stewart until I saw him in the diner window. And then I realized I had a choice. I could keep running…or I could face him and put this mess behind me. I chose a public place where he couldn't hurt me. I was smart, I swear."

He ground his teeth so hard his jaw hurt. Pride in her bravery warred with lingering fear for her safety. He couldn't listen to her rushed rambling for another minute without feeling for himself that she was safe.

He grabbed her by the shoulders and pulled her hard against him, covering her lips with his. She melted into him, wrapping her arms around his neck, kissing him back.

Everything next happened in a blur, thanks to the blood rushing through his head—and to other body parts. He devoured her with his mouth, relief that she was home safe firing up his blood along with her eager, hot response.

He pulled her hat off her head and tossed it onto the floor, freeing the long curls from confinement. She yanked her glasses off and then she was back, kissing him again.

Undressing him.

She pulled his shirt up and over his head. Lowered his jeans and briefs around his ankles, leaving him long enough to grab a condom from his wallet, step out of one pant leg, then the other before she plastered herself against him once more. But it wasn't enough for Mike.

He needed to feel her heat, her warmth. He pulled her T-shirt up for skin-to-skin contact and realized she wasn't wearing a bra.

He gazed appreciatively at her full breasts and darkened nipples before he yanked her against him with one hand. Flesh against flesh, heat seared him.

His groin pulsed between them, throbbing against her stomach. "Do you feel what you do to me?" he asked gruffly.

She grazed the head of his shaft, liquid coating her fingertips. She grinned. "Yeah, I feel it." She tipped her head back and met his gaze, wickedness burning in hers. "Now it's your turn." Her hands shook as she unbuttoned her jeans and quickly peeled them off along with her lacy underwear.

God, she was gorgeous.

"Feel what you do to me," she ordered.

He slid one finger into her warm, feminine heat, finding her slick and wet. Ready for him.

He reached behind him and turned the lock on the front door, assuring them nobody would walk in. "You sure you want to do this here and now? Isn't it disrespectful?" he asked, only partially teasing.

She'd felt that way before and if he took one more step, he wouldn't be able to stop.

She pushed him against the wall and practically climbed him to get closer. "That was then. Edward was around the house somewhere. This is now. And trust me, if Clara actually managed to get him out, she won't bring him back for hours." Amber treated him to a warm, wet, lingering, seductive kiss. "Are you sure you want to keep talking?" she asked.

Everything in him screamed for release. "Talking's overrated." He picked her up and carried her to the nearest couch, only to find it too narrow.

Amber laughed, the sound cushioning his heart in warmth. "At this point the floor works," she said, panting with desire.

He lowered himself onto his back, shielding her from the hard surface. He took care of protection, then held out his hand.

She took it.

Amber lowered herself over him, positioning her thighs over his until her feminine cleft sat poised over him. Her eyes never leaving his, she slid home.

Inch by sweet, delectable inch, she enveloped him in wet heat until he couldn't think. He thought he groaned out loud, but he couldn't be sure, so hard was the blood rushing through his head, his ears.

And then she squeezed, contracting her internal muscles, pulling him into her very essence and he couldn't control the wave of emotion filling his body, his mind, his heart.

If only everything between them was this perfect, Mike thought.

And then she began to move, and rational thought fled with the silky-smooth viselike grip her body had on his. He cupped her breasts in his hands as she rode him, up and down, fast, seeking release. He was damn close himself.

But suddenly he didn't want it fast. He wanted to savor it and her. In case this was the last time.

Shaking off that thought, he bent his knees slightly, slowing her tempo. Her eyes opened wide and as she met his eyes, she must have read his mind.

Because as he slowly lowered his legs, she eased her rhythm. Changed it slightly. Slid down, milking him hard, then up again, pulling his shaft with her. She came down again, leaning forward as she did so, joining their bodies more firmly, intimately.

A soft sigh escaped her lips. "I like this," she murmured, rocking against him before sliding up again.

Down, rock forward, back up.

Down, rock forward, back up.

Until her inner walls began to contract on their own, building everything inside him to an intense crescendo. Higher, higher, until she exploded around him, inside him, through him.

She'd taken him on the slowest, sweetest, most heart-stopping ride of his life.

One he'd never ever forget.

WITH THE KING BOBBY threat neutralized, there was no longer any reason for Amber to remain in Stewart. Whether there was a reason for her to stay with Mike remained to be seen. Amber dressed slowly, prolonging the moment and imprinting every second of making love with her husband in her brain and deep in her heart, which already belonged exclusively to him.

She glanced over her shoulder to see him pulling on his jeans in silence. The only sound was the ticking of an old clock and their own heavy breathing.

She knew what she had to do. Amber had been brave once today. She looked at Mike, the long line of his back and his stiff shoulders, and knew she'd have to gather her courage one more time.

Because she wasn't leaving him without putting it all on the line, without taking the ultimate gamble. She drew a deep breath. "Mike?"

He turned to face her.

"You already know I'm a gambler, right?"

He met her gaze, his expression confused. He was obviously unsure of her point. "Right."

She stepped up to him and tipped her head back to meet his eyes, to put herself on some kind of even footing. "We met in Vegas and gambled on marriage and the slots, so I guess it's only fitting I'm standing here now, gambling on you."

"Amber..."

"No. Don't interrupt and don't panic. Just pretend you're back in Vegas and willing to take a chance." Her heart squeezed tight in her chest, but she pushed on. "You already know how great we are in bed. Or out of it." She pointed to the floor where they'd made love and laughed.

He didn't.

She knew then she didn't have a prayer. But her father hadn't raised a quitter. "It isn't just that we started off strong sexually, though hey, that's a bonus. And we also like the same TV shows." She searched his face for a glimmer of emotion, but all she found was the wall she'd come back to in Boston.

"Look," she continued anyway. "Somewhere between you rescuing me from Marshall the first time and now, we've discovered something good. Fun. Something that could be real and lasting if we gave it a chance." She reached for him, but his stiff posture never changed. She let her hand fall uselessly to her side.

Her heart, which minutes before had been full of hope, seemed to be shriveling into a small ball of nothing. Pain shot through her, but she forced herself to go on.

"Mike, even if we can't have anything lasting—"

Her voice nearly cracked on the words. "Can you at least find it in your heart to forgive me for leaving you in Vegas? Taking the money? Knowing me the way you do now, can we at least part as friends?"

The word nearly killed her. Friendship was the last thing she wanted from him, but it was better than the disgust he'd felt for the woman she'd once been.

He cleared his throat and the pain in his eyes matched the hurt inside her. "Amber, being with you has been—"

She raised her hand in the air, cutting him off, unable to bear hearing more. "Please don't say anything else."

"I have to. Because you need to know that I do care about you." His expression was tight and tortured, his eyes bleak and devastated.

Yet whatever pain she glimpsed inside him didn't change the fact that he was obviously going to end things. "Don't tell me you're afraid of the curse. I won't believe it." She tried to laugh, but couldn't.

"Of course not. That's my father's job. He's the one who ran away from life." Mike glanced away from her.

"And what are you doing, if not running away?" she accused, trying to pull him back.

He shook his head. "It's not the same. You see how my father is. That's how he's been for as long as I can remember." Mike paused and cleared his throat.

Amber caught the fullness in his voice and didn't push him further. She had to let him tell her in his own time.

"I couldn't live with the ups and downs he caused when I was a kid. I hated it. So my mother took me away, making sure I had stability. I need that stability."

Amber swallowed hard. She'd understood his feelings about Edward, his fears about living with someone whose actions and moods he couldn't count on from one minute to another. It was the way she'd felt living with her father after his diagnosis.

"I can give you that," she said softly. "Maybe I haven't so far, but once things are settled in my life, that's exactly what I want, too." She touched his face, turning him toward her. "I lived the same way once. I had a steady job I loved working for the Crown Chandler Hotels and I was great at what I did. I want you to see that part of me!"

"I want that, too, but it can't work. We're different, you and I. You said it yourself in Vegas. You need that thrill every once in a while and frankly, I don't. The ups and downs you bring with you… they're just not how I want to live."

Amber's heart beat hard and a sick feeling settled in her stomach. "I don't need those kind of ups and downs. I was talking about how you make me feel. That's all the thrill I need."

"You like unpredictability, you thrive on it. I saw how easily you left me in Vegas. No matter what your reasons were, you jumped first and explained later."

She pulled in a deep breath and tried to think. He was right. Abandoning him in Vegas and taking his money had ripped the foundation out from under any relationship they might have had. "I would never do that again."

But she already saw in his bleak expression, her words didn't matter. Her past actions did.

"You don't think so now. But you don't know what the future holds." He grabbed her hands. "Being with you, though it's fun and exhilarating, it's also like a roller-coaster ride."

She remembered his words in Vegas all too well. *"I really don't like roller coasters. In fact, I hate them."* And hearing them now applied to her was like a punch in the stomach.

She stiffened and turned away. "I get it, Mike. We both know how you feel about roller coasters." She paused and forced the pain back down her throat before continuing. "It's too bad though, because we could have had it all."

Gathering her pride, she turned and headed for the bedroom to pack. "Make sure you call the psychiatrist for your father," she said before closing herself alone in the room.

She needed to get the hell out of Stewart and let Mike Corwin return to his safe, certain, stable life.

The one without her in it.

KING BOBBY PRIDED himself on being as good as his word. Unless something happened to change the circumstances during which he gave it. He'd been planning on leaving town and heading back to Texas. Yes sirree Bob, he had. He already knew there wasn't a hotel room available in this town or any surrounding it thanks to the press.

But then, as he was walking on back to his car, the King felt it again. A presence. A distinct feeling of being shadowed.

More than once, he'd turned back around only to find no one behind him, but King Bobby knew something was off. So he wandered for a while, finally ducking out of sight and peering out to see who was there.

Hot damn! Marshall, the lying, cheatin' SOB!

Unbelievable, King Bobby thought as he weighed his options. He could grab him now, but he had a feeling the coward would scream bloody murder before King Bobby ever found out where his cash was. Or he let him go and turned the tail on the weasel, following Marshall instead.

King Bobby had no idea *why* Marshall would

be following *him,* but it had to have something to do with the pretty filly in denial about her ex-part-ner's feelings.

Between the two, one of them had the King's cash. All King Bobby had to do was let things play out. Even if it meant going back on his word and spending more time in this rinky-dink town.

CHAPTER SIXTEEN

MIKE SAT in front of the television in his father's family room scarfing down a microwaved bowl of mac and cheese, wondering why the hell he felt so damn bad. He'd accomplished everything he wanted. Well, almost everything. Amber was safe and out of his life, he was single again—or at least, he would be—just the way he liked it. And if he didn't have her half of the hundred fifty grand, who cared? It wasn't the money that had been important to him anyway.

Then what was?

Before he could reflect on that question, he flicked on the television set and turned the channel to the local news, hoping for some sort of diversion from his thoughts.

"And now, here is our own Cathy Carmichael, reporting live outside the Diner on Main Street in the small coastal town of Stewart, where reporters have flocked seeking information on disgraced Olympic hopeful Jason Corwin."

"Oh, shit," Mike muttered. So much for diversion.

"To date, there hasn't been any sign of Jason Corwin, but his uncle Edward was spotted inside the diner with a lady friend. But that's news, too, due to the infamous Corwin curse and the fact that Edward Corwin has been a loner…" The reporter's words droned on, but Mike didn't hear the rest of what she said.

He was glued to the sight of Edward and Clara trying to make their way through the throng of reporters. His father appeared pale, hanging on to Clara's arm for dear life.

Suddenly Gabrielle appeared, looking beautiful as ever in a flowing dress that resembled one of Clara's outfits. A rosy, determined glow stained her cheeks. "Leave him alone!" she yelled to the crowd, pushing her way through.

When his cousin Derek got a load of this, he was going to hit the roof, Mike thought. He rose, wanting to go help, but needing to see how things played out here first. He'd never get there in time anyway.

"What a treat! Our local celebrity author, Gabrielle Corwin. Have you heard from Jason? Is he guilty of doping? Where is he hiding out?" the reporter asked.

As she spoke, Mike noticed Clara led Edward a few steps away from the large group of people.

Thank heavens for that woman. Mike couldn't believe his own thoughts, but they were true.

Gabrielle's eyes narrowed at the reporter. "My standard answer would be no comment, however your stupid questions warrant a different response. Jason Corwin has never done drugs in his life. And if you did more than make your money off of this town, if you *knew* this town, you'd be rallying behind him and not hurling stupid questions that sound like accusations!"

Mike chuckled. "Go, Gabrielle," he said, proud of her.

The way he'd been proud of Amber when she stood up to his uncle Thomas to protect Edward. Like a woman loyal to her man, Mike realized, the thought coming unbidden. He rolled his head back and forth, seeking relief from the building tension.

"Does that mean you've spoken with Jason Corwin since the scandal broke?" the reporter asked, nonplussed at Gabrielle's outburst.

"Where is he?" another reporter asked, pushing the microphone into Gabrielle's face.

Another reporter shouted yet a different question and suddenly Gabrielle was being jostled from all sides.

Mike hoped she wasn't wearing those stupid high heels. She'd break an ankle trying to remain on her feet.

"Everyone, *step back!*" a woman shouted.

Amber.

Mike bent down to get a better look at the screen. Sure enough, Amber had joined Gabrielle, shoving reporters out of the way. "Move it. Back off. The Corwins have no more comments!"

Gabrielle shot an appreciative glance at Amber.

"Who are you?" a reporter asked.

Amber glanced away. "Just a family spokesperson."

"Just a family spokesperson?" Mike asked aloud. "What the hell? *You're my wife,*" he yelled at the screen.

The sound of his voice and his vehemence took him off guard. Where had such possessiveness come from? Hadn't he just sent her packing? So why did her minimizing her position in the family bother him so damn much?

"Just one more question," a reporter asked as he sidled up to Amber from behind. He tripped and fell headlong into Gabrielle.

Amber pulled Gabrielle out of the way before the man's big body could fall against her. "I said back off! She's pregnant!" Amber shouted, and clapped her hand over her mouth, obviously regretting her words.

As far as Mike knew, nobody in the family had been aware of that fact. Except Amber.

Mike shook his head and reached for his cell phone to call his cousin, then grabbed his keys.

He had to get to town before his father, standing in the background, went crazy over the news. And he needed to thank Amber for protecting the people he loved.

"You're such an ass," Marshall said to himself as he sat in a seedy bar on the water in a town named Perkins. He couldn't find Amber, even though she was like a needle in a very small haystack. Somebody ought to have seen her and yet…nada.

It was his own damn fault. He'd lost track of Amber after she'd left the diner with that cop husband of hers. Since Marshall couldn't risk being seen, he'd decided to follow King Bobby, figuring the big man would be in touch with Amber Rose again soon. But for now, following the Texan was useless. He'd somehow found himself a motel on the outskirts of town, probably paying off a reporter while Marshall was left biding his time.

With the couple of bucks he had left in his pocket, he bought himself cheap beer on tap and wondered what the hell had happened to his lucky streak.

He'd used his winnings with Amber to pay off the loan shark he owed. Marshall had found another game to make some cash, but without Amber, his luck had gone south.

Unlike King Bobby, Marshall didn't have money

to burn. He'd been stuck sleeping in the car he'd rented with a stolen credit card.

He glanced up at the television on top of the bar and nearly choked on his beer. There she was, Amber Rose, pretty as a picture, on Main Street in Stewart. Beneath the screen, the tag read LIVE!

He slapped a couple of bills onto the bar and walked out whistling. His luck was changing after all. Once he had Amber back by his side where she belonged, money would follow.

MIKE PARKED HIS CAR behind the diner and ran to find his family. The first person he asked sent him to Derek's office. When he arrived, chaos ruled. But the only person he didn't see was the one he most wanted to lay eyes on.

"Where's Amber?"

No one answered.

Mike glanced at his father.

Edward paced the floor, muttering about curses. He seemed worse than before Mike had left.

"Dad, are you okay?"

"I'm fine. The curse doesn't care about me right now. It's them you should be asking about." He pointed to Derek and Gabrielle on the other side of the room.

"Don't you worry, I'm taking care of him," Clara assured Mike.

"Thank you," he said. Mike glanced around quickly. "Dad, where's Amber?" Mike asked.

"Why do you care?" Edward didn't look up as he answered. "The curse is going to get you two anyway," he muttered, continuing his pacing.

Knowing a lost cause when he saw one, Mike stepped over to Clara who sat at Derek's laptop, typing on the keyboard. "Clara, where's Amber?" Mike asked.

"Just a minute, son. I think I'm onto something here. Do you know your father's exhibiting signs of paranoia and bipolar disorder?"

Mike nodded. "We're going to see a psychiatrist on Friday." He just hadn't told his father yet.

Edward stopped in his tracks. "The hell I am! There's nothing wrong with me that won't be cured by me staying away from people."

"Dad, we'll discuss this later," Mike said, patting him on the shoulder. He'd planned to spring the psychiatrist appointment on him at the last minute, preferably in the car when Edward was already on his way there.

"No, we won't," he said, clearly angry. "And missy, if you want to protect your baby, you'll listen to me," he said to Gabrielle.

Gabrielle turned from where she sat in Derek's big, comfortable chair behind his desk, gripping the old wood so hard her knuckles turned white.

"Uncle Edward, I don't want to hear another word about curses. Please!"

Derek shot Mike a look, silently warning him to get Edward to back off. Then Derek glanced at his wife. "How is your ankle? You know better than to wear those high heels when you're pregnant! That reporter could have knocked you over," he said, obviously concerned.

"Well, he didn't, because Amber took care of things, didn't she?" Gabrielle asked her husband. "I'm pregnant, not sick. Not an invalid. I can wear heels and—"

Mike stepped between them. "Speaking of Amber, where is she?" he asked again, hopefully for the last time.

"If you'd told me about the baby—" Derek interjected.

"You would have driven me crazy for an extra couple of days," she said. "Can't you just be happy?"

He stopped in front of her and knelt down. "I'm thrilled, sweetheart, you know I am."

Mike had a lump in his throat watching them, knowing how much they loved one another, how they'd do anything to protect each other.

An unaccustomed feeling of envy welled up in his chest, along with thoughts of Amber.

"I hate to ruin the moment, but can someone

please tell me where the hell Amber went?" Mike asked in a low, level, *I mean business* tone.

He just wanted to make sure she was okay. That was all. Really.

Finally, everyone turned to face him.

"She's gone home, no thanks to you." Gabrielle spoke first. "She said now that she was safe, it was time to leave, since according to you, there was no hope for anything lasting between you two." Gabrielle's voice held a wealth of accusation.

Mike didn't blame her.

"Tell me you didn't say that to her face," Derek said to Mike.

"I may have led her to believe it was over." He shifted uncomfortably on his feet.

"Is it?" Gabrielle asked.

"It needs to be." And he wasn't going to reiterate all the good reasons he'd been trying to convince himself of.

"Then there's no need for you to go to the bus station," Clara said. "She was taking a bus to Boston and then catching another one home to Las Vegas."

"I can't believe you'd let a woman like that go," Derek said at last.

Mike's cell phone rang and he answered on the first ring. "What?" he asked, glad for the distraction.

"Hey, there, Detective, it's King Bobby. I got me

some information you might want. Seems I was followed when I left the diner."

Mike raised an eyebrow. "I'm sure you've made a few enemies in your day. Why is this of interest to me?"

The other man let out a booming laugh. "You got me all wrong. The King's a lover, not a fighter. And this isn't my fight. The man followin' me is Marshall Banks, and I'm thinkin' he's not after me, but your woman."

Mike's stomach cramped. "Why would you think that?"

"'Cause I'm not blind, man. I've seen how he looks at her. I also have a hunch she was the brains behind the operation so he needs her. He's not just going to let her go."

Mike had seen the same thing in Marshall's eyes back in Vegas. "How long has he been tailing you?"

"I realized it when I left the diner earlier."

"And you're just calling me now?" Mike asked, annoyed.

"Don't get your knickers in a twist. I knew the little lady was with you, so she'd be safe."

But she wasn't with Mike now. She was alone. And he was to blame.

"Anyways, I'm just calling to ask you to keep an eye out. If you see Marshall, make sure you let me know so I can collect my money," King Bobby said.

"Where are you now?" Mike asked the other man.

"I got myself a hotel room in the next town over. Why?"

Mike drew a deep breath and let it out slowly. "Meet me at the bus station in Stewart," he instructed the Texan. "It's on the far side of town."

"Why?"

"If you want your money, just be there." Mike disconnected the phone and faced his family. "I'm out of here," Mike said.

"What's wrong?" Gabrielle asked.

"That guy who was after Amber is in town." Mike clenched his jaw, furious at himself for not seeing this coming.

Derek rose from behind the desk. "If you need backup, I'm there for you."

Mike shot his cousin a grateful glance. "I can handle it, but thanks. You take care of your wife."

Gabrielle stood. "You'd better call the minute you find Amber. I want to know she's safe."

"I will."

"Goddess speed," Clara called.

Mike looked at her curiously. Sometimes her words were so odd. "Thank you."

"Dad?"

Edward paced, but didn't answer.

"I've got him," Clara promised.

Torn, Mike nodded and turned to leave. His father was in caring hands.

Mike didn't know whether or not Amber was in

trouble, but he wasn't ignoring his gut. If Marshall was in town, Amber had to be his target. He already had his money. Who else would he be looking for?

And if her ex-partner had seen her meeting with King Bobby in the diner, he might assume Amber had betrayed him. Marshall hadn't struck Mike as being the nonviolent type when they'd met in Vegas. He had to get to Amber and make certain she was safe.

BY THE TIME Amber had extricated herself and Gabrielle from the reporters, Derek had arrived in town to retrieve his wife. Along with Clara and Edward, they'd retreated to Derek's office for privacy. Mike's cousin was furious Gabrielle had kept him in the dark, ecstatic she was pregnant and worried that Edward would snap at any moment. His office was the nearest place to calm everyone down. Although they'd invited Amber to join them, she'd declined. She wasn't family and never would be, something she needed to accept sooner rather than later.

But to do so, she needed to leave town and get away from Mike, his family and the memories she'd created in such a short time.

To let go, she needed to *go*.

So she'd walked down Main Street alone and finding it difficult to breathe, the pain of loss overwhelming. She didn't have a plan, but she had ideas. Careerwise, she'd definitely go back to work for the Crown Chandler if they'd have her, preferably in Vegas near her father. She'd rent a small room instead of paying a mortgage or rent, and cut back on the luxuries. Anything to keep her father comfortable and still enable her to live her own life.

Without Mike.

She shook her head, caught her breath and continued to walk along the sidewalk, heading for the bus station. Since she was no longer trying to hide her whereabouts, she could use her credit card to go home, but flying was out of the question. She still needed to be frugal since she'd have to save as much as possible in order to keep her father in his current home. But she didn't have to panic.

At this point, she had time, knowing her savings would keep him there for a few months more while she came up with a plan of action. Those savings were the cushion she hadn't had when Sam had been diagnosed. The reason she'd contacted Marshall, which had set her on this painful course.

But she didn't regret meeting and marrying Mike. This past week had been the best of her life. She knew now she could never settle for less than everything. She understood what it meant to care so much she'd come to think of his family as her own. And she discovered how her past could affect the future. Her choices would be made with greater care from this point on.

She strode into the Greyhound station and paid for a bus ticket to Boston. From there she'd travel home over the course of three transfers and three days.

Her bus didn't leave for over an hour so she wandered outside. On the sidewalk outside the station, a few people milled around, but overall, the place was pretty empty.

A car honked, taking her off guard.

She turned. For a foolish moment, her heart tripped as she looked, hoping Mike had come after her. Instead, she saw Marshall pull up beside her in a burgundy rental car.

She narrowed her gaze, surprised he'd resurfaced.

"What are you doing here?" she asked.

Now. After she'd settled her problems with King Bobby and no longer needed him.

"That's no greeting, baby. Get in so we can talk."

She shook her head. "I have a bus to catch."

"No problem, then I'll get out." He parked his car in front of the station in a No Parking zone. But then in Marshall's mind, the rules never applied to him.

She started to walk toward the door, hoping to lead him inside where she felt safer.

But when Marshall joined her, he hooked his

arm through hers and steered her straight along the sidewalk outside the bus station. "You've been a busy girl, running off on me, getting married, and then hiding out here in a small Podunk town. What's going on with you?"

Amber stopped in her tracks. "Are you crazy?" She looked him over. In his jeans and mock short-sleeve turtleneck and leather jacket, he looked overdressed for the heat, but every inch the slick Marshall she knew. "You know exactly what's going on with me. You left me high and dry while that big Texan came after me for money *you stole,*" she said, her voice rising.

He shook his head and laughed. "Come on, that's water under the bridge. I knew King Bobby wouldn't hurt a woman. I was just waiting until the heat was off to come find you."

"So you hid behind my skirts? That's low, even for you," she muttered.

He gripped her arm tight and she realized her mistake. She'd let his friendly veneer fool her into thinking she was safe.

"Drop the tough-guy routine, Marshall, it's me. We can talk this through." She hoped. "What is it you want?"

"You. Me. Things back the way they were." His voice held a hint of desperation, but he released his grip, which told her he was sure he could reason with her.

He'd kidnapped her father and used him as leverage. Even if Amber hadn't opted out of the life for her own reasons, there was no way in hell she'd trust Marshall on any level now. She may have once viewed him as her salvation, but now she saw him as he truly was—a shell of a man, a pathetic con artist, and nothing more. But she knew better than to let her true feelings slip again. Especially when she looked into the dark depths of Marshall's eyes and saw nothing there.

She decided to humor him. "Didn't you pay off the loan shark?" she asked.

He nodded. "But there's always the next score. You know that. And I need you."

She wondered if he was in more trouble and didn't want to admit it to her. "We can talk," she promised him.

He exhaled a long breath. "That's my girl." He not so subtly patted the pocket of his jacket and she realized there was a bulge there.

He had a gun.

Her heart pounded in her throat, fear rising like a wave but she refused to panic. She knew now to keep him calm—she wouldn't give him any reason to use the weapon. Her next priority was to get inside where she wouldn't be alone with him.

"You must be roasting in that jacket. Let's go in where it's cool. I'll buy us each a bottle of water and we can figure out a plan." She started for the door.

To her relief, he followed. "I knew you'd come around. You're heading home anyway. What happened? Prince Charming turned out to be a frog?" He laughed.

She bit the inside of her cheek to keep from telling Marshall that Mike was one hundred times the man he'd ever be. "He didn't understand me," she said instead.

He nodded, obviously pleased. "Not like I do, baby. We're partners, you and I."

"We've had our moments." She stopped short of agreeing, too busy trying to figure out how to get away from him once they were inside the bus station.

"Amber!"

She whipped around at the sound of her name.

Beside her, Marshall froze as Mike walked toward her from one side.

"How y'all doing?" King Bobby called from the other.

"Shit," Marshall muttered. Without warning, he grabbed her arm once more, stopping her from running away.

"Let her go, Banks," Mike said, his voice low. Deadly.

Amber wouldn't think of crossing him when he sounded like that. But Marshall always had an inflated sense of self. He was also holding a grudge against Mike for coming between him and Amber in Vegas. She knew this wasn't going to be pretty.

She broke into a sweat, as much from fear as from the sun overhead.

"Everyone relax," King Bobby said in his long drawl. "Listen, son, I just want to talk to you."

"Bullshit," Marshall said. "You want your money and he wants *her*." He yanked Amber closer to him.

"Don't hurt her, Banks." Mike's warning was loud and clear.

Amber tried not to grimace and give Mike a reason to act, but Marshall's fingers dug into her arm painfully.

"Don't tell me what to do with my lady, Detective," he said with a sneer. "She was leaving you anyway, so you've got no rights where she's concerned. Isn't that right, baby?"

Amber swallowed hard. She never tore her gaze from Mike as she repeated the words Marshall needed to hear. "That's right." Anything to keep Marshall from turning on the man she loved.

Loved.

Oh, God, she loved him.

She didn't just want a chance, she wanted him. Now, forever. Nothing else mattered. They'd work out the little details over the next fifty-plus years.

But Mike didn't love her. He'd protect her when necessary, like now. But then he'd let her go.

"You heard her, man. Go home. She's where she wants to be."

"Then why do you have a death grip on her?" Mike asked sarcastically.

Marshall's hold turned to a bruising pinch. Amber couldn't stop herself from groaning out loud.

Mike immediately pulled out his gun, prompting Marshall to do the same.

CHAPTER SEVENTEEN

"HOLY MOLY, BOYS, everyone take a deep breath," King Bobby said, keeping a careful distance from Mike's and Marshall's guns.

Mike couldn't breathe. Not until he got Amber away from that psychopath. She was a champ, and refusing to show Marshall any fear. But Mike could see it in her eyes. He could feel it in his gut. And he wanted to kill the man with his bare hands.

Marshall was a wild card. He shook like the pansy he was, which made Mike nervous he'd fire by mistake. And while Mike's gun was trained on Marshall, Marshall's alternated between Amber and Mike.

"Come on, Banks. Be smart," Mike said. "Put the gun down before someone gets hurt."

He let out a laugh. "I am smart. I've got the girl. You've got nothing."

Mike ignored the dig. "Then do the math. You've got what looks like a .22 and I've got a .38. Anything you shoot is just going to piss me off. On the other hand, *you'll* be sprawled on the pavement bleeding out, with no chance to spend all the money you've been winning."

"*My* money!" King Bobby shouted.

"Shut up," Mike hissed at him. He didn't need the big Texan stirring up Marshall's already volatile temper.

"Marshall, I was on my way home to Las Vegas. Why don't we work out our problems there. Put the gun away," Amber said, her voice strong despite his grip on her.

"You hear that?" he asked Mike. "She wants me, not you. We love each other. We're going to have a good life."

Mike stared.

Even Amber, who was trying to keep Marshall calm, looked at the man as if he'd lost his mind.

"Tell him you love me, baby, and he'll just walk away," Marshall said.

Amber winced. She could only do so much in the name of keeping everyone safe, and as much as she tried, the words Marshall wanted to hear wouldn't come. Not even in a patronizing tone.

"Tell him you love me." Marshall's grip tightened so hard she thought her arm might break.

Amber looked from Marshall to Mike, digging down to find strength she didn't realize she'd had. "Marshall, are you crazy? We never were more than partners. And that was only so I could pay for my father's nursing home."

"There's different kinds of love. We had an understanding! Now tell him!" He waved the gun at Mike.

"I can't! Because I don't love you, I love *him!*" Amber pointed to Mike.

At her declaration, Mike's throat went dry. Stars spun behind his eyes. Her words shocked him, although he should have known, should have realized it before.

At the same moment, the sound of sirens filled the air as police cars pulled up around them. In a small town, Mike was surprised they hadn't attracted notice before.

"Damn cops. They'll take the bastard and I'll never get my money," King Bobby muttered. "Of all the damn, rotten luck…"

"Drop the gun, Marshall. Before you find yourself in a situation you really can't win," Mike ordered.

"Marshall, please." Amber spoke directly to her ex-partner, pleading. "I don't want anything bad to happen to you. Neither would my father. The worst the police have on you now is possession of an illegal weapon. That's minor. It can still work out. Just give it up," Amber begged him.

King Bobby groaned. "I'm goin' back to Texas. You kin' keep your money for when you get out of the can," he said to Marshall, clearly fed up with the whole situation.

"Oh, hell. I'm probably safer in the joint here than in Vegas where the loan sharks can find me," Marshall muttered. Then he lowered the gun, tossing it onto the ground.

Mike scooped up the weapon and seconds later, the local cops had surrounded them, demanding Mike's attention, preventing him from dealing with Amber and her declaration.

I love you.

OTHER THAN A FEW BRUISES where Marshall's fingertips had dug into her skin, physically Amber was fine. Emotionally was another story. But as soon as she boarded the bus for Boston, she'd be able to put this ordeal behind her. Putting Mike there, too, though, wouldn't be quite as easy.

When the police had arrived, one officer had taken care of Amber, steering her toward a waiting ambulance over her objections. Standard procedure, they'd said. And Mike had been occupied giving his statement.

He hadn't looked for her at all, not that he'd had much of a chance in all the commotion.

King Bobby had disappeared, probably to avoid any possible scandal that might upset his so-called associates. And Amber knew Mike wouldn't bring up the man's name to the local authorities. The simpler the story, the faster this mess would all go away. Simple. Since Mike was a fellow cop, they'd taken his word for what had gone down.

A man from Amber's past had followed her to Stewart and tried to force her to go with him at gunpoint. She assumed they'd both told the same story, because the police seemed satisfied with her answers, asking only for her personal information so they could find her if they had any more questions. She supplied her Las Vegas address, home phone and cell.

A quick glance at her watch told her she could still make her bus. Another told her Mike was still busy with the local cops.

She could get on the bus and go home without a messy confrontation. He'd probably appreciate that, since her I love you declaration had gone unanswered. Besides, she hadn't said it to him, she'd said it to Marshall.

About Mike.

After he'd shut the door on them.

Amber was many things but she wasn't a martyr. She knew he cared for her, but he'd made it clear he could never forgive what she'd done. To stick around where she wasn't wanted wasn't her way. Mike had saved her and she was grateful. Beyond that, there was nothing more to say.

IT WAS OVER.

No sooner had Mike grabbed Marshall's gun

from the sidewalk than the local cops took over. They cuffed Marshall and read him his rights. The paramedics, who'd been called out along with the police, presumably by someone who'd witnessed the standoff, had reached Amber before Mike had a chance to get close to her. It was just as well. Anything they had to say to each other was best done in private.

At that moment, Mike hadn't a clue what he was feeling beyond relief and an overwhelming desire to kiss her until she melted into him, his body joined with hers, and he forgot the fear that had consumed him watching Marshall holding her in one hand, a gun in the other. But as Amber had pointed out earlier, that was just sex. Anything physical between them had always been spectacular. He wasn't ready to delve deeper.

So with the paramedics seeing to Amber, Mike put all his energy into making damn sure Marshall Banks didn't slip through any procedural cracks. Although Stewart wasn't his jurisdiction, Mike prided himself on being thorough, and he wanted the local cops to handle this booking the same way.

Only when the squad car carrying Marshall had pulled away did Mike turn to look for Amber. He glanced around, but he didn't see her anywhere. The ambulance had left and only one cop remained, scrawling notes while he sat in his car.

"Hey, man. Do you know where Amber went?" he asked.

The guy shook his head. "No clue." Then his radio beeped, capturing the cop's attention.

Mike headed for the bus station. He asked a few people if they'd seen her based on description, but no one had. Finally, he walked over to the young woman selling tickets behind the counter. "Have you seen the woman who was being held hostage earlier?" he asked.

"Yep. She took the number ten." The woman hooked her thumb toward the bus stop far from where the drama had taken place.

Mike's heart nearly stopped. "She *what?*"

"Bought a ticket before the ruckus and took the bus after." The woman glanced around him. "I'm sorry, but you're holding up the line."

Mike looked over his shoulder. One person stood waiting to buy a ticket. Some line. "Sure, sorry." He stepped aside and glanced toward the front door, slowly making his way out.

Gone.

She'd up and left him.

Because he'd told her they were through.

Because even after Marshall had released her, he had avoided dealing with his feelings for Amber by immersing himself in work.

Because…he was no better than his father. The truth hurt. In trying to avoid the trap his father had fallen into, Mike had landed there anyway *and* he'd probably lost his only chance at happiness. The only difference was that Mike claimed sanity while avoiding what frightened him. Only now that Amber was gone did Mike have the courage to face his fears.

Her words, the ones she'd used when she'd refused to tell Marshall she loved him, "I don't love you, I love him," ran through his mind nonstop.

Taunting him.

I love him, she'd said.

And at the moment when Mike thought he might lose her to Marshall and his gun, Mike had gone cold inside. Because though he hadn't verbalized it, he'd realized *he loved her, too.* And that love scared him, causing him to avoid her. He'd still been running, holding tight to the reasons he'd sent her away—the fear of instability, roller coasters and insanity.

Mike looked at the empty street where the bus had once been and realized those reasons suddenly meant very little when compared to losing her forever.

He'd been a fool, he thought, running a frustrated hand through his hair. He'd been too afraid to face his feelings before, because if he let himself love her… His thoughts trailed off and he broke into a sweat.

Afraid if he let himself love her…*what?*

Alone, Mike walked to the end of the sidewalk where the bus station ended. He and his friends used to hang out in the empty lot here. For Mike, the place had been an escape from his tense family life—at least until he and his mother had moved out. An escape from the arguments between his parents and the uncertainty of his father's mood swings. Mike had never known what he'd come home to. He'd always been afraid of ending up just like Edward, pushed to the edge by the curse. Or loving someone too much.

Amber had pushed and pulled. She'd abandoned him in Vegas, taken his money, left him alone only to show up again in Boston. With every lie by omission, every little truth finally revealed, Mike had suffered one punch to the gut after another.

He shoved his hands into his jeans pockets. His father had the power to put him on that painful roller-coaster ride because Mike loved the ornery old man.

Amber had the same power over him, he realized now, because he loved her, too.

He glanced at his watch and wondered if he could get to Boston before her bus. If not, he'd probably be able to head her off before she boarded the next bus out West.

He ran for his car only to be stopped by the cop he'd questioned earlier. "Corwin!" the other man called.

"Yeah?" Mike turned, trying not to sound annoyed.

Now that he'd made his decision, he wanted to find Amber immediately.

"Dispatch just radioed in. Your father was taken to the county hospital. Possible heart attack," the officer said. "I'm sorry, man."

"Thank you." Mike glanced up at the sky and swore aloud. When in the hell would he catch a break?

He dialed Amber's cell phone, but it went directly to voice mail. He didn't leave a message. What he had to say could only be done face-to-face.

After he made certain his father was okay.

With the police car leading the way, Mike sped to the hospital, raced into the emergency entrance and ran through the doors leading to the patients. All the while, his heart was lodged dead center in his throat. Because, for all the aggravation that went along with being Edward Corwin's son, Mike loved his father. And he did not want to lose him.

He heard his family's voices immediately and zeroed in on his cousin Derek's, the one person he could trust to be a voice of reason.

"What's going on?" Mike asked, winded from his panic.

"He's okay," Derek assured him first. "After you took off, his agitation increased. He started complaining of chest pains in between his ranting about the damn curse again. I brought him right over."

"Thanks." Mike sapped his cousin on the back. "What'd the doctors say?"

"They ran some blood work and said Edward hadn't had a heart attack. But they need to check it two more times. Some kind of protocol. He's hooked up to a monitor."

Not a heart attack. Thank God.

"What do they think it is?" Mike asked.

"Too early to say, but my guess is a panic attack." Derek shook his head. "I'm only surprised it hasn't happened sooner."

"I know. I'm sure it was the stress of being in public with Clara, the reporters surrounding them…"

"Finding out about Gabrielle's pregnancy, Amber leaving, you going after her because she was in trouble," Derek continued. "Your father's had a lot to deal with today in the one area of his life he doesn't cope with well."

Mike nodded. "I'm just glad he'd okay. I've made an appointment for him with Dr. Shelby."

"You might not need to go. Dr. Shelby was called in to consult. She's going to evaluate him before they let him go home, assuming the rest of the tests come back negative, too."

Mike exhaled a long breath. "I need to see him."

Derek pointed to the closed curtain. "They gave

him something to calm him down and he's sleeping. Gabrielle's standing watch outside as you can see, and Clara's sitting beside him inside."

"I take it there was no telling her 'family only'?" Mike asked, laughing. The other woman had reinvaded his father's life and obviously decided she was staying.

Mike was grateful. His father needed someone to love him. After all his years alone, he deserved that. Mike just hoped Edward would be able to enjoy it someday.

"I hate to bring this up, but what happened with Amber?" Derek asked.

Mike shook his head, still in shock himself. "When it rains, it pours, my cousin." He filled Derek in on the events of the last hour, including how Amber had taken off before they could connect.

"In other words, she bolted before you had the guts to face her."

He laughed at Derek's uncanny accuracy. "That's right. Now shut the hell up and let me think."

"About?"

"About the fact that I can't get out there until I get Edward settled. Which means Amber's going to have a three-day bus ride to build up her walls and begin to hate my guts." His stomach tightened at the unavoidable thought.

Derek hung his arm around Mike's shoulder in

a show of support. "Look, she's smarter than you are. Maybe she won't hold it against you."

"Funny. She's female, isn't she?"

Derek grinned. "Last time I looked."

"Then she'll hold it against me," Mike said. He'd earned any grudge Amber chose to hold on to.

She'd offered him everything and he'd turned her away. Why would she believe in him now?

THREE DAYS AFTER Edward was admitted and evaluated, Dr. Shelby discharged him. Mike was relieved and met the doctor in his father's room when she told him the good news.

"Mr. Corwin, we'll be releasing you today," Dr. Shelby said to Edward, who was sitting up in his hospital bed. "I'm sorry it took this episode for us to meet. But as I explained to your son earlier, I'd like to start you on a medication for mild anxiety. We'll meet at my office next week and see how you're doing on it, if that's okay. I'm hopeful that with weekly visits and the proper medication, we can improve how you've been feeling," she said.

Edward, normally blustery and talkative, remained sullen and quiet.

"Dad?" Mike sat down on the chair close to the side of the bed.

For the last few days, Edward had refused to even look at Mike. Yet despite his behavior, Mike held out hope that his father was finally getting the treatment he needed and that things would finally improve for the older man.

"Did you hear that? Your heart's fine and you're going home," Mike clarified.

Silence.

"Edward, your son's talking to you," Clara said, no edge in her tone.

Because she wasn't immediate family, she hadn't been permitted to spend the nights at the hospital. But she'd been by his side every waking minute since Edward had been admitted.

Edward shrugged. "I got nothing to say to him. He thinks I'm crazy."

"No, I think you're sick and you need help," Mike said with much less patience than Clara exhibited.

The doctor stepped up to Mike and tipped her head toward the door. "Can we talk?"

Mike followed her into the antiseptic-smelling hallway.

"Don't worry," she said after she shut the door quietly behind her so Edward couldn't overhear. "Your father is fine. He's now on an anti-anxiety medication, which has calmed him down and let him *feel* for the first time in ages," the doctor explained.

"So he's feeling anger. Toward me. The only person who's stood by him?" Mike asked in disbelief.

Confusion, frustration and anger overwhelmed

him, an impotent mix of feelings he didn't have the first clue how to handle. Because along with those feelings came the guilt for being angry at a sick man.

"Welcome to the world of therapy, Detective Corwin." The psychiatrist placed a hand on his shoulder. "It's always really bad just before it gets better. But it *does* get better."

"I'll have to take your word for it."

"Sometimes counseling can help family members, too. It's not easy to deal with the changes in their loved one."

Mike let out a rough breath. He didn't need counseling, he needed Amber.

Needed to tell her he was sorry, that he loved her. That he didn't want to end up like his father, alone and afraid. He should never have sent her away. Mike wanted Amber in his life now and forever. And the sooner he told her those things, the better, as far as he was concerned.

But Edward was his first priority. And as much as that frustrated him, it was the way it had to be. "What does he need from me now? Can he stay alone?" Mike asked the doctor.

She shook her head. "But his friend Clara offered to move in and make sure he takes his medication and things like that. He seems to respond well to her so I have no objection if you don't."

The knot in Mike's stomach eased. Not just because he wanted to hop a plane to Vegas, but because Mike feared for his own sanity if he had to move in with his father.

"Selfishly, that works for me," he admitted.

The doctor nodded. "I understand. It saves you having to disrupt your life until we know if his medication is correct and he's able to function on his own." She scribbled a few notes on her chart as she spoke. Then she glanced up at Mike. "Any other questions?"

"Actually, yes. About my own life…" Mike paused, feeling extremely self-centered for what he was about to ask. "I need to go out of town for personal reasons. But I won't go until you say it's okay."

"Detective—"

"Mike, please." He had a feeling they'd be seeing a lot of one another.

"Mike. Your father is going through a rough time, and clearly he's taking his anger out on the one person he trusts enough not to abandon him. That's you." She smiled, reminding him of his warm, caring mother. "That said, because he is angry, it wouldn't hurt if you put a little distance between you. As long as Ms. Deveaux makes sure he takes his medication and contacts me if there's a problem, you can feel comfortable taking your trip."

Her words took him off guard. "Really?"

She nodded. "As much as you feel responsible for your father, he's safe. He's cared for. And he's on the road to being healthier than he has been in years. I can't promise, but I can say with ninety-nine percent certainty based on experience, he will come around. Edward knows he can count on you." She touched his shoulder. "You're a good son."

Unbidden, a lump formed in his throat. "Thank you." He forced the words out.

She inclined her head. "I'm just telling you like I see it. You're a good influence and your father needs you."

Grateful, Mike shook the doctor's hand.

He'd help Clara get his father settled at home, then he'd see about booking a flight to Las Vegas, Nevada. The state where he'd met Amber, the city where his lucky streak had begun. With everything inside him, Mike hoped the streak didn't end in the same place it had started.

His fate was in Amber's hands.

CHAPTER EIGHTEEN

By THE TIME the bus pulled into Vegas, Amber's body ached from the long hours of travel. Her heart ached even more, but she would have to learn to live with that. She didn't go home first, but took a cab to the nursing home to visit her father. She doubted he'd know she'd even been gone, but she needed to see him and pretend for a little while that he was healthy and she was still his best girl.

Because it was the summer, his floor nurse had taken him outside for some fresh air, and after checking in, Amber wandered out back. She found her father sitting in a lawn chair, staring out at nothing.

She pushed aside the expected pang of sadness and put on her brightest smile. Pulling up a chair, she seated herself beside him. "Hi, Dad."

She took his hand. As she'd gotten into the habit of doing, she didn't wait for a reply.

"I'm sorry I haven't been here in a while. My life got a little crazy." She laughed at her bland description.

Also keeping with her promise to always keep things positive with her father, she omitted any mention of her problems with Marshall or King Bobby.

"I met a man," she said instead. "A good man. You'd like him." Visions of Mike entered her head.

Mike, looking sexy in his navy T-shirt as he'd rescued her from Marshall in Vegas. Mike, his face in shock when he'd found her sprawled on his bed in Boston. Mike, holding her after they'd made love. No matter how hard he fought it, he'd always come back to her.

Until now.

"Anyway, things between us didn't work out," she said to her father. "Guess what, though? I'm going to put out feelers to see if I can get a concierge job at one of the big hotels in Vegas. That's what you always wanted, right? Me working close by?" she asked, a lump in her throat.

She breathed in deep. She'd only been East for a short time, but she realized she liked looking around and seeing green trees instead of desert. And she'd have even come to terms with the humidity and frizzy hair if it meant being with Mike.

In the end, the choice hadn't been hers.

"I have to go now, Dad. But I promise I'll be back soon. Hopefully, I'll even have news about a new job." She forced exuberance into her tone that she wasn't really feeling.

Leaning over, she kissed his cheek and as she rose, she tried to tell herself she'd accepted the fact that he could no longer hug her back.

She lied.

She couldn't accept losing her father any more than she could accept losing Mike. Not in her heart. Where she felt more alone than she'd ever felt before.

AMBER SLEPT WELL and woke up the next morning with a plan. As she glanced around her father's old apartment, she realized she had to let the place go if she wanted to move forward. On a notepad she began a to-do list, starting with the intention to give notice on his apartment lease and find a new place of her own to live.

Amber glanced around her father's home and realized she'd also have to begin sorting through his belongings if she really intended to move out—and on. Parting with his things wouldn't be easy. She dreaded the task and knew she'd put it off until the very last moment.

Instead, she focused on herself. Next up, she needed a job. She called her old boss and let him know she was ready to return to work if there was a job opening in Las Vegas. He promised to look into things and get back to her as soon as possible. Amber then created a wish list of the top five hotel chains she'd like to work for, in case the

Crown Chandler fell through. But her boss in Beverly Hills had really loved her and she knew he'd do everything in his power to find her a position within the chain.

Knowing the business, Amber could put a solid guesstimate on what her salary would be—which forced her to face her father's situation. The reality was, she could not afford the high-end home she'd placed him in. She was ashamed of what she'd done with Marshall to cover those costs to begin with.

Any job she obtained now would allow her to put him in a nice home, but one where she'd have to compromise something in exchange for affordability. Like most people in the world, she had no choice. She wished she'd accepted the truth from the beginning, but she'd been in such a panic, and his illness had progressed so unexpectedly fast, she'd turned to Marshall and the life her father had taught her.

She couldn't regret her choices, because without those, she wouldn't have met Mike.

And how could she regret him?

Amber showered and dressed for the day. There wasn't a thing to eat in the apartment, so grocery shopping was definitely in order. Amber didn't mind the ordinary routine, but it made her realize just how alone she really was. More than once she caught herself talking out loud, expecting Edward Corwin's muttered answer.

She hoped Mike had taken her advice about his father's mental health to heart. Maybe she'd call Clara and find out how things were going. Amber reached for her cell phone, then paused.

She'd needed to make a clean break. By keeping in touch, she was only prolonging her agony. Instead of people from Mike's life, she ought to be contacting people from her own.

She reached for her cell again, flipped it open and saw an incoming text message she hadn't noticed before. A glance at the number caused her heart to race.

Mike.

Her hands trembled as she struggled to press the buttons to bring up the note. Finally, she was able to read Mike's message: Circus Circus, Adventuredome, Canyon Blaster. Noon. If you're willing to take the ride of your life with me.

He was here? In Vegas? Now?

She glanced at her watch and saw she had just one half hour to get to his assigned destination. All the while, she struggled to breathe as she contemplated what this meant. Because Amber knew the coasters in Vegas like the back of her hand. The Canyon Blaster was the world's only indoor double-loop, double-corkscrew coaster.

She told herself not to hope.

She found it impossible not to.

MIKE GLANCED UP at the huge double loops and wanted to vomit. He'd rather face a bullet than buckle himself into that death trap, letting some stranger push a lever that sent him soaring into oblivion.

Being with you, though it's fun and exhilarating, it's also like a roller-coaster ride, he'd said to Amber. He hadn't meant it as a compliment.

And she hadn't taken it as one.

So Mike stood in front of this monstrosity now, waiting to see if Amber would put her trust in him one last time. He could think of no other way to prove he was willing to give one hundred percent to their relationship, and to her.

Assuming she showed up.

Mike needed a drink to calm his nerves, but he was afraid to put anything into his stomach before going on the ride. Unlike the last time, he wanted to be stone-cold sober for this particular meeting in Vegas.

He recognized her from far away, the long legs, flowing blond curls and the determined stride as she came closer. He wanted to reach out and pull her into his arms, but her shoulders were back, her gaze wary.

"I wasn't sure you'd come," Mike said.

Helluva greeting, but he didn't know what else to say.

She smiled. "What can I say? I'm a gambler. But

you already know that about me." She paused, then added, "You know everything now." She didn't break eye contact.

There were no more secrets, lies or omissions between them. He knew who she was. What she was. And he loved her for all of it.

He extended his hand. "Take that ride with me?" he asked, not surprised his voice was low and rough. He wasn't scared of a future with Amber, but he was petrified he wouldn't survive the night-marish ride that awaited them.

"You don't have to do this for me," she said, her gaze warm and soft.

He appreciated the gesture and leap of faith. "Maybe I have to do it for me."

Without another word, she placed her hand in his and let him lead her to the roller coaster that went fifty-five miles per hour. He hadn't missed that fact in the online description, either.

She didn't let go of his hand as the ride took off and raced toward nothing. His heart lodged in his throat as they climbed the loop, higher and higher, upside down, then he was flying in a downward spiral. He didn't remember if he screamed or re-mained quiet, shut his eyes or watched every last moment. His body vibrated with the motion and thrill of the ride.

And with Amber by his side, it was a thrill, Mike realized as the cart finally, blessedly, came to a halt. He didn't know how he stood up or walked off without falling over or making an ass of himself. He only knew he'd not only survived, he'd conquered the Canyon Blaster, a ride that had lived up to its name.

Having proved that to himself, he grabbed Amber's hand and led her to a quiet corner. His pulse still raced, but for positive reasons.

Good reasons.

Solid reasons.

"Amber—"

"Mike—" she said at the same time.

He laughed. "I'd like to say ladies first, but I really need to tell you something."

She grinned, her smile easing the knots in his stomach. "You traveled three thousand miles and a double loop, double corkscrew. Somehow I think you've earned it."

"I appreciate that, but first—" He reached out and cupped her head in his hands, pulled her toward him and covered her mouth with his, the way he'd been dying to since the moment he saw her again.

Amber didn't hesitate. She kissed him back, looping her arms around his neck and aligning her body with his. The kiss went on and on, his tongue delving deep into her mouth, devouring her as if they'd been apart years instead of days. He couldn't get enough. Would never get enough.

And he didn't want to.

She piqued his arousal, his interest, she tugged at his heart and found a place inside him forever.

It wasn't easy, but he broke the kiss, leaving her panting. His own breath wasn't steady. "I was such an idiot," he told her. "Pushing you away when you were everything I ever wanted."

Amber's throat filled. Her heart swelled. But fear still managed to work its way through. "What about that little problem with you and roller coasters?" she couldn't help but ask.

He stroked her cheek with his hand. "I just didn't understand them before."

She blinked back tears. "And you do now?"

He inclined his head. "That ride wasn't so bad," he said, teasing her.

She didn't laugh. "That's not enough, Mike. You can't go from hating something to *that wasn't so bad.* You can't settle."

"Have I said or done anything since stepping onto that roller coaster that indicates I'm settling?" he asked incredulously. "*I love you,* Amber. I. Love. You. I flew here to tell you just that. I rode the roller coaster to prove that not only do I want the fun and the exhilaration that being with you brings, but I can handle it."

She couldn't tear her gaze from his clear blue eyes, so full of love and hope. She'd never seen the combination burn so bright in them before.

"Say that again."

"The whole mouthful?" he asked in horror.

She laughed, her heart full. "No, silly. Just the three most important words."

"I don't know. You haven't said them yet to me." A smile worked at the corners of his mouth.

"I said them back at the bus station!"

"You said to Marshall, 'I don't love you, I love *him*.' That's not the same thing."

She opened her mouth, then closed it again. He was right. Even when she'd come to him and asked for a chance to make their marriage work, she'd never said those three words.

"I love you, too, Mike. I love you and your father and your cousin Derek and his wife, Gabrielle. I love your life and I want—" She realized what she was doing and she clenched her jaw shut tight.

"Go on," he said, laughing.

She shook her head. "No. Not this time. You came out here, you say what you need to first." Because she didn't want to misread or misinterpret what *he* wanted for their future.

"I love you," he said, giving her what she'd asked for. "And in case you aren't sure what that means…" He paused and reached into his front jeans pocket, pulling out the large, gaudy ring he'd won for her, the one he'd found in his father's house after she'd left. "So here is your engagement ring, back on your finger where it belongs. On your wedding-ring finger," he clarified as he slipped it onto her left hand.

Laughing, she admired her bauble. "I do love it," she said.

"And this is the wedding ring I hope you'll wear from now on." Taking her completely off guard, he pulled a small pouch from his other front pocket and removed a diamond band.

"I… Wow… When…"

"A lot's gone on since you left, but there's time to fill you in later. Let's just say, I wasn't coming to get you without a concrete symbol of commitment. Something beyond this." He pointed to her huge fake diamond.

Amber grinned. "I love it, but how did you ever afford it?"

"Are you forgetting the money we won in Vegas?" he asked.

At the reminder, she sobered. "Have you forgiven me?" she asked softly.

"For what? Being you? Loving your father so much you'd do anything for him?" Mike wrapped one arm around her waist. "You've already invested so much of that infinite love into me and my family. There's nothing to forgive."

"Thank you." Eyes damp, she brushed her lips over his. "Can I wear my wedding ring now?" she asked.

He shook his head. "Not yet. Not until I ask your father for his blessing."

His words took Amber off guard and she fell in love with him all over again. "I want you to see him, but you do realize that he can't give you an answer?" she asked, saddened at the notion.

Mike nodded. "I know. But he deserves the respect due him as your parent. I want to ask."

Proof, Amber thought, that this man knew what was most important to her and would always go out of his way to make her happy. Just as she'd do for him.

"What about Edward? Can he handle a real marriage between us?" she asked, equally worried for Mike's father.

Mike let out a groan. "That's something else we need to talk about. Good thing we'll have those long hours on the flight home."

Home.

The word settled in her heart, warming her straight to her toes. "I have so much to take care of here before I can leave for good. And my father…"

"I have Gabrielle researching good-quality facilities close to Boston. She'll have a list and we can go check them out together." He pressed a long kiss against her forehead. "It'll be okay," he promised. "I'll fly out weekends to help you get things wrapped up here and we'll come back often so you can get your fix of roller coasters and Las Vegas excitement."

She blinked, dizzy with how fast her life had turned around. "I just called my old boss and asked him to find me a concierge position in Vegas."

Mike shrugged as if there was no problem. "Call him back and tell him you need a hotel in Boston instead."

She laughed. "I think I'll do that. I just hope there's an opening available."

"There will be," Mike said as he looked into her eyes.

She frowned, not as certain. "How do you know?"

"Simple. We're on a lucky streak, sweetheart. Nothing's going to stand in our way." He sealed his certainty with a kiss that left no doubt in Amber's mind.

They were meant to be.

EPILOGUE

AMBER THREW a belated wedding reception for herself and Mike. Family only and extremely casual, the event took place in Edward's backyard. With the lake in the background, the early fall provided a beautiful backdrop of green leaves that hadn't yet been touched by color. Amber couldn't wait to experience her first autumn season out East. For now, though, she was happy just to celebrate the present.

True to his word, Mike had presented her with a list of facilities for her father. They'd visited all and chosen one, settling him in with no problem. Things in the job department had also gone well. The Crown Chandler corporate offices had been so excited to have Amber back on board, they'd created an executive position in Boston just for her. Her increased salary enabled her to choose one of the better homes where she knew her father would be cared for and she'd be able to visit often.

Since his move to Boston, Sam hadn't been so agitated, which Amber took as a sign her father was content. In a new suit, he attended today's reception along with a private nurse she'd hired for the occasion. Amber wanted to believe somewhere inside him, her father understood what was happening and he was not only happy for her, he heartily approved.

Mike's family was more complicated, but then they always had been. Gabrielle, now safely out of her first trimester, had begun to show and beamed with happiness. She also arrived in her favorite pair of heels, prompting Derek to remain close by with a hand beneath her elbow to steady her. As much as the other woman claimed to hate his hovering, she clearly reveled in the attention.

Derek's daughter from his first marriage, Holly, had come for the party. She wore skinny black jeans with a T-shirt that emphasized her teenage body, along with a fringed linen scarf wrapped around her neck. A minifashionista at thirteen, and already beautiful, she clearly idolized Gabrielle. Derek definitely had his hands full with the two women in his life.

Jason Corwin had turned into a sullen man, frustrated by the turn his life had taken, and angry that he hadn't made any progress in clearing his name. With the Olympics only a few months away, it looked as if he'd never have his chance to compete. The family tried to fix him up with women, but he wasn't interested. Not that they'd stop trying, anyway. The Corwin women liked to defy the curse and they were determined to find Jason his own happily ever after.

Then there was the older generation.

Amber had been horrified to find out about Edward's panic attack, but it had all worked out in the end. He was responding well to his new medication and life was starting to look much brighter. Unfortunately, like all Corwin men, he liked to hold a grudge for too long. Though he'd agreed to all the psychiatric tests at the hospital, he was still annoyed with his son for imposing the psych consult on him at all. Even if he was improving daily.

Clara had moved in with him, a situation that necessitated daily adjustment on both Clara's and Edward's parts. And as Edward emerged from the fog he'd lived in for years, he had trouble coming to terms with his lost years and past behavior. His embarrassment led to angry outbursts, something Edward, his doctor and Mike were dealing with.

Amber's only concern with today's party were Edward's brothers. She and Mike couldn't exclude them, but when all three were in one place, trouble was likely to follow.

So when Hank Corwin arrived along with his brother Thomas, Amber prayed that common sense would win out.

But Hank immediately zeroed in on Clara and Edward, and headed their way. Thomas walked after him.

Amber quickly followed in an attempt to head off a confrontation that would ruin the family gathering. She hadn't forgotten Thomas's interest in Clara or how fragile Edward still was.

She intercepted them before they reached the couple. "Hi, Hank, Thomas. I'm so glad you could make it," Amber said, greeting them each with a kiss.

"Wouldn't miss it for the world!" Hank said. "We're all still praying the curse won't touch you and Mike, or Derek and Gabrielle—"

Amber cleared her throat. "We don't discuss the curse here. House rules," she reminded him, as she had each time she'd seen him since her return.

A quick glance at Edward told Amber he wasn't paying attention to his brothers. He was looking out toward the lake. He still tended to withdraw into himself. The doctor explained his behavior as being a combination of fear, anxiety and embarrassment. And they were still trying to get the right medication for his conditions. Therapy and medication could take a long time to work correctly and in sync.

"Is everything okay here?" Mike walked over to his family. He placed an arm around Amber's waist.

"We're all great!" Amber said. "Isn't that right?"

Hank nodded. "Where's the beer?" he asked.

Mike gestured to the bar area they'd set up, and

Hank ambled over. "Uncle Thomas, thank you for coming."

"I couldn't be happier for you two," he said sincerely. "How's your father doing?"

"It's a slow process, but he's coming along."

"Would it be all right with you if I said hello to them?" Thomas tipped his head toward Edward and Clara who sat a few feet away.

"As long as you behave," Amber warned him in her sternest voice.

Thomas gave her a salute and a kiss on the cheek. "I do like this lady," he said to Mike.

"Me, too." Mike squeezed her tighter.

Thomas turned and walked away. "Edward, Clara, it's so nice to see you!" He headed straight for Clara first, kissing her on the cheek a bit too long.

Amber took a step toward them, but Mike held her back. "It'll be okay. Let it play out," he said.

She narrowed her gaze. "I don't like how Thomas gets around Clara. It's as if some kind of spell or something comes over him and he can't resist her."

"Like I can't resist you?" Mike asked, nuzzling her cheek with his lips.

"Mmm," she murmured, loving the feel of his warm touch. Her body tingled in anticipation. "Stop trying to distract me or I'll have to lure you to the boathouse so I can have my way with you," she said, only half-kidding.

"Promise?" He slipped his hand beneath her shirt, easing his fingers into the waistband of her jeans.

Like newlyweds, they couldn't keep their hands off each other. Amber hoped the honeymoon period never ended.

"No! I'm kidding. We're surrounded by family."

"I forgot what a prude you are when there are people around." He often teased her about the way she'd acted the first time she stayed in this house. Because now that they were happy and officially together, he knew she'd have her way with him anywhere, anytime, as long as they were discreet.

She turned into his arms and a feeling of pure happiness and contentment washed over her. Surrounded by *their* family, the people who meant the most to them, and secure in each other, Amber's lucky streak had indeed continued.

"I love you, Detective Corwin."

He grinned. "I love you, too, Amber Rose."

Her entire body melted at his words.

Until a loud shout interrupted them. When they turned to look, they saw Edward standing on a chair, shouting at Thomas. "You want her so badly, take her. She's yours. Maybe then the damn curse will leave me alone and start working on *you!*"

"Eddie, you get down at once before you fall and break your hard head," Clara yelled up at him.

Amber grabbed Mike's hand and they ran toward the ruckus.

"Dad, I warned you not to go near Clara," Jason said, approaching his father.

"I didn't do anything except compliment the lovely orange color of her dress, dammit," Thomas exploded.

Mike rolled his eyes and glanced at Amber. "Are you sure this is what you want to deal with for the rest of your life?" he asked his wife.

The woman he'd traveled across the country to reclaim.

A female shriek reverberated around them.

Amber and Mike turned fast.

"Daddy, that's a *skunk!*" Holly shouted as she leaped onto the rectangular buffet table. The extremely portable, unstable table came crashing to the ground, the food along with it. Holly got up, fine but embarrassed.

Mike winced.

Amber laughed.

"Just what is so funny?" he asked, tension mounting.

Amber placed her hand on his shoulder to calm him. "Your question? You wanted to know if I wanted to deal with this for the rest of my life."

Mike clenched his jaw. "Maybe I shouldn't have asked."

She shook her head. "I'm glad you did. Because you need to know, I love *our* loud, crazy family and I wouldn't have it any other way. My old life was sad and lonely." She met his gaze with a warm, re-assuring one. "I'm lucky to have you."

Relieved, Mike shook his head and tipped his head toward hers. "I'm the lucky one."

And that was something he never intended to forget.

* * * * *

We hope you enjoyed reading

LUCKY STREAK

by *New York Times* bestselling author
CARLY PHILLIPS

If you liked reading this story by
CARLY PHILLIPS, then you will love
Harlequin® Blaze.

Harlequin® Blaze stories sizzle with strong
heroines and irresistible heroes playing the game
of modern love and lust. They're fun, sexy
and always steamy!

Enjoy four *new* stories from
Harlequin® Blaze every month!

Available wherever books and ebooks are sold.

New York Times bestselling author
Vicki Lewis Thompson is back with three new
sizzling titles from her bestselling miniseries
Sons of Chance.

Riding High

"Caution. Proceeding with it."

"You want to proceed?"

"I do." Her eyes darkened to midnight-blue and her gentle sigh was filled to the brim with surrender as her arms slid around his neck, depositing mud along the way.

As if he gave a damn. His body hummed with anticipation. "Me, too." Slowly he lowered his head and closed his eyes.

"Mistake, though."

He hovered near her mouth, hardly daring to breathe. Had she changed her mind at the last minute? "Why?"

"Tell you later." She brought his head down and made the connection.

And it was as electric as he'd imagined. His blood fizzed as it raced through his body and eventually settled in his groin. Her lips fit perfectly against his from the first moment of contact. It seemed his mouth had been created for kissing Lily, and vice versa.

He tried a different angle, just to test that theory. Still perfect, still high-voltage. Since they were standing in water, it was a wonder they didn't short out. He couldn't speak for her but he'd bet he was glowing. His skin was hot enough to send off sparks.

She moaned and pressed her body closer. She felt amazing in his arms—soft, wet and slippery. He'd never imagined doing it in the mud, but suddenly that seemed like the best idea in the world.

Then she snorted. Odd. Not the reaction he would have expected considering where this seemed to be heading.

He lifted his head and gazed into her flushed face. "Did you just laugh?"

She regarded him with passion-filled eyes. "That wasn't me."

"Then who—"

The snort came again as something bumped the back of his knees. A heavy splash sent water up the back of his legs.

She might not have been laughing before but she was now. "Um, we have company."

Although it didn't matter which pig had interrupted the moment, Regan had his money on Harley. Whichever one had decided to take an after-dinner mud bath, they'd ruined what had been a very promising kiss.

Pick up RIDING HIGH by Vicki Lewis Thompson, available June 2014 wherever Harlequin® Blaze® books are sold!

And don't miss RIDING HARD and RIDING HOME in July and August of 2014!

It feels good to be bad!

Good girl and preacher's daughter Melanie Knowles has lived a sheltered life in Blackfoot Falls, Montana. No one could ever imagine she has a secret thing for bad boys... that is until ex-con Lucas Sloan comes to town.

Don't miss the latest in the
Made in Montana miniseries

Need You Now

by reader-favorite author
Debbi Rawlins

Available June 2014 wherever you buy
Harlequin Blaze books.

Fires aren't all that's sizzling for this smoking-hot firefighter!

Firefighter Dylan Cross, aka Mr. June in the annual "hottie" calendar, is used to risking his life to save others. But he's not about to risk his heart—or his bachelorhood!—when it comes to sexy Cassie Price....

From the reader-favorite miniseries *Last Bachelor Standing*

The Final Score
by *Nancy Warren*

Available June 2014 wherever you buy Harlequin Blaze books.

Available now from the
Last Bachelor Standing miniseries by Nancy Warren

Game On
Breakaway

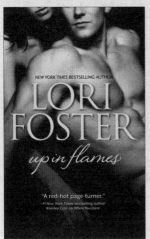

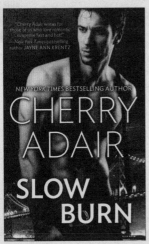